"I overheard you tonight. You knew DeWitt had done underhanded things before—I heard you discussing it."

"Underhanded?" He looked puzzled. "Roxanne, it really . . ."

"Lymond, I heard you." I wrenched myself from his grasp. "Besides, I was going to tell you that I had seen DeWitt looking at the scroll. He was at this very desk looking at it. He even commented on the fact that it contained household accounts."

"A good reason not to use it then, wouldn't you say?" Lymond reached for me again, but I went behind the desk. I wanted some space between us. He looked at me strangely, turned his back to me and took a deep breath. Then he turned to face me again and took a moment to light another candle. I noticed the knuckles of his hands were white and rigid.

"Damn it, Roxanne," he said in a flat voice, "just think about it. That scroll was substituted while Woodbury was outside during the fire at the stables. That fire was set to draw everyone out. DeWitt wasn't even in the house at the time."

"It could have been a ruse." I stared hard at him. "Why are you defending DeWitt so, Lymond? Could it be that you have a guilty conscience?"

He laughed shortly. "I thought we were agreed, Roxanne, that I had no conscience at all."

ELEGANT LOVE STILL FLOURISHES —
Wrap yourself in a Zebra Regency Romance.

A MATCHMAKER'S MATCH   (3783, $3.50/$4.50)
by Nina Porter

To save herself from a loveless marriage, Lady Psyche Veringham pretends to be a bluestocking. Resigned to spinsterhood at twenty-three, Psyche sets her keen mind to snaring a husband for her young charge, Amanda. She sets her cap for long-time bachelor, Justin St. James. This man of the world has had his fill of frothy-headed debutantes and turns the tables on Psyche. Can a bluestocking and a man about town find true love?

FIRES IN THE SNOW   (3809, $3.99/$4.99)
by Janis Laden

Because of an unhappy occurrence, Diana Ruskin knew that a secure marriage was not in her future. She was content to assist her physician father and follow in his footsteps . . . until now. After meeting Adam, Duke of Marchmaine, Diana's precise world is shattered. She would simply have to avoid the temptation of his gentle touch and stunning physique — and by doing so break her own heart!

FIRST SEASON   (3810, $3.50/$4.50)
by Anne Baldwin

When country heiress Laetitia Biddle arrives in London for the Season, she harbors dreams of triumph and applause. Instead, she becomes the laughingstock of drawing rooms and ballrooms, alike. This headstrong miss blames the rakish Lord Wakeford for her miserable debut, and she vows to rise above her many faux pas. Vowing to become an Original, Letty proves that she's more than a match for this eligible, seasoned Lord.

AN UNCOMMON INTRIGUE   (3701, $3.99/$4.99)
by Georgina Devon

Miss Mary Elizabeth Sinclair was rather startled when the British Home Office employed her as a spy. Posing as "Tasha," an exotic fortune-teller, she expected to encounter unforeseen dangers. However, nothing could have prepared her for Lord Eric Stewart, her dashing and infuriating partner. Giving her heart to this haughty rogue would be the most reckless hazard of all.

A MADDENING MINX   (3702, $3.50/$4.50)
by Mary Kingsley

After a curricle accident, Miss Sarah Chadwick is literally thrust into the arms of Philip Thornton. While other women shy away from Thornton's eyepatch and aloof exterior, Sarah finds herself drawn to discover why this man is physically and emotionally scarred.

Available wherever paperbacks are sold, or order direct from the Publisher. Send cover price plus 50¢ per copy for mailing and handling to Zebra Books, Dept. 4337, 475 Park Avenue South, New York, N.Y. 10016. Residents of New York and Tennessee must include sales tax. DO NOT SEND CASH. For a free Zebra/ Pinnacle catalog please write to the above address.

The Secret Scroll
Dawn Aldridge Poore

ZEBRA BOOKS
KENSINGTON PUBLISHING CORP.

ZEBRA BOOKS are published by

Kensington Publishing Corp.
475 Park Avenue South
New York, NY 10016

First Printing: October, 1993

Printed in the United States of America

Chapter 1

"Marriages may be divinely inspired, but they're devlish hard on all concerned," I said to Aunt Henrietta as I totaled up the expense column again. Unfortunately, I got the same result as before. "And do you think Cassie cares a whit about this?" I frowned at Aunt Hen and tossed my papers onto the table in front of her. We were involved in going over the guest list and expenses for Cassandra's wedding to Captain Owen Amherst.

"Sh," Aunt Hen said, looking around quickly. "You don't want poor Cassandra to hear you. Your sister can be so sensitive." Aunt Hen rolled her eyes upward. "Much as I hate to agree with you on this point, Roxanne, I suppose I must. This is becoming a traumatic experience."

I made a face. "And we still have to go to London for the ceremony. I don't see why Cassie couldn't have decided to marry here in Brighton, at the house. Papa would have loved to know his daughters were all married here at Bellerophon."

"Poor George," Aunt Hen sighed. From the time Papa was killed, that's become her catch phrase. It's rather automatic with her. I wondered occasionally if she really knew she said it. "It's too bad we couldn't have found the treasure so Cassandra could have had a proper dowry," she said. Aunt Hen was always talking about the supposed treasure of Agamemnon that Papa had left somewhere. Since his untimely death, we'd looked for it in and under every nook and cranny at Bellerophon.

"There is no treasure, Aunt Hen." This was my usual response. Still, no matter how many times I said it, she never seemed to believe me. Aunt Hen was rather like a homing pigeon—once set on a course, she seldom deviated. "We've been over this dozens of times and there is no treasure."

"If you'd only put your mind to it . . ." Aunt Hen's voice trailed off as I gave her a frowning glance. She seemed to think that all I had to do was think about the treasure, and its whereabouts would come to me in a vision. Catching my glance, she tried another tack. "Dear Robert thinks there is," she said, as though that settled everything. I frowned again. Robert Lymond again. For reasons that completely escaped me, Aunt Hen thought Robert Lymond was the most marvelous man this side of the Prince. Of course, with that worthy as competition, there was little argument.

Lymond was the chief reason we were in this uproar. He had come to Bellerophon to discover a thief and had introduced Captain Amherst into our midst. Cassandra and Captain Amherst had been immediately attracted to each other and were soon betrothed. However, the captain had broken his leg so the wedding had been postponed until he was able to stand in front of a minister.

They were not be delayed any longer. Their wedding was only a fortnight away and Aunt Hen, my other sisters, Julia and Olivia, and I were all inundated

6

with work. Cassandra, however, was above all this—she spent all her time floating around looking ethereal and in love. We had given up asking her to make decisions since no matter what we asked, she gave us a vague smile and a beatific look, then told us to do whatever was best. I had, I confided to Julia and Aunt Hen, decided the best thing would be to ship both Cassie and Captain Amherst to a tropical island somewhere and dispense with all this wedding business. Aunt Hen had promptly come down with the vapors.

Aunt Hen was still thinking of the Treasure. "You recall, Roxanne," she said with a sniff, "that Robert helped us search for the treasure. He specifically said that he believes it's here."

"Umm." I pulled one of my lists back in front of me, pretending to be absorbed in it. When Aunt Hen got on the subject of either Robert Lymond or the treasure, there was no stopping her so I had learned to try and divert her. She pulled some of my papers up close and peered at them. "Ah, a list of things to be done after we get to London!" Aunt Hen turned to me and, as I had feared, wasn't content to let her mention of Robert Lymond end. "This could be you planning a wedding," she said coyly, giving me a sidelong look. "After all, you're the oldest sister—I know poor George would have wanted you married first." She smiled. "I know in my heart that dear Robert would declare himself if you gave him the slightest encouragement, Roxanne. You could be Mrs. Lymond." She paused and savored the moment. "He's such a wonderful man."

"Aunt Hen," I started, then stopped. There was no use trying to convince her. Instead I tried another tactic. "I'll take care of these myself." I gathered up our letters and left to post them in Brighton. I could have sent Woodbury or one of the grooms, but when Aunt Hen began using the words "marriage" and "Robert Lymond" in the same breath, I knew from bitter experience that it was time to absent myself.

Actually, I admitted grudgingly to myself, Lymond wasn't really a bad sort. I had even fancied an emotional entanglement with him before. I had thought he had an interest in forming an attachment, but then he left for London and I heard nothing from him. He did send a short note that he was off to Brussels, but that was all. No hints, no encouragement. I decided if he didn't wish to pursue an association, then I certainly didn't plan to make a cake of myself. The only word I had had about Lymond lately had come through Cassie who heard about him from Captain Amherst. I had privately decided to put the man entirely out of my thoughts.

In reality, there was no point in my pursuing any kind of attachment. I certainly wasn't the marrying kind. Some were, and my sister was one of them. I wished Cassie well. She and Captain Amherst would have a wonderful life, I knew. Or at least they would when they got over this sentimental phase.

I was delighted to get away from wedding plans, my sisters, and Aunt Hen for a short while. I needed to get into Brighton alone. Lymond had leased our house, Bellerophon, for a quarter, and now that quarter was up. I wanted to see our agent, Mr. Miffle, again. I had asked him several times to see about finding us another tenant, one to whom we could lease Bellerophon on a yearly basis. After adding up the expenses for Cassie's wedding, I knew we needed the money and we needed it sooner rather than later.

That had been the reason we had let the house in the first place. Papa had wonderful taste, expensive

8

taste. Bellerophon and its grounds were a monument to his fascination with the ancient world. The house itself looked on the outside like a Greek temple, the mausoleum resembled an ancient tomb, and there were artifacts everywhere. Hundreds of artifacts, but no money.

After Papa's death, we weren't destitute, but we certainly weren't affluent and there were dowries to think of. I had decided to let the front part of Bellerophon so we would have enough money to send Cassie to London for a season. That wasn't necessary now, but paying for the wedding was. Besides, my other two sisters, Olivia and Julia, were getting older every day. With Papa gone and my half brother Edward having nothing to do with us, it was up to me to get them fired off.

After I posted my letters, I hurried to Mr. Miffle's. On the way, I could have sworn I saw a familiar carriage heading out of town, but I looked again and the color seemed wrong. Surely Lymond wasn't in Brighton. I would have known.

Mr. Miffle wasn't in but his wife told me he was meeting with a very important person. She hinted it was about our lease. "I really can't tell you Mr. Miffle's business," she said coyly, "but I can tell you that you're going to be more than pleased."

"Has he found us a permanent tenant, then?"

She smiled again, just as coyly. "I wish I could tell you, but I can't spoil his surprise. You know how Miffle is."

I had no idea what Miffle was like, but I didn't press her. Still, I went on my way quite satisfied that Miffle was negotiating for us and we would soon have another tenant. It would be good to have a tenant other than Lymond with us. I hoped our new person or family might be one with connections that Livvy or Julia could make use of. However, the more I thought about it, the more I wished Mr. Miffle would discuss the particulars with me before he did anything. Miffle had very little perception about people, and our tenant could be someone completely unsuitable. After all, Mr. Miffle was the reason we had been stuck with Robert Lymond.

When I got home, there was a dusty green carriage in front of the door, the same carriage I had seen in Brighton. I looked at it again: the lines were right, but the color was wrong. I hurried into the house.

"Roxanne, dear, just look who's here." Aunt Hen was purring like a well-fed cat. Only one person could put that smirk on her face. Robert Lymond was standing beside the fireplace, leaning negligently against the mantel as though he owned it.

He looked just as he had when I first saw him: dressed in black, his boots slightly dusty from travel. His hair was the same, brown with a touch of curl in it, sunstreaked because he usually forgot to wear a hat, and still longer than fashionable because he was too busy to get to his barber regularly. He was as tanned as usual, and this made his eyes seem all the more blue. "Miss Sydney," he said, walking towards me, giving me his charming, slightly lopsided smile. "I'm delighted to see you again."

"We're all delighted to have dear Robert back again," Aunt Hen said, nodding vigorously to include me, Livvy, and Julia. Cassie wasn't there—she was probably upstairs dreaming about Owen Amherst.

"Delighted," I murmured, sitting down hard. My knees were weak. I had driven too fast from Brighton, I supposed. "Are you just passing through, Lymond?"

"No." He and Aunt Hen spoke at the same time. He paused and sat down across from me, still smiling.

10

Aunt Hen jumped into the breach. "Robert has the most wonderful news, Roxanne. Tell her, Robert." Aunt Hen didn't even pause for breath. "I'm so delighted." She turned to Lymond and smiled. "Are you hesitant to share your news?"

Lymond started to share whatever it was, but Aunt Hen didn't give him a moment's pause. "Roxanne," she said, "you'll never guess what! Robert is going to be with us permanently!"

I felt my jaw drop open. Unladylike, I knew, but I couldn't help myself. "What?"

"Permanently. Isn't it wonderful? Mr. Miffle came by a short while ago with Robert and we signed all the papers. He has—what kind of lease is it, Robert?"

Lymond gave me a wolfish grin. "Five years."

I would never have thought it, but my heart almost stopped for a moment. I took a deep breath to steady myself. "Five years?" I couldn't credit my ears. "Impossible. Completely impossible."

Aunt Hen handed me a copy of a signed lease. "I just knew, Roxanne," she said, "that you'd want me to sign this. After all, I am acting somewhat as your guardian."

I refrained from telling Aunt Hen that she couldn't guard a chicken coop. Instead, I concentrated on reading the lease carefully. It was ironclad—Robert Lymond was indeed going to be with us for five full years, with an option for another five. I opened my mouth to protest, but then I saw the amount of rent he was paying. I was completely speechless.

I handed the copy back to Aunt Hen. "I suppose this was all your doing," I said to Lymond. "The rent you're paying amounts to charity. I won't have it."

"Nonsense," he said, smiling at me again as though he had never been away. "I can afford it and it's the going rate for a house in Brighton on a permanent basis. Mr. Miffle told me so."

"I don't believe you."

He shrugged. "Ask Miffle."

"I intend to. I intend to ask him about a great many things." It was futile and I knew it. I tried another tack. "It won't work, Lymond. I know you wouldn't do anything that would breach propriety in any way, and you know you can't stay here alone with us. Our reputations would be quite ruined."

"Aunt Henrietta is a wonderful chaperon," he said, smiling at me. It suddenly occurred to me that he was enjoying this.

"Oh my, yes," Aunt Hen said. "Roxanne, I can't believe you'd think that I would allow anything compromising at Bellerophon." She took a deep breath and looked on the verge of the vapors. Aunt Hen can summon an attack at will. Julia spoke up quickly to divert us.

"Mr. Lymond has asked all of us to stay at his family house in London when Cassie gets married," Julia said, giving me a quick nudge with her elbow. "All of us."

"We couldn't," I said without considering his offer at all. I realized as soon as the words were out that they sounded rag-mannered, and I tried to patch things. "Thank you for asking, Lymond, but we certainly don't want to impose."

Lymond smiled at me again. I hated it when he did that. He had the most charming smile in the world and didn't hesitate to use it when he needed it. "It won't be an imposition at all. I have a cousin getting married in Scotland then, and most of my family plan to attend, so the house will be almost empty. I expect my mother to be there and I know she wants to meet you." He

12

looked directly at me and I felt myself begin to blush, then caught myself. I couldn't believe his behavior. After all, there had been no word from him at all—other than his message about Brussels—the whole time he had been away. Now he was acting as if he had never been gone.

"We couldn't . . ." I began, but Aunt Hen, seconded by Julia and Livvy, interrupted me. "We certainly can," Aunt Hen said firmly. "Only Robert would make such a generous offer and it would be most unmannerly of us to refuse him."

"Besides," Livvy said, "we certainly don't want to batten ourselves on Matilda and Edward." She shuddered as she said it. We have not been close to our half brother, known familiarly in our family as Pompous Edward. His wife, Matilda, could be charitably described as a prude and an obnoxious upstart. Uncharitably, we have described her—and him—in worse terms.

"That's absolutely true," Julia chimed in before I could remedy things. "And as far as us staying with cousin Lydia—to be blunt, I don't think Lydia will want all of us barging in on her either."

"Julia!" I said sharply, giving her a speaking look. "We can discuss this later." Sadly, there wasn't very much to discuss. The girls were right: our options for lodgings in London were severely limited. I had already discussed with Aunt Hen the possibility of staying at a hotel. Nothing would do for Cassie but to be married in London. After all, that's what Owen Amherst wanted and Cassie seemed to want whatever he did. Captain Amherst had inherited a home in London and had invited us to stay with him, but after discussing it, we didn't think it would be suitable.

"I wish you'd consider staying at the family's Lon-

13

don house," Lymond said smiling again. "You know I've asked you several times to visit and I assure you it will be no imposition. I would consider it a pleasure." He gave me a look that made me slightly dizzy. Lymond sometimes had that effect on me.

I sighed and accepted a cup of tea from Aunt Hen. "All right, Lymond, you win. We'll come to London for the wedding and we'll stay at your family house." I fixed him with a stare. "But only because they'll be gone to Scotland. I would never impose."

"I assure you, the house will be empty except for my mother."

"In that case, we'll be delighted to stay, but only for a short while. We'll need to come home right after the wedding."

"I'm delighted." He smiled at me over his teacup. "By the way, I'll be glad to escort all of you to London when you go. I plan to stay here until then." He took another sip of tea. "An old friend of mine plans to visit me here for a few days."

I lifted an eyebrow but said nothing. As long as he leased the front of the house, there was little I could say about who came or who went. Aunt Hen, the girls, and I all lived in the back of the house and had no claim on the front, other than the kitchen. We had reached an understanding with Lymond about that. While he had been living there, he had asked us to take meals with him since he didn't care to eat alone. Aunt Hen had pointed this out as a tidy saving since we didn't have to pay either the cook's wages or the grocer's bills. I told her we weren't that far under the hatches, but we wound up eating at Lymond's table. It was good social practice for the girls, I supposed.

"I'm delighted you're having friends in," Aunt Hen said, helping herself to yet another piece of fruitcake.

"It's good for you to be social. It's too bad that we don't have people in—I've told Roxanne dozens of times that she needs company."

"Perhaps I can remedy that." Lymond smiled at me again and I cast about for a topic to change the subject. It was not to be.

"Do we know your guest?" Julia asked, trying to balance her teacup. Julia had an unfortunate tendency to either spill, drop, or break whatever was at hand. She was probably the prettiest of my sisters, but simply had no grace. She had dark hair and very dark blue eyes. Papa had called her his little Aphrodite, although I had always pictured Aphrodite as blond.

In truth, Julia did look like Aphrodite except for the times she was sprawled over the back of a chair trying to keep from falling or the times she was constantly mopping up spilled tea or soup from her dress. Then she looked rather like a drawing from the acid pen of a caricaturist. This time, she almost caught the teacup but it eluded her and teetered precariously on the edge of her saucer.

Lymond reached over and snatched Julia's teacup from sure destruction and put it on the table with a careless grace. "My visitor? A friend of mine from my school years," he said, handing Julia a napkin to mop up the drops of tea on her skirt. "His name is Kenyon Gwynn and I haven't seen him in several years, although we've corresponded infrequently. Kenyon's been in America for the past three years, so I'm looking forward to seeing him and hearing about the country and his adventures."

Livvy frowned. "America? South America? Canada? Surely he hasn't been in the United States. I thought all loyal Englishmen had either come home or gone to Canada."

15

Lymond judged Julia sufficiently recovered and handed her teacup back to her. "That was back during their war, I think. That's been over for years. Kenyon went to one of the states—South Carolina, I think—to assist his uncle on his estates. They were rice planters, I believe."

"Rice?" This was Aunt Hen. "But, Robert, I thought rice came from China or some such place. Perhaps from one of those islands with volcanoes that one is always reading about. Where Robinson Crusoe was."

Lymond looked at Aunt Hen with perfect gravity, not even a hint of a smile. "Yes, rice comes from those places, but it's also grown in the Americas. I believe South Carolina is a major rice-growing region."

"Who would have thought it?" Aunt Hen's eyes were wide. "And we fought the colonies for a muddle of rice paddies?"

"You were telling us about your friend," I said, to get the conversation back on track. Aunt Hen has never been much of one for either geography or politics.

"Yes," Lymond said. "Kenyon came back to England some months ago when his father became gravely ill. His father is much better and I thought Kenyon would enjoy some time away from his responsibilities, so I invited him for a short visit." He smiled. "I also had a selfish motive: I heard from Owen that Kenyon had had some amazing adventures in the Americas. He's visited west of the Mississippi River and I want to talk to him about it."

"I can only hope Bucephalus likes him," I murmured, giving Lymond a look as the dog walked into the room and fell heavily to the carpet, drooling as his tongue lolled to one side of his mouth. Bucephalus is

16

my dog, a huge mastiff. Bue and Lymond had not been the best of friends.

Lymond glanced first at Bue then at me, rather uneasily, I thought. "I need to talk to you about that. Kenyon doesn't care at all for dogs."

"I'm sorry," I said firmly. "You know Bue almost has the run of the place. I'll try to keep him out of Mr. Gwynn's way, but I certainly can't promise anything. You really should have taken that fact into account, Lymond."

Aunt Hen dismissed Bue with a wave of her hand and probed for the fact she considered most important. "Tell me, Robert," she said in her usual subtle way, "does Mr. Gwynn have a wife?"

"Aunt Hen!" This was from me and Livvy in unison.

She refused to be embarrassed. "Well, it's certainly something we need to know. It isn't as if any one of you three couldn't use an eligible *parti.*" She frowned at me. "Some people refuse to take advantage of opportunities."

I felt my face flame. The only suitable retort was throttling Aunt Hen and that wasn't possible right now. Worse, she was still speaking. "I really don't think any of the girls can refuse an introduction to an eligible gentleman." She turned back to Lymond. "Well? Is he attached or not?"

Lymond tried unsuccessfully to suppress his laughter. "No, Kenyon isn't married—or at least, he wasn't, the last I heard. As of last week, he wasn't attached at all."

"Then I'm sure Roxanne will make arrangements to have Bucephalus kept on a chain," Aunt Hen said, nibbling more fruitcake. She had lately decided that fruitcake was good for her. "It's all settled." She smiled around at all of us.

There was no arguing with Aunt Hen when she was on the trail of an eligible bachelor for any of us. "I'll do my best," I said, "but you know Bucephalus doesn't take kindly to being chained up. The last time we tried it, he pulled up the stakes and dragged them around until Holmwood managed to catch him."

"Tie him to a tree," Julia suggested.

I gave her a withering look; that suggestion didn't deserve a reply. "Tell me, Lymond," I said in reply, "is Mr. Gwynn coming to Bellerophon immediately?"

"He's coming here right away and then going to London with us. I suppose he'll go home from there."

Aunt Hen nodded. "Wonderful." I could see she already had one of us married off to Mr. Gwynn. I tried to give her a warning look but she ignored me. I made a face at Livvy and she made one back. To keep Aunt Hen from saying anything else that might embarrass us, Livvy started chattering about the wedding plans.

After some desultory conversation, Lymond got up. "Are you going to London to get your things and then come back?" I asked, more for information than because I really wanted to know.

Aunt Hen, Lymond, Livvy, and Julia looked at me in surprise. "I'm here now," Lymond said.

"Well, I can certainly see that, Lymond," I said with asperity. "I wanted to know when we need to expect you to move in."

"Now." He looked at me and smiled broadly. "You weren't here when I came. I had my things taken upstairs to my room. I'm here to stay, Roxanne." He took a step towards me and stepped on Bue's tail. Bue set up a howl that would wake the dead from their tombs and leaped to his feet, knocking over the tea table and tea set. He braced on all four feet and bared his teeth at Lymond, snarling and drooling.

"Nice doggie," Lymond said, backing up into me. "Roxanne, call off your beast."

"I can't do a thing with him lately," I said, smiling as I left the room. As I went along the hall towards the back and my room, I could hear Lymond trying to talk above Bue's snarls. "Nice doggie, nice Bucephalus." It didn't seem to be working.

I tried not to chuckle until I got inside my room and shut the door.

Chapter 2

We were spared the visit by Mr. Gwynn—he wrote Lymond that some sort of pressing business had detained him, but that he would meet Lymond in London. Lymond himself was no bother this visit. He spent most of his time in Brighton visiting his friends stationed there with the dragoons. The rest of the time he spent with Aunt Hen and the other girls. I think several hours were spent with Cassie discussing the various excellent traits of Captain Amherst. Cassie never tired of hearing about her betrothed.

I saw very little of Lymond. I had decided—finally—to force myself to complete Papa's translation of Xenophon. I had worked on it off and on—mostly off—since Papa's death and wanted to finish it as something of a memorial to him. I worked on it during the mornings, spent the afternoons reading and working on either the wedding plans and announcements or the household accounts, and worked on the Xenophon again at night. Some nights I was persuaded to spend with Lymond, Aunt Hen, and the girls, playing cards or listening to music, but not often. I was still put out with Lymond for completely ignoring me.

Xenophon was not completed when it was time for

us to go to London and I abandoned it once again. Cassie was in alt, Aunt Hen was in a dither, and Lymond was horrified at the thought of having to escort a whole carriage full of females by himself. I was still worried about the invitation to stay at his family's house.

"You're sure, Lymond, that we won't be imposing?" I asked for the dozenth time. "I couldn't bear to just barge in on anyone."

"No one's there except Amelia, and you know her well," he said patiently, just as he had every time before. "Everyone else has gone to Scotland for the wedding—even Mother, although I had hoped she'd stay in London." I ignored his look at this point, and he continued. "Wyricke was relieved that we were going to stay in the house because he thought it would keep the staff in trim if we were there. You know how staff get lax when the house is empty."

I didn't know, but I nodded in agreement. "All right," I said with a sigh. "I won't ask again."

"It won't do much good since we're already on our way," Julia said. "I, for one, am looking forward to it." Everyone nodded in agreement except Cassie. She just sat there and looked ethereal. No doubt she was thinking of Captain Amherst.

Lymond's London house actually belonged to his brother, the earl of Wyricke, but Lymond's family seemed to be one of those large, cheerful families where everyone is always welcome and they come and go at will. The house itself was located on Berkeley Square and was much larger than I had expected. Actually, it would hold all of us, Lymond's entire family, and perhaps a half dozen of Lymond's army friends. We got out of the carriage and looked up at it. I tried not to appear impressed, but the other girls—there's no other word for it—gawked like country misses.

"Come along," I said, to get them off the sidewalk. "We'll send someone out for the baggage." I herded them inside and Lymond came in behind us. The butler reminded me a little of Woodbury, all stiff and formal, but he certainly didn't have Woodbury's human touch. "See to the bags, Carlsen," Lymond said, moving us right along to have the housekeeper show us to our rooms.

"Mr. Lymond," Carlsen murmured in the perfect butler voice—authoritative, yet unobtrusive. "May I have a word?"

He and Lymond conferred for a few seconds in a corner while we stood in the hall. Lymond came over to us. "It seems there's been a slight change in plans," he said, "but it's really of no consequence." He hesitated. "It seems that my Uncle Harley is here for a very short visit. I'm sure it won't matter a bit."

"Did I hear someone out here?" I recognized the voice immediately. It was Lymond's sister-in-law, Amelia. In a second, she came rushing into the hall. "Robert! Aunt Henrietta! Cassandra! Julia! Olivia! Roxanne!" Amelia had a regrettable tendency to speak in exclamation points. "How delightful! I'm so glad to see you!"

Lymond gave her a brotherly peck on the forehead. "I thought you'd be off with everyone else at the wedding. You're not"—he searched for the right word—"indisposed?"

Amelia laughed. "No, Robert, I'm not indisposed. When I heard you were bringing all the Sydneys and Mrs. Vellory up for a visit, I purposely stayed home. I promised to attend Cassandra's wedding anyway." She smiled at us as she spoke, then turned to Lymond

22

with a small frown. "Did Carlsen tell you that Uncle Harley is here?"

Lymond nodded and they both looked at us. It was time for me to take the lead. "Do we know your Uncle Harley? I hope we're not intruding on his visit."

Amelia sighed and took Aunt Hen's arm to lead us to the drawing room. "Let's go in here and have some tea while your baggage is carried up. Robert and I will tell you all about Uncle Harley."

We had all settled down to tea and cakes and were just beginning to be comfortable when the door was thrown open. It banged against the wall with a crash that caused all of us to jump. A large man stood in the doorway, dressed all in grays and black. His hair was a frizzy gray and stood out around his head as if it had a life of its own. He had a high forehead and rather bushy black eyebrows. Those brows were drawn together quite ferociously as he glared at each of us in turn.

"All right! Who moved my copy of Dr. Johnson's *Dictionary?* I want it and I want it now! Which one of you touched it?" The gentleman stood, filling the entire doorway as he pinned each of us in turn with a questioning stare.

"Uncle Harley," Lymond said under his breath to me as we waited for the stare to pass us by. "Curmudgeon of the clan." He stood and smiled at Uncle Harley. His smile, which usually stood him in good stead, especially with females, had no effect whatsoever on Uncle Harley.

"I'm sure no one here knows about your *Dictionary,* Uncle Harley," he said in the level, reasonable tone most people use for wayward animals. Lymond used the same tone on Bucephalus. "I'm sure it's just been misplaced. Have you looked in the library?"

"Misplaced! I've never misplaced a book in my life. And as for that inane suggestion— Have I looked in the library? *Have I looked in the library!*" His voice reverberated from the walls. "Of course I've looked in the library! It was the first place I looked! I tell you, someone's taken it and I may never see it again."

Amelia stood and tried to make the introductions. "Uncle Harley, we'll search for your book in a moment. In the meantime, let me introduce you to Robert's guests."

"I don't have time for guests. Don't know the lot of them anyway. Besides, Robert's a fribble. Don't know a book from a brick, I'd wager. I want my *Dictionary!*" He glared at us once again and stamped out of the room, slamming the door closed behind him. We could hear him yelling at some poor unfortunate down the hall.

"Do you think you need to come to someone's rescue?" Amelia said to Lymond, listening to the din. "I worry about Uncle Harley chasing off the servants."

Lymond, the fribble, listened at the door and then returned to his seat beside me. "He's just yelling at Mowbridge. I think Mowbridge is accustomed to Uncle Harley by now." He turned to us with an apologetic smile. "Mowbridge is Uncle Harley's personal librarian."

"Uncle Harley is a bibliophile," Amelia explained.

Lymond sighed. "Not just an ordinary bibliophile. Uncle Harley is a bibliophile of the first water. Uncle Harley's whole life is his books. He collects them and has one of the most extensive and valuable collections of rare books in England."

"In the world, to hear him tell it," Amelia said.

"I suppose that's true, Amelia." Lymond paused as though to say something else. He evidently thought

24

better of it and contented himself with smiling at us again. "Carlsen tells me that Uncle Harley will be here for a few days. He's on the track of another rare book so he'll probably be out of the house most of the time. We may see him at meals or we may not. Just bear with him when he's here." Lymond smiled again and I could see Aunt Hen melt. Lymond's smile usually had that effect on her.

"I understand," Cassie said. "Papa was rather caught up in his collections."

Lymond squirmed slightly. "Uncle Harley gets more than just caught up. He's rather like a bloodhound on the trail once he hears of a rare book for sale."

"I would imagine that since so few rare books exist, collectors must be clamoring for every one of them." Livvy said. "It must be rather difficult for him if he misses one."

"Difficult isn't the word," Amelia said fervently, giving Lymond a significant look.

"Hell hath no fury like Uncle Harley thwarted," Lymond said. "Perhaps if he misses whatever he's after this time, he'll simply go back home and lick his wounds."

"We can only hope." Amelia lowered her voice and glanced anxiously at the door.

Aunt Hen looked around at us. "I thought he seemed a very nice man." We all looked at her as if she had taken leave of her senses. "Well, I did. As Livvy said, collectors are occasionally temperamental. Poor George had his quirks, you know."

I raised an eyebrow. Papa would never have acted so before company, but I refrained from commenting. Instead, I steered Cassie to the topic of her wedding and we shortly went up to our rooms to supervise the unpacking and rest for supper. Cassie, I believe, also wanted to write a note to inform her beloved that she was now in London.

Supper was uneventful, Captain Amherst came over later and he and Cassie spent the evening gazing into each other's eyes. All in all it was a rather boring evening for the rest of us. Lymond and Amelia were on tenterhooks all evening. Uncle Harley still had not found his dictionary and, worse, he was miserable over a bid he was preparing on a rare book. It seems Uncle Harley was ordinarily something more than frugal, but he wanted this particular book badly. The poor man was torn between twin evils: losing the book or parting with his money. He didn't join us for supper or later; Lymond said he was closeted with Mowbridge, discussing the bid proposal. Amelia allowed as it was just as well and I gathered Uncle Harley was not a favorite for social evenings.

I rose early and dressed to go down for breakfast. Julia came out of her room as I exited mine. She looked wretched. "Whatever is the matter, Julia?" I asked, concerned. She didn't look particularly ill, just sleepy and bedraggled.

"It's that man," she whispered, pointing to the door next to hers. "He ranted and cursed all night. I could hear him through the fireplace. He must have spent an hour or more berating that poor Mr. Mowbridge, then he cursed someone named Spencer for another hour. All in all, I scarcely slept all night."

I patted her on the shoulder. "Let's eat breakfast, then you can go back and get some more sleep this morning. Lymond told me his uncle was going out to bid on a rare book of some kind or the other." With that, we went downstairs to eat.

To Julia's horror, a very personable young man was sitting in the breakfast room, having a cup of coffee with Lymond. He stood as we entered. He was of average height, well built and wearing a blue coat that showed off his shoulders to advantage. His skin was dark and tanned. I thought he must have been in the sun quite a bit as his dark hair still showed the effects of sun streaks, especially on the ends. His eyes were a warm brown. He would have been a very handsome man except for a scar which ran down one side of his face. It ran down his forehead, through one eyebrow, giving that brow a satanic arch, then finished on his cheek, near his ear. It was a thin white line on his tanned face. When he stood, I noticed that his hand was scarred as well. It looked as if the back of his left hand had been slashed several times across.

Lymond stood as we entered. "Miss Roxanne Sydney, Miss Julia Sydney, may I present my friend, Kenyon Gwynn." Mr. Gwynn nodded at us and we sat. I could hear Julia's sharp intake of breath and knew she must be regretting her appearance. It was a shame she looked so wretched this morning.

"It's a pleasure—" Mr. Gwynn began, but was interrupted by a bellow from the hall. "Mowbridge! Mowbridge! Do you expect me to wait all day! You know that damned scoundrel Spencer will beat me to that book if we dally. Come on!"

"You remember Uncle Harley," Lymond murmured to Mr. Gwynn.

"Boots's father?" Gwynn asked with surprise. "He's still alive?"

"Still alive and bellowing," Lymond said with a sigh. "Boots stays away as much as possible."

Lymond could be so rag-mannered at times. It was time to remind him we were present. "I don't believe

27

I know someone named Boots," I said, getting my breakfast and some for Julia. She was too mortified to get up.

Lymond and Mr. Gwynn looked at each other. "Boots is my age," Lymond said with a grin, "and is Uncle Harley's son. His mission in life is to spend every penny of Uncle Harley's money, a difficult thing to do since Uncle Harley is equally determined to hold on to every shilling."

"Sinclair's still a little clutchfisted?" Mr. Gwynn asked with a smile.

Lymond rolled his eyes upward. "Clutchfisted is hardly the word. Right now, Uncle Harley is in agony. He's bidding on a very rare edition of Boccaccio—a 1471 I believe he said—and it's going to cost a pretty penny. Lord Spencer wants it as well, so Uncle Harley is going to have to top Spencer's price."

Gwynn laughed. "He must be in agony."

"To put it mildly."

"He was up all night," Julia offered. "His room is next to mine and I heard him most of the night."

Lymond looked at her quickly, then looked again at her red, puffy eyes and assessed the damage. "I'm sorry, Miss Sydney. I'll find another room for you until Uncle Harley leaves. I should have thought of that."

"Mowbridge! I'm leaving!" It was almost more than a bellow. The door slammed, but in just a moment we heard someone muttering in the hall and then going out. "Mowbridge." Lymond leaned back in his chair and let out a long breath. "I think poor Aunt Lenore died in self-defense. Life with Uncle Harley can be hectic."

"Unless you're a book," Kenyon Gwynn said with a laugh. We all joined him. I was glad to see Julia laughing and enjoying herself.

After breakfast, we spent the day seeing to wedding arrangements, buying all those little things that can only be found in London, and writing notes to our relatives scattered around London, reminding them of Cassie's wedding. We all gathered for tea in the late afternoon, thoroughly glad to sit and relax for a short while. Even Cassie, who had floated through the day, was exhausted.

Amelia had asked Aunt Hen to be the hostess, and she had just begun to pour our tea when the door was flung open again. Uncle Harley was there, glowering at the lot of us. Mr. Gwynn, who wasn't staying at the house, had stopped by to arrange for an evening with Lymond at his club, and he was, unfortunately, closest to the door.

"Are you the one who took my *Dictionary?*" Uncle Harley bellowed, pinning poor Gwynn with a look. "Or are you the spy in our midst?" He shifted his gaze to include the rest of us. "I know one of you is a spy and you might as well admit it. Spencer is paying one of you to tell him what I'm doing." He walked over and tapped Mr. Gwynn on the chest with a forefinger. "Did you? Well, man, answer me. Did you do it?" Before waiting for an answer, Uncle Harley turned to Lymond. "It's all your fault, Robert. You've brought a nest of vipers into my bosom. Which one is the traitor?"

Lymond, to my surprise, didn't cower before this onslaught. "None of us, of course," he said coolly. "Am I correct in assuming, Uncle Harley," he continued, offering a rather stiff glass of whiskey, "that your bid on the Boccaccio wasn't sufficient?"

Uncle Harley snatched the whiskey and downed it at one gulp. "Damned Spencer beat me out of it. Someone had to have told him what I planned to bid.

Now it's his. A 1471 Boccaccio. It would have been the jewel of my collection." He sat down heavily and extended the glass for a refill. "I won't take this sitting down, I tell you. I intend to find a book that will turn Spencer green with envy. He'll come crawling to my library just for a look at it."

"I've seen your library, Mr. Sinclair," Gwynn offered, "and I would think anyone would be proud of your collection."

Uncle Harley relaxed a bit. I wasn't sure if it was the whiskey or the praise, but suspected the whiskey. "I am proud of it. What did you say your name was?" Before Gwynn could answer him, he turned to Lymond. "I'm getting damned old. I used to remember names just like that." He snapped his fingers. "That must be why Spencer beat me out—he's a trifle younger. The mind goes first." He extended his empty glass to Lymond once again.

Lymond took the lull in Uncle Harley's remblings not only to refill the glass, but also to make introductions all around. We all made polite noises, but only Kenyon Gwynn struck up a conversation.

"I saw your library some years ago and it was a marvel then," Gwynn said, risking a chair beside Uncle Harley. "I believe you had several extremely rare books then."

"I have more now," Uncle Harley said, sipping the whiskey. "When were you there? I don't remember you at all. Do you collect books?"

Gwynn shook his head and the light seemed to catch the white line of his scar and highlight it. For a moment, it made him look rather sinister. "No, I don't collect books. I enjoy them, but that's all. I visited your house several years ago. Boots took me home with him during a school holiday."

30

"Boots." Uncle Harley said the word with obvious disdain. "The pup doesn't know a book from a brick. The only things he knows about are the denominations of money and the faces on cards. He knows those well." He drained his glass and gave Gwynn a look. "I can't say that knowing Boots is any recommendation."

Gwynn smiled and took no offense. "It just takes some men longer to grow up than it does others." He changed the subject before Uncle Harley could comment further on his son. "Tell me, Mr. Sinclair, what have you acquired lately? Do you have any prospects other than the Boccaccio?"

Uncle Harley was off and running. We heard more about books than I had ever wanted to know. It seemed there was a rather fine edition of the Koran he had spotted and he intended to beat Spencer to it—if someone didn't warn Spencer first. This was said with a glare that included the lot of us.

"Books are so interesting," Aunt Hen said finally, smiling at Uncle Harley. "I've often told dear Roxanne so."

I tried not to stare at her. The only thing Aunt Hen knew about books was that they had to be dusted regularly. "Poor George was always buying old books and things." Avarice hit Aunt Hen full force and she turned to me with wonder in her eyes. "You've got shelves and shelves of old books at Bellerophon, Roxanne. One of them might be worth a fortune. Didn't George say that one of those scroll things was very old?"

Uncle Harley jumped to his feet, ran across to Aunt Hen, and seized her hands in his. "What's that? What books? Scrolls! You have scrolls! Tell me about them! Whatever you do, let me look at them first. Spencer will be after them if he hears about them. Where are they?"

"Really, Aunt Hen," I began, but it was too late—Uncle Harley was like a bloodhound on the scent. He left Aunt Hen and came to stand in front of me. "They're yours? You own these scrolls and books?" An amazing transformation came over him. He sat down beside me, leaned back comfortably, and gave me a winning smile. He looked amazingly as Lymond always did when he asked for something. "Tell me about these books and scrolls," Uncle Harley said, smiling. "Where are they?"

Aunt Hen was not to be denied. "They're at our house, Bellerophon, in Brighton. Poor George left a whole library—boxes and shelves full—of books and scrolls." She smiled and leaned back in her chair. "Just think, Roxanne, this may be the Treasure. It would be just like poor George to keep his money in books. We may have books worth thousands and thousands. Didn't you once tell me you had one of those ancient—what was it?—an *Illyrian?*"

"*Iliad.*" I corrected her without thinking. Aunt Hen's education had been sadly neglected. "But I don't think . . ."

"A copy of the *Iliad?* In scroll form?" Uncle Harley was more than genial—he was effusive. "Could you describe it?"

"I really haven't seen it in a while," I told him, concentrating on the last time I had run across the scroll. "Actually, I haven't seen it since right before Papa was ki- . . . before Papa died." I looked around at the other girls. "Have you seen it anywhere?"

No one seemed to have seen it, and like me, hadn't really missed it. "I suppose it's in the library somewhere," I told Uncle Harley. "I really don't know. It's probably nothing."

32

"But it may be important," he persisted. "Tell me about it. Do you know anything about its history?"

I really didn't wish to encourage him. "No, nothing definite."

"Now, Roxanne," Aunt Hen said, still on the trail of some cash, "didn't George tell you it was from some city and had belonged to someone famous? I seem to recall that. George was rather proud of having acquired it."

"I think Papa was more proud of his edition of William Blake. He had one of the original watercolored ones," Livvy said, looking at me. "Didn't he have a Milton as well?" Livvy and Julia were looking just like Aunt Hen, avarice gleaming in their eyes. "Then there were those boxes and boxes of scrolls," Julia said. "Perhaps the *Iliad* is in one of those."

"Boxes and boxes?" Uncle Harley could scarcely restrain himself. "Do tell me about them. I want to know exactly what you know about the history of the *Iliad* scroll."

"It's probably nothing," I said wearily, giving up. "Papa was always collecting artifacts and things, most of them quite worthless. As for this scroll, he was somewhere in Turkey looking for a trace of Alexander the Great and an old man sold him a box of scrolls, none of which we can decipher. He also sold him one scroll encased in a leather bag of its own. That one seems to be the *Iliad* written in Greek. The old man swore that it came from the old city of Samarkand and belonged to Alexander the Great." I paused to allow Uncle Harley to control himself. He was breathing heavily. "Of course, I don't believe for a moment that a scroll could have survived from the time of Alexander the Great. It just isn't possible. I can translate the Greek myself, so it's probably a rather modern copy. Papa didn't check it—he was the quintessential gullible tourist. He bought anything and everything.''

"But it could be Alexander's," Aunt Hen said. "Stranger things have happened."

"Really, Aunt Hen," I began again, but was stopped. Uncle Harley had regained his breath and he turned and grabbed my hands. "When can I see it— see them? I want to see everything you have. Why don't we leave tomorrow? I have time."

I looked at Lymond in supplication, but he was grinning. He was actually enjoying this. I looked back at Uncle Harley. "I don't really . . ." I began, but Uncle Harley forestalled me.

"As for accommodations, I hear Robert has leased a house in Brighton. I could stay there." He turned to Lymond. "You won't mind a house guest or two, I'm sure, Robert."

This wiped the smile from Lymond's face. "I really don't know, Uncle Harley. I don't plan . . ."

"Wonderful," Uncle Harley said. "I knew there'd be no problem." He looked back at me. "When can you leave? Brighton isn't overly large, so I'm sure Robert's house will be close by. What did you say the name of your house was—Bellerophon?''

I nodded, enjoying the rather distressed look on Lymond's face. Perhaps he could deal with Uncle Harley and I wouldn't have to be bothered. "You'll have to discuss this with Lymond. Actually, he leases Bellerophon, or part of it at any rate, from us. Since he has the lease, I insist that he be there if anything is touched. As for our family, we have a wedding coming up shortly, so we need to stay in London for a while." I smiled at Lymond as Uncle Harley released my fingers and turned to begin on Lymond. "I'm sure Lymond would be delighted to take you to Bellerophon and show

34

you the library while we're here." I looked around at the girls. "I believe we need to go upstairs and rest for dinner."

"Wait a minute, Roxanne," Lymond said, peering around Uncle Harley. "We need to discuss this."

It was too late. I gave him a sweet smile as I herded Aunt Hen and the girls out the door. He would have to deal with Uncle Harley. I had things of my own to say to Aunt Hen.

Chapter 3

Once upstairs, I rounded on Aunt Hen. "Now Roxanne, dear," she said mildly, "what's the harm? After all, Mr. Sinclair seems to be quite knowledgeable, and I have it on good authority that he's rich. We might have the treasure right in the library."

"You know how Papa collected junk," I said. "I'm sure it's nothing but another copy of the *Iliad*. We must have a dozen."

Cassie smiled at me. "It won't hurt to find out, Roxanne," she said. "After all, one or two of those things might be valuable. I agree with you that it's unlikely the scroll belonged to Alexander, but it still might be worth something."

Julia and Livvy agreed, and Julia didn't hesitate to point out that we could use the cash if there was any. We were in the middle of our discussion when there was a knock at my door.

"Roxanne," Lymond said from outside the door, "I need to talk to you."

"I'm sorry, Lymond," I called back. "I'm indisposed."

Julia looked at me scandalized and started to say something, but I quieted her. "Roxanne," Lymond said again, his voice low, "we need to talk about Uncle Harley. He's hell-bent on going to Bellerophon. Preferably within the hour."

"You'll just have to take care of it, Lymond," I called back. "I really can't do anything until after the wedding is over."

"Roxanne," he said again, "are you clothed? If not, you'd better get that way by the time I count five, because I'm coming in. You have to get Uncle Harley off my back. One, two . . ."

Aunt Hen looked at me with round eyes. Before I could stop her, she dashed across the room and flung the door open. "Do come in, Robert," she said. "We were just discussing the situation."

"And what did you conclude?"

"We think it's a good idea for your uncle to look at Papa's library and tell us if anything is valuable," Julia said, knocking over my powder box. She and I started sneezing as powder wafted over both our gowns. It took a good five minutes to brush us off. By that time, Lymond had appropriated my chair.

"I think it's a good idea as well," Lymond said, continuing the conversation. The rest of us were seated on the bed, lined up like students in a nursery. "Uncle Harley may be eccentric, but he does know his books. I don't know why I hadn't thought of it before, but he would be able to tell you if there was anything valuable in your father's library."

"I knew it," Aunt Hen said triumphantly.

"Very well, Lymond," I said. "I told you that you could take him to Bellerophon. Just don't bother me with it."

Lymond shook his head. "I may have the house leased, but I'm certainly not going to prowl through your father's library when you aren't there. I think I can persuade Uncle Harley to wait a fortnight until after the wedding. I'll go along—and a sacrifice on my part this is—but you'll have to show him the library.''

I looked at Lymond closely and saw the corner of his mouth twitching. "You did this on purpose," I accused him. "You just want us to be there so you won't have to deal with your uncle.''

"We'd be delighted to," Aunt Hen said, "wouldn't we, girls?''

They all agreed, and Lymond rose to leave. "Thank you, ladies," he said with the same engaging smile I had seen Uncle Harley employ when he wanted something. He started to say something else, but contented himself with smirking in my direction. I really wanted to do something childish, like stick out my tongue at him. Actually, I did, after the door was closed.

Aunt Hen looked at me sternly. "Now, Roxanne, what's the harm of having a houseguest once in a while? This will be to our great benefit and, after all, Mr. Sinclair is certainly someone we'd be proud to invite to stay with us.''

"Besides," Livvy pointed out, "he won't be staying with us. he'll be staying with Lymond, so we won't see him that much.''

"He'll still be at Bellerophon," I noted, "and rummaging through everything in the library. You all know that Papa didn't like to have his things bothered.''

"All the more reason to invite him," Aunt Hen said illogically. I looked at her in surprise and she explained. "Roxanne, I know you've hesitated to examine anything in the library since your father was mur- . . . since poor George's death. It's time to look through it and weed it out.''

"That's not true." I was indignant. "We've turned

every book and every artifact in that library over a dozen times looking for the treasure.''

"That's why I think the treasure is that book," Aunt Hen said, a smug smile on her face. "It would be just like George to do that. Mr. Sinclair may recognize it immediately and we'll be rich, rich.''

"What we'll be is insane by the time Uncle Harley spends two nights under our roof," I said, but I was ignored in the general hubbub. The word "rich" seemed to have settled the matter for everyone except me.

When we went down for supper, we discovered that Lymond had, by some miracle, managed to talk Uncle Harley into going back to his home, then joining us in Brighton after the wedding. "I could just imagine him throughout the wedding, urging the minister to hurry so he could get at your books," Lymond whispered to me as we watched Uncle Harley try to discover from Aunt Hen what wonderful items might be in our library. Uncle Harley had no idea that Aunt Hen hadn't read a book in years unless it came from the Minerva Press.

"I suppose I should thank you for that, at least," I murmured back to him. "Aunt Hen and the girls are convinced that Uncle Harley is going to discover Agamemnon's treasure. They now think it's in the form of a rare book, no doubt written by Agamemnon himself." I surveyed the lot of them, hanging on to Uncle Harley's every word. "Lymond, I blame you for this whole fiasco.''

"I," Lymond said stiffly, "am not to blame for Uncle Harley. Believe me, I dodge him at every opportunity.''

I regretted my tone and smiled at him. "I didn't mean that, Lymond, and you know it. I imagine having to entertain your uncle at Bellerophon will be something of a trial for you."

"If I'm near you, I can bear it."

I glanced at him sharply, but he didn't seem to be smiling. In fact, he wasn't even looking at me—he was staring off into the distance, looking at nothing. I decided I hadn't heard him correctly and almost embarrassed myself by asking him to repeat what he had said. I caught myself just in time and changed the subject to cover my confusion.

We spent the remainder of the evening discussing the latest *on-dits*. While the rest of us were unpacking, Livvy had gone out for a few minutes to visit our cousin Lydia and tell her we were in London. Livvy now had all sorts of gossip to share with us. Lydia was better than the *Morning Post*.

The next morning, Uncle Harley left us, rather reluctantly. He didn't seem at all happy to leave, and kept asking if we intended to let Spencer look at Bellerophon's library first. After the better part of an hour, while his carriage and horses stomped impatiently outside, I finally wrote a note granting Uncle Harley first crack at the library and signed it. Uncle Harley carefully gave it to Mowbridge with instructions to file it. Behind Uncle Harley's back, Mowbridge rolled his eyes heavenward and gave me a look that spoke volumes.

"I'm surprised Mowbridge stays with him," I said to Lymond as their carriage finally rolled away. "It seems poor Mowbridge is quite put upon."

Lymond laughed. "I don't think Mowbridge would work anywhere else. Life with Uncle Harley does have its moments."

"But what kind of moments are they?" Julia asked at my elbow. "The poor man must never get any sleep." Julia was still red-eyed.

We laughed, but one thing still puzzled me. "Lymond, didn't you say that your uncle was somewhat frugal? I would think an excellent librarian like Mowbridge could ask his own wage."

"He can, and does," Lymond said with a grin. "Uncle Harley pays him quite well and almost goes into apoplexy every payday. However, he knows Mowbridge's worth. Besides," he added with a laugh, "Spencer once offered Mowbridge a position. Uncle Harley would keep the man or die." Lymond reached out and took my hand, much to my surprise. "Would you like to tour around London with me today?"

Instinctively, I pulled my hand away. "I need to help Cassie," I said and fled up the stairs, leaving Lymond and Julia there. I glanced back to see Julia staring at me with round-eyed wonder while Lymond chuckled.

Actually, Cassie didn't need me at all, but I needed some time to think. I had once thought Lymond had been interested in an attachment, but then he seemed so distant. I certainly didn't want to appear to be chasing him, but on the other hand, neither did I want to be just a momentary dalliance while we were in London. I wasn't really sure of my feelings for him, anyway. Perhaps, after the wedding, I could organize my thoughts. Until then, I determined to stay clear of him.

That was easier said than done. During the following days, Lymond was always at my elbow, always organizing some trip or other. He, of course, had Captain Amherst along to escort Cassie, and Kenyon Gwynn usually came along to entertain the rest of us. Lymond seldom walked beside me, however; he customarily escorted Aunt Hen, a courtesy she enjoyed tremendously. She almost played the coquette around him. Since Livvy was more often with cousin Lydia than with us, Julia and I were usually in Mr. Gwynn's company.

There was an unexpected problem in this quarter: Julia seemed quite ill at ease around Mr. Gwynn. I was surprised, since she was usually most agreeable and affable, so I asked her why, and her answer was doubly puzzling. She blushed profusely, stammered a great deal, but couldn't give me a reason. So, on our outings, I acted as a buffer and spent most of my time in conversation with Mr. Gwynn. I couldn't understand Julia's discomfort since I found him most personable and a good conversationalist. He told us stories of life in South Carolina, laughing at our notions of a dangerous land inhabited by Indians It seemed South Carolina was a place of genteel plantations, lively social life, and a great deal of hard work. He never mentioned his scar and I often wondered about it. I thought of asking Lymond, but the opportunity didn't present itself.

As the day for the wedding drew nearer, Cassie seemed to become calmer and calmer as I grew more and more frantic. There were so many things to do, but she didn't seem to notice. "You take care of it, Roxanne," she said to whatever I asked of her. Livvy and Julia seemed also to believe that every detail would take care of itself. As the date drew nearer, I felt rather like a mouse scurrying from one thing to another while everyone else sat and watched me.

At last the wedding day arrived. Livvy and Julia produced their handiwork and I was surprised at what they had done. They had done much more than I had given them credit for. They had made Cassie a beautiful dress. She had always fancied light or white clothing—a difficult choice on laundry day—and the girls had fashioned her a dress in pure white. It was in the

Grecian style that suited Cassie, and Julia bound Cassie's hair up with ribbons and flowers. "There," Julia said, standing back to admire her handiwork as Cassie spun around in front of us, "doesn't she look just like Diana?"

"I think you mean Aphrodite," I said, "and yes, she does." In truth, Cassie was the most beautiful bride I had ever seen. Part of her beauty was the radiant glow that seemed all around her. The same glow seemed to suffuse the ceremony. Captain Amherst was the perfect, handsome groom and when they looked at each other, they saw no one else. It was a fairy-tale wedding.

As the carriage rolled away taking them to the coast, Cassie waved good-bye to us and, I confess, I had a feeling of great sadness. One part of my life seemed to be over. Livvy and Julia must have felt the same thing as we all looked at each other with the same understanding. "She'll be back soon," I said. "After all, they're merely going to Italy for their honeymoon."

Julia and Livvy nodded, but said nothing. They knew as well as I that even when Cassie returned, things would never be the same. Aunt Hen, however, put things in perspective for us. "Well," she said briskly, going back into the house, "that's one fired off. Now we've got to see about the rest of you. Roxanne, you . . ."

"Enough, Aunt Hen," I said. "No more talk of weddings."

She gave me a look and I knew I hadn't heard the last of it. "Now, Roxanne, you must agree with me. Weddings are quite necessary and so beautiful."

"Necessary, perhaps, but they're nothing but a great deal of bother. All of us have worked our fingers off to make this wedding beautiful."

"The next one will be easier for you, Roxanne. Unless, of course, it's your own, and then, naturally, the work will be on the rest of us."

"Aunt Hen," I said in warning, "don't start on me now. My nerves are frazzled enough as it is."

"You'd make a beautiful bride."

I felt the urgent need to go to crawl into a quiet, dark corner with a cup of tea and did just that.

We stayed in London two more days as Mr. Gwynn and Lymond had planned to escort us to the theater. There, as we were sitting in our box, Lymond's friend Debenham stopped by and asked him outside for a private conversation. Lymond looked rather grim when he rejoined us. "Do you tell us what's going on, or must we guess?" I whispered to him as the play resumed.

"Nothing." He sat back and appeared to concentrate on the play, but was really scanning each member of the audience, apparently looking for someone. He excused himself after a few minutes and left us. I kept my eyes on the audience, but didn't see him. He still hadn't returned by the time the play was over. "We'll need to wait on Lymond," I said to Mr. Gwynn as we rose.

Gwynn shook his head. "He told me to escort you back home. I think he saw someone he knows and plans to visit for a while."

I lifted an eyebrow. "Rather rag-mannered of him. I wouldn't have thought it of Lymond."

As we were getting ready to leave our box, a man came in. He was about Gwynn's height, and was slender. His hair was fair—more blond than brown—and his eyes seemed to be a pale blue that almost made them look a slate color. He was pale, as though he seldom went out in the daytime. He walked in rather arrogantly, looked around, and dismissed us with a glance. "Is Robert Lymond with you?" he asked of Gwynn. "I thought I saw him."

"He was with us, but he left a short while ago," Gwynn said, looking at the man carefully. "Boots? Is that you?"

Boots looked surprised, then took another look at Gwynn. "Yes. Gwynn, isn't it? Edward?"

"Kenyon."

Boots nodded the briefest of acknowledgments. "I was looking for cousin Robert. I have something rather important to discuss with him." Before he could say anything else, another man appeared behind him, taller than Boots, and much darker. The man nodded at us pleasantly, smiled, and touched Boots on the arm. Boots jerked involuntarily, then steadied himself. "Tell Robert I'll see him later," he said and left without introducing the other man.

"Bad manners must run in the family," I muttered to Aunt Hen. She frowned at me. As far as she's concerned, Lymond can do no wrong, and that extends to his family as well.

"Was that Mr. Sinclair's son?" I asked Gwynn after we were in our carriage.

He nodded. "Yes, and I almost didn't know him. I know I've been away a while, but I've recognized most people. Boots has changed a great deal. He's still very fair, of course, but I remember him as being rather plump."

"He doesn't seem to resemble Harley," Aunt Hen said absently. I stared at her use of Mr. Sinclair's name. Evidently they had become better acquainted than I knew. No one else seemed to notice it.

"He doesn't at all," Gwynn said, "and I think that's

45

one of the reasons they don't get along. He doesn't resemble his father in looks or temperament."

To my surprise, Lymond was already at home when we arrived. He acted as though nothing was wrong with his disappearing and leaving us in the lurch. No one else remarked it either. In fact, we all had a cup of tea together and Gwynn went home. The rest of us started to bed. "By the way," I said, turning on the stairs, "your cousin Boots came by to see you at the theater."

To my surprise, Lymond paled and stopped dead in his tracks. The others had gone ahead, and he touched my arm to detain me. "Did he say anything?" Lymond's voice was low.

"Nothing at all. Although there was a man with him. What is it, Lymond?"

With a glance to see that the others were gone, he motioned me back into the drawing room and shut the door behind us. "All right, Lymond," I said, sitting down and pinning him with a look, "what's going on? You and Debenham are after some criminal again, I take it."

He sighed, sat down across from me and nodded. "There's been a murder," he said bluntly. "One of Uncle Harley's friends—a man named Havilland. Oh, it looked natural enough all right—the man was run over by a carriage and the body mangled until the real cause of death was almost unnoticed. Everyone thinks it was just another unfortunate accident."

"Who, what, where, when, and why?" I asked, knowing full well that I would have to drag every word from Lymond. Since he works for Debenham, he has this strange notion that only Debenham and the Home Office should know of his activities.

He glanced at me, clearly reluctant, and waved my

46

questions away. "I think I may have a clue to the murderer," he said. "I saw one of my informants at the theater. Debenham had seen him there and thought he might be looking for me. My informant thinks he might be able to discover a thing or two for me. He needed to talk to some people tonight and I'm to meet him again tomorrow."

"With a large amount of cash," I said dryly. Lymond nodded and I continued. "You still haven't answered my questions, Lymond. Who, what, where, when, and why?"

He leaned forward. "Listen to me, Roxanne. I'm only telling you this much so you won't become curious and start asking about things you shouldn't. You do seem to have an unfortunate tendency in that direction. I want to know about the man with Boots. Who was he?"

I shrugged. "I really don't know. Boots didn't introduce him to us. Actually, Boots didn't introduce himself either. Kenyon recognized him."

"Describe the man."

I grimaced. "Really, Lymond, why all this cloak-and-dagger pretense? He was simply an ordinary man. Slightly taller than Boots, much darker. I really didn't notice much of anything else."

Lymond stood up and paced the floor a moment, then sat back down. "Roxanne, I want you to go back to Brighton and entertain Uncle Harley and keep him there."

I laughed. "Lymond, you can't be serious. Your uncle is your problem." I paused, looking at the expression on his face. He wasn't teasing at all—he was deadly serious. "Do you think your uncle is in danger? You said his friend had been murdered."

Lymond shook his head. "I don't think he is, but I

don't really know. It may be only a coincidence that Havilland was also a book collector—or it may be a link. I just don't know." He paused. "Havilland's the second book collector to die within the space of a few days." He looked at me and gave me his appealing smile. "Please, Roxanne, just go to Brighton and entertain Uncle Harley. This is probably nothing, but I'd feel better if you could keep him there for a fortnight or so until Debenham and I solve this puzzle."

"A fortnight! Lymond, is this a trick to evade having to play host to your uncle? How can you ask me to do this? I hardly know the man." I rose to my feet. "I certainly will not! You'll come to Brighton and entertain him while he's there. I don't mind popping into the library from time to time, but that's all I intend to do. Do I make myself clear?"

"Perfectly." Lymond stood, his voice icy. "I should have known you'd be as stubborn as usual."

I started to reply to that, but he walked out of the room, leaving me standing there. I sat down hard on the chair, completely amazed at his manners, or rather his lack of manners. I was so overset that it took me until after midnight to realize that Lymond still hadn't answered a single one of my "who, what, where, when, and how" questions.

I was up early the next morning, determined to intercept Lymond and discover what was going on. We were due to leave for Brighton the next morning, so I wanted also to make sure that he planned to go. I neither wanted nor intended to be the hand that reined in Uncle Harley.

I had to wait until evening to see Lymond. He had gone out early, Carlsen told me. Thwarted by Lymond again, I spent the day packing and getting ready to return to Bellerophon. In the afternoon, Aunt Hen,

Julia, Livvy, and I visited Lydia and had a comfortable chat. We left early to return to Lymond's as we had planned an early supper and bedtime so we could get up and get started to Brighton. As we were at her door, Lydia turned to me in surprise. "Oh, Roxanne!" she exclaimed—Lydia also speaks in exclamation points—"I didn't know you had priceless objects of art at Bellerophon. Hendrix told me that your house was full of the most exquisite treasures."

All of us stared at her. We didn't know that either. "Who is Hendrix and how on earth did he know anything about Bellerophon?" I asked, dumbfounded.

"He's Wentworth's heir. I did think to ask him how he knew about it. He heard it from Brummell who had gotten it right from Cooke." She frowned as I prompted her, then she continued. "Yes, Cooke got it directly from Boots Sinclair. It seems his father is going to buy the whole lot for shillings." She looked at me. "Here I have been thinking you were . . ." She stopped, blushing.

"Your poor relations," I finished, laughing.

"Not really poor, but . . ."

Julia and Livvy looked at each other. "Imagine us being an *on-dit*," Julia said, making a face, "and not a word of truth in it."

Lydia stood there in her silks and looked at us in our muslins. "It isn't true, then? I wondered. Frazee tweaked me all evening about having such wealthy relatives."

"You've been to Bellerophon," I told her. "You know what's there."

"But then there's the tre—" Aunt Hen began, but Livvy kicked her sharply as I grabbed her arm. Lydia was better at disseminating news than the *Post* and the last thing we needed was gossip and word bandied about concerning a treasure. If that kind of story got around, we'd have thieves all over the place. They wouldn't find anything valuable, but door locks and windows were expensive to repair, not to mention the bother.

That evening, Lymond seemed distracted at supper. After supper, Amelia, Aunt Hen, Livvy, and Julia all gathered to say their good-byes, but I had other things to do. I slipped down to the library where I thought Lymond might be closeted. I started to knock, but at the last second, decided to just barge right in and pretend I was looking for a book. I opened the door casually and sauntered in, but stopped in shock. Lymond was in there with another man, handing over a sheaf of bank notes. The man wheeled and, with a gleam, a knife appeared almost magically in his hand.

"Put it away, Turner," Lymond said quietly, stepping between the man with the knife and me. In a second, the knife disappeared along with the bank notes and Turner brushed past me on his way out the door. He said nothing at all.

Lymond waited until Turner shut the door behind me. "I wasn't expecting company," he said in mild reproof.

I resorted to my first plan. "I was just coming down for a book to read. I'm not particularly sleepy."

Lymond had the audacity to laugh at me. "Roxanne, I know you all too well. You realized I hadn't answered your questions last night, so you came down here to badger me." He gave me his best smile and indicated a chair across from him. We both sat. "You might as well admit it."

"All right, Lymond," I said, "I admit it. I want to know what's going on. Now will you answer my questions?"

"No."

I thought I hadn't heard him correctly. "What did you say?"

"I said no." He leaned towards me. "Roxanne, I think the best thing you and your family can do is return to Bellerophon. I told you that Debenham and I think Havilland was murdered. The fact that he was a book collector and a close friend of Uncle Harley disturbs me. I'd prefer both you and Uncle Harley at Bellerophon where no one knows your location."

"Then you'd better tell me what you know, Lymond," I said, looking straight at him, trying to ignore his smile, "because everyone in London knows your uncle is coming to Bellerophon to search for rare books. Lydia told us all about it. She heard it from Hendrix who heard it from Brummell who got it from Cooke who was told all about it by Boots. We, your uncle, and our library are the *on-dit* of the day."

To my surprise, Lymond leaned back against his chair and began muttering. Only after a moment did I realize that he had fallen into an old habit: Lymond was cursing softly to himself. Lymond happens to be quite fluent in profanity, probably as a result of his days in the army.

"Really, Lymond!"

He glared at me, but stopped. "Do you know what this means, Roxanne? It means that you and Uncle Harley could be in danger."

"Don't be melodramatic, Lymond." I tried not to laugh at his distress. "What's really oversetting to you is that you're going to have to entertain your uncle for a while. I do hope you enjoy yourself at Brighton, Lymond." I stood up and looked down at him. He was rather florid from the stress of controlling himself.

"I'll leave so you can curse to your heart's content, Lymond," I said, leaving him with a dazzling smile.

It wasn't until I was already up the stairs that I realized that, once again, Lymond hadn't answered my questions.

Chapter 4

Early the next morning, I went to hunt up Lymond. I was going to insist that he accompany us to Brighton, or at least get his word that he would be there shortly. Thoughts of us coping with Uncle Harley were not to be borne. Besides, I still needed to get some answers to my questions.

Lymond was in the breakfast parlor, dressed for riding, and Kenyon Gwynn was with him. Questions were out, but I could still insist he go to Brighton. I sat down across the table from him and helped myself to chocolate and a muffin. "Lymond," I began, subtle at usual, "I insist you be at Bellerophon when your uncle is there. I want your word on it."

"I'm going with you," he said, a touch grimly, I thought. "If all of London thinks you're sitting on the greatest treasures this side of the Mona Lisa, I'd better be there to protect you."

I found this irritating. "I do not need your protection, thank you. I need you to entertain your family." I stressed the last two words. In truth, keeping a rein on Uncle Harley certainly wasn't my responsibility.

Lymond let this pass. "Kenyon's going with me,"

he said. "If I have to, I'll get some recruits from the dragoons in Brighton to help if we need them."

I stared at him. "I do not intend to be overrun by strangers, Lymond. Furthermore, I don't want . . ." I caught myself just before I said too much and looked at Mr. Gwynn. "My apologies, Mr. Gwynn. I was speaking of Lymond's threat of the dragoons; I certainly didn't mean you. You're welcome at Bellerophon." It sounded rather hollow, but he didn't seem to take offense.

Lymond ignored me. "I sent word to Kenyon last night after we talked, and he came early this morning. We'll escort you down and stay until after Uncle Harley gets there. After that, I'll decide."

"Oh, and I'm to have no say in these high-handed arrangements?"

Lymond grinned at me. "No."

I debated about getting up and flouncing out, but decided that would be rather undignified. Instead I calmly buttered my muffin. "We'll see about that," I said casually to Lymond, then I chatted aimlessly with Mr. Gwynn. I hadn't managed the witty repartee I wished, but at least my calm acceptance seemed to have confused Lymond. He looked at me warily. I just kept smiling until everyone had come down for breakfast and my departure went unnoticed.

We were to leave right after breakfast and I was ready, still smiling, as we assembled in the hall. As usual, Aunt Hen hadn't been ready, so the footmen were just now bringing some of our trunks down. Lymond had provided another carriage since he and Gwynn were going along, so new arrangements had to be made for all the packing.

Lymond, Gwynn, and I stood impatiently by the door while Aunt Hen and Amelia cried on each other's shoulders. Finally I took Julia by the arm, hoping to speed up the process, and suggested we go ahead and get in the carriage. Carlsen glided in front of me to open the door and I shoved Julia on out. She almost fell down the steps as she stumbled over something. She turned to look just as I stood in the doorway. Julia dropped on the steps in a dead faint just as John Coachman came running toward us. "I never saw that, and I was here just a minute ago," he said, staring in horror. "That" was a very dead man, the man I had seen in Lymond's study. I searched my memory for his name. "It's Turner," I croaked, turning to Lymond. He elbowed by me and pulled the door closed behind him so the rest of the group couldn't see.

Turner was quite dead and blue. His shiny knife was protruding out of his chest, and the money Lymond had given him was stuffed into his mouth, the ends of the notes sticking out. For a moment, I thought I was going to be sick, and then I knew I was. I hung my head over the iron railing and cast up my accounts right there. Lymond stood and held my head. "Steady, Roxanne," he said, but I noticed his hands weren't any steadier than mine were. He glanced down at John Coachman, holding Julia up, her head and arms trailing. We were gathering a curious crowd.

Lymond held on to me with one hand as he tried to move Turner aside with the other. The body had fallen completely across the doorway. "Kenyon! Carlsen!" he yelled, dragging me across the body and pushing the door open with his shoulder. My knees refused to work. "Get Julia," he said to Gwynn, then turned to Carlsen. "Get some men to move Turner and see that the crowd is dispersed. Send a message to Debenham that I need to see him immediately." He looked at

Aunt Hen, Livvy, and Amelia standing in the middle of the hall. "If you don't mind, please go upstairs."

Gwynn and John Coachman walked in carrying Julia, her arms and head dangling dangerously. Aunt Hen took one horrified look, made an inarticulate cry, and promptly fainted into a crumpled heap on the polished marble of the floor. "Oh, God," Lymond said, looking around, "there's nobody to pick her up."

"I'll get her," I said. My knees were beginning to work again. "You take care of Turner and get Debenham; I'll take care of everybody in here." I stood carefully on my own and sent Gwynn upstairs with Julia, had John Coachman pick up Aunt Hen and carry her up, sent Amelia in search of cold compresses, and had Livvy go in search of feathers to burn. As I started up the stairs, I turned back to Lymond, catching him just as he opened the outside door. "I want to talk to you, Lymond, just as soon as things calm down. This time, I expect some answers."

"I'm not sure I have answers." He paused and leaned against the doorframe as he ran his fingers through his hair and looked weary. "All right, Roxanne, I'll tell you what I know, which isn't much. Let me talk to Debenham first though. Send Kenyon down as soon as you can." With that, he went outside. I could glimpse Turner's body as Carlsen and a footman tried to pick up the dead weight. I closed my eyes for a moment, visualizing the man the night before. All I could remember was the fear in his eyes and the gleam of his knife. Mentally, I shook myself hard, then went upstairs to oversee my brood.

It took the better part of an hour to get everyone on the way to recovery. Aunt Hen got on her feet, then promptly fainted again. We had to use every restorative we knew to bring her around. When I heard the hall clock chime twelve, I left her in Amelia's care and went to check on Julia. Livvy was sitting with her. Julia was propped against the pillows and was almost as white as they were. "Who was that?" she said with a shudder.

"A friend of Lymond's," I said noncommittally. "I'm going down now to discover what happened." I paused at the door to look at her again. "Julia, are you all right?"

She nodded. "I'm fine now. Mr. Gwynn was so comforting." Did I see a spot of color on her cheeks? Hastily, she went on, "How is Aunt Hen? Livvy said she was completely distraught."

"She was, but she's all right now. Amelia is with her, rubbing her temples with lavender water. You know Aunt Hen—with some attention, she'll rebound in no time." I smiled at both of them. "I think we should still plan to leave for Brighton as soon as possible. Would you be able to travel first thing in the morning?"

Julia shuddered. "Yes, the sooner away from here, the better."

Downstairs, everything seemed as calm as usual. Carlsen indicated to me that Lymond was in the library. This time I made sure to knock first.

"I really expected you earlier, Roxanne," Lymond said. "Is everyone all right? I sent up to ask and was told that Mrs. Vellory wasn't rallying. I understand Julia is all right."

"She is, and, with attention, Aunt Hen has recovered." I sat down in the chair in front of his desk and found myself eye to eye with a sheaf of dirty, scattered bank notes. It took me a second to realize that these were the notes that had been stuffed in Turner's mouth.

I felt nausea rising. "Lymond, please . . ." I closed my eyes and waved my hand towards the notes.

Lymond covered them with his handkerchief and moved them, placing them in a large envelope before he put them in his desk drawer. "I'm sorry, Roxanne. I had forgotten those were there."

"I suppose he's dead. He *looked* dead."

Lymond nodded. "Yes. He was supposed to get some information for me. Someone must have discovered that."

"Was that why the notes were in his mouth?"

"Yes." Lymond sat down, not behind the desk, but in the chair beside me. He reached over and touched my hand. "Are you sure you're all right? You look pale."

I forced a smile, trying to get the picture of the bank notes out of my mind. "I'm fine." He looked at me with a little more than concern, and clasped my hand in his. Much as I would have liked to explore this avenue, this wasn't the time. I pulled my hand away on the pretext of pushing my hair back. "Lymond, I think I'm—we're—due some answers. Do you want to tell me what's going on?"

He sighed and leaned back in his chair, wearily closing his eyes as he laced his fingers together in his lap. "I had hoped to keep you and your family out of this, Roxanne." He paused.

"After this morning, I don't think that's possible, Lymond." Another thought hit me. "Just how do you think we're involved, other than finding bodies on your steps? I certainly don't know what's going on, and I know Aunt Hen and the other girls don't."

"*Body.* Only one body on the steps, Roxanne."

"You're quibbling at trivialities, Lymond. Exactly how are we involved?"

"You may not be involved." He ran his fingers through his already tousled hair. "Debenham and I simply don't know enough to know what's going on. I wasn't even sure there was any kind of a link until this morning. Turner's death seems to prove that." He paused and then continued. "I thought perhaps Havilland's death might be connected in some way to Uncle Harley. There have been two other book collectors murdered on the continent—one in Brussels, one in Paris. We—Debenham and I—weren't sure if the murders were connected or not but now I suspect they are."

I was thoroughly confused. "And you think your uncle may be involved?"

He stared at me, startled. "Involved? Lord, no! I thought he might be a target in some way."

I nodded and thought about it. "And when I told you that everyone in London knew he was coming to Bellerophon, you thought that our family might be targets as well."

"Yes." He sighed again, sat up a little straighter, and looked at me. "I don't think there will be any danger to you or your family in Brighton. However, considering what happened to Turner, I'd like you to wait a few days until I can go to Bellerophon and see how things look."

"That's ridiculous, Lymond. I gave the staff time off while we were in London. Holmwood, some footmen, and some grooms stayed to watch the place, so I know everything has been guarded. Besides, I wrote to Woodbury last week and told him to have everything in readiness and gave him the date we'd be returning." I paused while he digested this. "So, I've already talked to the girls. Julia in particular doesn't wish to stay here any longer. We're leaving first thing in the morning."

"I refuse to allow it."

I stared at him for a full minute, incredulous. "*You* refuse to allow it! Since when are you in charge of me or my family! I'm telling you right now, Lymond, that we'll go where we please and do what we wish, whether you *allow* it or not!" I stood to leave.

He leaped to his feet and reached for my hand. "I'm sorry, Roxanne, I didn't mean to anger you. It's just that . . . that . . ." He stopped and ran his fingers through his hair again. "Sit down and let's talk."

I sat down on the edge of my chair and glared at him as he sat down. "Roxanne, I apologize. I wouldn't presume to order you or your family to do anything. What I was going to suggest before I completely made a cake of myself was that you and your family stay here for just a few days until I can go to Bellerophon and make sure everything is secure. You could leave in three days. Surely you could grant me that."

"Perhaps if you told me the facts, Lymond, I might be more amenable. I've asked you several times, but you seem more than reluctant to tell me."

He looked at me and took a deep breath. "All right, Roxanne, I'll tell you what I know, which isn't much. As for being reluctant, I wasn't really—I simply didn't think it was necessary to tell you since it didn't concern you in any way. I'm still not sure it does, but I don't want to take the risk." He went over to the sideboard and poured two glasses of wine.

"A little early for wine, isn't it, Lymond?" I said as I accepted the one he handed me.

He nodded and sat. "Yes, although this day already feels a week long." He finished his in one gulp and put the glass on the table. "In the beginning, I didn't think much of it when Uncle Harley told me that his friend, M. LeFoucald, had been found murdered in a street in Paris. LeFoucald and Uncle Harley had traded books for years, as well as visited each other frequently. Then Debenham and the Home Office received word that LeFoucald's murder might be part of a larger scheme—that's all we knew at the time. Then, a month ago, Uncle Harley's friend in Brussels, M. Moncure, was murdered in a particularly savage way. His library was also sacked, and again, Debenham was warned to be on watch for thieves of rare books. Last week when Havilland was murdered, we knew the gang—if there is one—had arrived in London. Immediately, of course, I began worrying about Uncle Harley. Debenham is watching Spencer, without his knowledge, of course. I wanted Uncle Harley out of London and back home. I had no idea that he'd take a wild notion to go to Bellerophon and perhaps involve you.''

I looked at him firmly. "That's it? That's all you know? What about Turner?''

He looked pained and picked up his empty glass. I handed him my untouched one and he drank it down. ''You really shouldn't rely on alcohol, Lymond. A good cup of strong tea would be better.''

"A vacation in Italy in the sunshine would be even better,'' he said with a short laugh.

"Turner?'' I prompted.

"Yes,'' he said with a sigh. "I should have known something like this would happen. Turner was a good man.''

He looked woebegone. "Lymond, I would think Turner knew the risks. You can't feel guilty about it.''

Lymond glanced at me. ''Turner wasn't a professional informer. What bothers me is that he has—*had* a wife and children.'' He looked bleak. "Debenham

61

and I will see to their care, of course, but nothing can take the place of a husband and father."

There was nothing I could say to this, so I stayed quiet until Lymond rang for some tea. We sat in companionable silence until it was brought. I poured for us as Lymond talked. "Turner was just trying to do the right thing. He thought he might have some information for me. He works—worked in a bookshop and had been recently approached by a man about a rare book. Turner knew I was looking because I had been by to talk to him some weeks back when we were looking for books from Moncure's library. Debenham had been told some of them were being sold in London."

"Did Turner know the man or what he wanted?"

Lymond shook his head. "The man said he'd return. He did, but called himself Smith, a rather obvious alias. We supplied Turner with some books to lure the man in, and hoped to discover his identity and if there was a link to the murders. After Havilland was killed, the man came to Turner with an offer to sell some books. He left one to be examined and said he'd be back for either money or the book. The book was one of Havilland's."

"Was Turner able to tell you anything?"

Lymond shook his head. "You can see from Turner's death that this man—or these men—are playing for keeps. That's why I'm worried." He gave me a long, level gaze. "Will you please just stay here until I can go to Bellerophon? I'd like to see for myself that the house is secure if only for my own peace of mind."

I glanced at him and gave way. Turner's death had obviously hit him hard. "All right, Lymond. Julia wants to leave immediately, but I think I can persuade her to stay here a few days." I paused and looked at him over the edge of my teacup. "Do you plan to leave for Brighton in the morning?"

He shook his head. "Late this afternoon. I've already talked to Kenyon and to Debenham. Kenyon will stay and keep an eye on things here. I'll leave today, spend the night on the road, and get to Bellerophon tomorrow. After I check on things, I'll probably return the next day." He smiled at me. "Just a few days. That won't be too long for you to wait, will it?"

I agreed, and it wasn't very difficult to persuade the others. Of course, I didn't mention the murders Lymond had discussed with me. Aunt Hen would probably have wanted to emigrate if she had thought anything at all was wrong. I merely said I thought Julia should recover her strength before we left. Aunt Hen thought that was wise.

I didn't see Lymond again until he returned from Brighton. In the meantime, we stayed in. Julia and Aunt Hen just didn't feel like getting out on the town, so we stayed at home and entertained ourselves. Kenyon Gwynn stayed as well, and he was a great help in keeping Julia's spirits up. He and Livvy became excellent friends and they did everything from sing duets to stage impromptu skits. By the time Lymond returned, we almost felt Mr. Gwynn to be a part of our extended family. He must have sensed our feelings, as he asked us to call him by his given name. Since he was going to be in Brighton with us for a while, we asked the same of him.

Lymond returned on the fourth day. Livvy and I were in the small parlor helping Amelia with some mending. Or rather, they were sewing while I was reading aloud to them from *Childe Harold*. I was never any good at needlework or any other of those housewifely things. I didn't know how Amelia could see her stitches—she was almost in tears over the adventures of Harold.

My back was to the door, and I didn't see Lymond until he came in and sat down with us. "Well, Roxanne," he drawled, "I didn't know you read anything later than Vergil. Imagine you waxing sentimental over Childe Harold."

"I am not waxing, Lymond," I answered. "Merely reading."

"With a tear in your eye." He laughed, and that was when I saw that his smile didn't really reach his eyes. He looked very tired.

"I have the tears, not Roxanne," Amelia told him. "Robert, you're filthy! Whatever has happened?"

For the first time, I looked at Lymond's clothes. He looked as if he had fallen in the mud and there was a large rip in the sleeve of his coat. There was also a large, purple bruise on his cheek.

He shrugged and smiled at us. I'd seen that smile every time he didn't want to reveal something. "I fell from my horse," he said, "but please don't bruit it about. I'll never hear the end of it."

Amelia and Livvy laughed at him, but I didn't. Lymond was as good or better in the saddle as anyone I had seen. His horse was a rather ordinary looking piece of horseflesh with extraordinary abilities. Lymond had named him The Bruce in honor of another Robert. Lymond and The Bruce moved and worked together, so under no circumstances could I imagine Lymond falling off him.

After everyone laughed, Lymond looked at all of us lazily. "Bellerophon seems to be fine. No one was there except Holmwood and some grooms, but we checked everything carefully. You can leave as soon as you wish."

I frowned. I had written Woodbury to have the staff return and get the house ready for us and had thought they would all be there. Perhaps they had already done everything and that's why Lymond didn't remark their presence. I started to ask him, but before I could, Livvy breathed a sign of relief. "It's so good to hear that. I don't want you to think I haven't enjoyed your hospitality—I have, and I thank you. I've really been delighted with shopping and visiting, but it will be wonderful to get back home."

Again, I started to ask Lymond about Bellerophon, but Livvy continued, "You'll have to come visit us, Amelia. We can't compete with the sights of London, but we'd love to have you."

Amelia smiled sweetly. "You know how much I love Bellerophon, and I'd love to visit you. However, I think I'll wait until after Uncle Harley leaves. You'll have enough to do while he's there," she said, laughing. "Robert, do you know when he plans to arrive at Bellerophon?"

Lymond sighed and got up. "Whenever it is, it's all too soon. I'll have to find out from Boots."

"Pay no attention to him," Amelia assured us as Lymond left us. "You'll love Uncle Harley once you get to know him."

Livvy and I exchanged looks. From what we had seen of Uncle Harley, we weren't nearly as sure of that as she was.

That night at supper, we agreed that we would leave for Bellerophon the next morning. Kenyon would accompany us, and Lymond would come down later. He promised to be there when his uncle arrived, no matter when it was. I waited until we could speak privately, then asked him again about his condition when he arrived and about the bruise on his cheek. He told me again that he had fallen from his horse.

"I don't believe you, Lymond," I said under my breath as we sat and watched Livvy and Kenyon sing. They sang well together.

"It isn't the first time you've doubted me," he whispered back. He gave me his smile that was guaranteed to melt opposition. I was expecting it, so it had no effect on me.

"No," I agreed, "and occasionally with just cause." I got no response from this, so I continued. "What happened to you, Lymond? Not only are you bruised, but I was sitting right beside you when you came in. Unless I was badly mistaken, that was blood on your shirt, where your shirt and coat were torn."

"You're imagining things, Roxanne."

We both smiled and nodded as Livvy and Kenyon finished their song, and at the urging of the group, began another. "I am not imagining things, Lymond," I whispered as soon as the music started. "I know blood when I see it."

"I fell on a stick."

I looked at him. He wasn't looking at me; he was staring at the pianoforte—a dead giveaway. Still, I didn't want to call him a liar. "You're prevaricating, Lymond," I said.

He looked at me in astonishment that changed to an expression of hurt. The man could have made an adequate living on the stage. "Roxanne, really!"

"Yes, really. Lymond, it's no use to try to fool me. Despite your cheerful demeanor, I've noticed you seem to be in quite a bit of pain. You could scarcely lift your glass at supper. Ergo, your arm is hurt much more than you're pretending."

"I'm not pretending—it was quite a fall."

I gave him the look that statement deserved. Still, I got no more out of him. He devoted his entire attention to the music and spent the rest of the evening talking about trivialities. Still, every time he moved, I saw that he had to control his expression to keep from grimacing. I was worried. When we started to our chambers, I started to ask him again, but he simply smiled at me. "I'll see you as soon as possible," he said, touching my shoulder with his fingertip.

"Lymond," I began, but he stopped me by turning to Aunt Hen to wish her good night. The man was becoming impossible. I decided to try again in the morning before we left.

The next morning, Lymond was not to be found. We sent the trunks down and they were packed and away before I asked Amelia about him. She knew nothing. In desperation, just before we were to leave, I turned to the person sure to know everything in the house. I asked Carlsen.

"I'm not at all sure where Mr. Lymond went," Carlsen said stiffly. I always got the feeling that he didn't approve of me or any other female.

"He didn't say anything? I really need to speak to him before I leave, Carlsen." I am nothing if not persistent.

"You could leave him a note."

"I don't choose to do that, Carlsen." I looked at him coolly, gauging his disapproval. I have dealt with butlers like Carlsen before. One must be very specific. They will always tell the truth, but only as much truth as they can get by with. "Tell me, Carlsen," I said pleasantly, "when did Mr. Lymond leave and did he leave with anyone?"

Carlsen glared at me, realized I was one up on him,

then grudgingly answered. "He left about six this morning with the earl of Debenham and the doctor."

"The doctor!" I felt my eyes widen. "Then he was hurt!"

"I know nothing of that, Miss Sydney," Carlsen said suavely, opening the door and holding it for me. Everyone else was in the carriage. "They're waiting for you."

They saw me in the open door and called for me. Carlsen smiled a rather superior smile at me as I went down the steps and was helped into the carriage. The man was as bad as Lymond.

Chapter 5

The trip home was uneventful, although tiring. Kenyon Gwynn rode on horseback beside us. Every time we stopped, I noticed that he and Livvy chatted with each other. The more I thought about it, the more a plan developed. Before I played matchmaker, however, I needed to find out a little more about his background, regardless of Lymond's claim of his eligibility. Still, Kenyon and Livvy made a handsome couple. Livvy had reddish-blond hair, rather like Cassie, and was very fair. She had been the closest to Papa's ideal of Greek beauty. Papa was convinced that all the Greeks of antiquity didn't look Mediterranean at all—they were tall, beautiful, and fair. The women of such a race would, of course, have luxuriant blond tresses. Papa always called Livvy his "little Achaean." I suppose it was some comfort to him—Julia was dark, and he certainly couldn't call me his little anything. I'm not fat, but I am a rather large woman. "Statuesque" was the word Papa always used.

By the time we reached Brighton, I was tired, so I knew the others must be exhausted. I was looking forward to nothing so much as some tea and my bed.

When we drove up, the grounds looked empty. In just a moment, Holmwood rounded the corner, followed by a bounding Bucephalus. Bue started for us joyfully, then stopped, every hair on end, as he growled at Kenyon. I got him by the collar and introduced them. Kenyon was rather reluctant to put out his hand to be introduced and I remembered that Lymond had told me that Kenyon didn't care for dogs. Besides, Bue is rather intimidating—he's a huge mastiff and, unfortunately, none too intelligent, but very possessive of his grounds and people. I had wanted a spaniel, but Papa, with his usual philosophy of bigger is better, had gotten Bue for me instead. Neither of us had realized the size Bue would become. Even for a mastiff, he was huge.

As soon as I convinced Kenyon that Bue wasn't going to rip him limb from limb, I turned to Holmwood, the gardner. "Where is everyone, Holmwood? Didn't Mr. Lymond tell you we'd probably be here today?"

"He told me. Woodbury said he'd gotten a letter from you." Holmwood is a man of few words. If Lymond had left word with him, that was as far as it had gotten.

The front door was open and we went inside. Woodbury was nowhere to be seen. Our trunks and bags were stacked in neat piles in the front hall. "Woodbury! Mrs. Beckford!" I called.

Woodbury came out of the dining room, a look of complete surprise on his face. For the moment, he seemed to be speechless. "What is it, Woodbury?" I asked. "Surely you knew we were coming."

"But not for two more days. That's what you said in your letter." He dashed to the tray on the sideboard where miscellaneous bits of paper were stashed. "Here. Isn't that what you wrote me?"

I glanced at the paper. It certainly looked like my handwriting, but some of the letters were slightly off.

One thing I did know for certain though—*I* had written no such letter.

"Where did you get this, Woodbury?" I demanded.

"I found it on the hall table right after Mr. Lymond left. He had told us you would be here in a few days, and when I found this, I assumed that you had sent him explicit news." He gestured towards the trunks in the hall. "I thought you had sent these ahead." He looked around. "Things just aren't ready."

I glanced at the others. They were as travel-weary as I was. Aunt Hen had staggered into the drawing room and fallen into a chair, no matter that the holland cover was still on it. "Woodbury, it's of no matter. This is obviously some kind of prank Mr. Lymond has played on us. If you can get something for us to eat— I could make do with bread and cheese if necessary— and remove most of the covers, I think we can manage until tomorrow."

"Has the staff returned?" Julia asked.

Woodbury nodded yes and then no. "Most of them. Everyone else will be returning tomorrow." He looked around in despair. "All we've done is get the dining room and library ready."

"I want my bed," Aunt Hen moaned. "Every joint in my body is in pain."

We sent the trunks to our rooms, got Kenyon Gwynn settled in a room that seemed only a little dusty, then went to our apartments in the back. My room looked fine, the covers were off the furniture, the bed looked slightly rumpled, but I decided someone had put my bandbox on it before placing it in the floor. I glanced around quickly, decided I would wait to unpack until Meggie arrived, and went to see about our supper and to soothe Aunt Hen.

Supper was a success. Aunt Hen had recovered and

our meal was more like a picnic. We had an enjoyable evening, tired as we were. Woodbury had exaggerated slightly—the staff was in place except for our maid, Meggie, and two of the footmen. We'd have everything to rights by midmorning.

There was little conversation after supper and we all went to our rooms early. I opened my trunk, rummaged around for a nightshift and closed it again. I was too tired for anything else. Bue scratched at the door and I let him in, then had to shove the trunk over so he could get to his rug. He looked at me with a look that told me he was happy we were back and flopped down heavily. I smoothed the bottom of the rumpled bed and pulled the covers down. That's when I discovered that someone had slept in my bed recently.

Stepping back, I looked at the indentation in my bed, and saw that the covers had been pulled up so that I wouldn't notice at first. I moved back for a better look and that's when I first saw the open book beside my bed. It was Papa's prized copy of William Blake's poems, and the page was open to the poem "A Poison Tree." An uneasy feeling came over me as I skimmed the familiar words:

> I was angry with my friend:
> I told my wrath, my wrath did end.
> I was angry with my foe:
> I told it not, my wrath did grow.
>
> And I water'd it in fears,
> Night & morning with my tears;
> And I sunned it with smiles,
> And with soft deceitful wiles.

And it grew both day and night,
Till it bore an apple bright;
And my foe beheld it shine,
And he knew that it was mine,

And into my garden stole
When the night had veil'd the pole:
In the morning glad I see
My foe outstretch'd beneath the tree.

I shuddered as I always did when I read that poem.
Worse, Papa's beautiful book had been desecrated. At
the bottom of the page, someone had scrawled the
words "For you, Roxanne."

Without touching anything else, I looked all around
the room. I saw nothing else out of place, but I felt
dirty all over. I felt as if not only my privacy, but my
whole being had been violated. Who could have been
here?

I mentally shook myself hard. "Roxanne, don't be
a goose," I said aloud as Bue opened one eye and
looked at me. "This had to be Lymond. No doubt he
thought it would be a great joke to do this." Briskly I
closed the book and began to strip the bed. I jerked the
quilts off and tossed the pillows to the bottom of the
bed. That's when I saw the torn page skewered to my
pillow with a large hatpin. I removed the pin and
looked at the page. It was another Blake poem, torn,
not from Papa's illustrated version of the book, but
from a plain, printed page. It was a poem by William
Blake as well, but this one was "The Angel." My flesh
crawled when I read it, but then I became angry. I
read it aloud in the empty room, just to make sure of
the words:

I asked a thief to steal me a peach:
He turn'd up his eyes.
I ask'd a lithe lady to lie her down:
Holy and meek she cries.

As soon as I went
An angel came:
He wink'd at the thief
And smiled at the dame,

And without one word spoke
Had a peach from the tree,
And 'twixt earnest and joke
Enjoy'd the lady.

Rage boiled up in me as I finished. I tossed the torn page down as though it were hot. Then the feeling passed and I reminded myself that this wasn't anything sinister—it was merely Lymond trying to be funny and failing miserably. He would hear about this! Without another wasted moment, I stepped across Bue and took my candle to my desk where I penned a scathing letter to Lymond, telling him exactly what I thought of him and why. It was not flattering in the slightest. I wrote for two pages, back and front, and included not only this gauche incident, but I threw in several other complaints as well. I felt quite vindicated by the time I sealed and sanded it. I would have Woodbury send a footman into Brighton to mail it tomorrow. Slightly mollified, I went back to put clean linens on my bed. "This had to be Lymond," I said again, speaking to Bue as I stepped back over him. "You would never allow anyone else in the house." Bue yawned and fell back asleep.

The first thing the next morning, I sent the letter

into Brighton so it would be on the first coach out, but I said nothing to any of the family about Lymond's tasteless joke. Aunt Hen would just defend Lymond, and I didn't want to hear it. I was thoroughly disgusted with him.

The footman brought our post back and we discovered that Uncle Harley would be arriving the next day. He said he would be bringing Mowbridge and his family. "I didn't know Mowbridge had a family," I said to Kenyon.

He shrugged. "I didn't either, but then I've been away so long that I know very little about anyone. Do you want me to lift that for you?" Gratefully, I accepted his help and watched as he easily lifted a chair. He was proving to be kind and helpful beyond measure. I watched him speculatively. He was well built, handsome except for the thin scar on his face, and intelligent. I knew little about his family, but I intended to find out. If his family was suitable, I intended to promote a match between him and Livvy. They seemed well suited. Her blond looks set his darkness off to advantage, and I had noticed they had many things in common. Still, before I actively did anything, I had to know more about him—those scars worried me. I knew by now that he hadn't been in the war, so it could mean he had participated in a duel although the scar seemed a little thick for a saber slash. The scars on the back of his hand didn't seem to be slashes either—they were jagged and rough. Still, if he had what Aunt Hen termed "A Past," he certainly wouldn't be the kind of man I'd want for Livvy.

I put Kenyon's past aside and concentrated on seeing how well he and Livvy rubbed along. Julia stayed with us as we helped get the house in order, and things went smoothly. We had everything cleaned and in place by the time Uncle Harley's carriage pulled up the next day. A second carriage followed, no doubt, I remarked to Aunt Hen, carrying Mowbridge's family. To our surprise—and horror, since we were not prepared for an onslaught—both carriages were full of Uncle Harley's family. The first carriage contained Uncle Harley and Mowbridge, who, as it seemed, was a confirmed bachelor. The second carriage—and the one following it—contained Uncle Harley's son Harley Clarke Sheridan, who had previously been pointed out to me as Boots. Boots had brought along the man who had come to our box at the theatre and had not been introduced to us at that time. This time we discovered that his name was George Gage and he and Boots were good friends. There was also Uncle Harley's daughter, Evelyn; Uncle Harley's valet, Lambert; Boots's valet, Ballew; Evelyn's abigail, Miss Lettice Hinchley; and— God help us, help Bucephalus—Miss Hinchley's very large calico cat, Precious. Aunt Hen stood beside me, took one long look, then sagged against me. "I feel faint, Roxanne," she said.

"Rally yourself, Aunt Hen," I muttered. "If you ever needed fortitude, the time is now." I forced a smile on my face and greeted Uncle Harley.

"I'd like to get started on the library right away," he said while we were still standing in the door. I fobbed him off on Aunt Hen until I could greet the others and make some order out of the chaos as they unloaded the baggage wagons. Evelyn must have brought every dress in London with her.

I dragooned Julia into seeing that enough beds were ready—we had prepared only three rooms. I assumed that Lymond would be here shortly so we couldn't use his room, Kenyon was occupying one, so we really didn't have enough beds cleaned and aired. Evelyn informed me that she wanted a suite, Boots didn't care although he wished to be next to Mr. Gage, and Miss Hinchley asked if it would possible for her to have a corner room since Precious preferred to jump from window sill to window sill, surveying the grounds. I looked at her in horror, wondered how Bucephalus would take to this, made a few inarticulate sounds, and left it at that.

Woodbury, imperturbable as ever, oversaw the baggage. Uncle Harley and Mowbridge appeared to travel light, as did Gage, but Boots and Evelyn had dozens of trunks and boxes. There were trunks and bandboxes everywhere.

Just as I thought we had everything in hand, Bucephalus came bounding into the hall, drooling and overjoyed at the thought of company. Precious, in what seemed to be her usual spot—clutched firmly to Miss Hinchley's bosom—took one look and bristled. Bue accepted the challenge and stopped dead in his tracks, every hair on his back straight up. Precious yowled, jumped over two trunks, ran up Woodbury's leg and onto his head. Using Woodbury as a launch, Precious jumped through the drawing room door, over the sofa, and up the drapes. I heard the drapes rip as she went up—Precious was not a small cat.

Bucephalus didn't hesitate. He jumped the trunks as well, sending Julia right into Kenyon Gwynn and both of them sat down heavily on the stairs. Bue knocked over tables and chairs trying to jump the sofa, tore Papa's Greek key upholstery, then stood on his hind legs trying to turn the cat's luxuriant tail into a trophy. Precious was by this time safely atop the cornice, every hair on end. She looked rather like an angry hedgehog.

With a calmness that amazed even myself, I walked to the door and called for Holmwood. The gardener is the only one who can handle Bucephalus at times like these. I would have asked Woodbury to do it, but he seemed to be in shock, standing in the middle of the hall, small rivulets of blood running down his face from the cat scratches on his head.

As Holmwood dragged Bue out the door and a footman tried to dislodge Precious from the cornice, I turned and smiled at Uncle Harley. "Quite an auspicious beginning," I said, trying to hide the beginnings of hysteria. Miss Hinchley was already having spasms.

Mr. Gage seemed rather amused, but Boots regarded the whole episode without changing his bored expression. As the excitement subsided, he turned to me, his face still blank. "Do you have anything to drink besides water, milk, or tea?" he asked.

We finally got everyone settled and had a rather sparse meal for supper. Cook hadn't stocked the larder yet, and even if she had, I doubt she would have been prepared for such an onslaught. However, no one seemed to notice except us. Uncle Harley had no clue what he was eating—I told Aunt Hen later that we could have served boiled oxhide and Uncle Harley wouldn't have noticed. Mowbridge didn't do anything except pick at his food and rearrange it in various patterns on his plate; Mr. Gage, however, tried to keep up a semblance of conversation. He appeared to be quite witty and personable. Boots was another matter—to our consternation, although no one else seemed to notice, he did nothing except drink. To our amazement, he went through a bottle of claret, a bottle of port, and some sherry—and was still on his feet. At the end of all that, he was as coherent as usual, which wasn't very much. Miss Hinchley didn't dine with us—she and her cat had taken a tray in her room.

Evelyn was the difficult one. She surveyed the company, complained that there was no one of any consequence at the table, and declared that she could eat nothing except French cooking. I wanted to invite her to take herself off to France, but swift kicks from both Aunt Hen and Livvy made me hold my tongue. It wasn't easy. Evelyn was medium everything—medium height, medium brown hair, medium looks. The only thing outstanding about her was her ability to find something to complain about in every situation. I noticed that Boots and Uncle Harley ignored her. I decided to do the same.

Everyone went to bed early, Evelyn complaining that her bed was lumpy and that her view was obstructed. I pointed out that she might see more in the morning when it was daylight, and went on to my bed. I was determined to dodge her at all costs. I would put Livvy on her as her companion. Livvy was patient and understanding and all those things I wasn't.

I was in the middle of a deep sleep when I was roused by a noise. At first I thought it was the rain, but then, as I came out of sleep, I realized it was a scratching at my window. In my groggy state, I thought it was Bue and got up to let him inside, but then I stepped right on him. I was awake instantly. Picking up the large statuette of a cat that I used as a doorstep, I moved to the window, standing at the side so I wouldn't be seen. I peered around the edge of the curtain, but couldn't see a thing. It was as dark as pitch out there. Bue got up, walked to the window, and proceeded to lap it noisily with his tongue.

"Roxanne," someone hissed. I turned around but could see no one. "Roxanne, let me in." This time I realized the voice was coming from outside the window.

"Who's there?"

"It's me. Robert."

I was still disgusted with Lymond. "Go around to the front," I whispered back. "You know the way inside."

"I need to talk to you." Bue kept lapping at the window. "What in heaven's name are you doing? What's that noise?"

"Nothing. Good night, Lymond." I replaced the statuette against the door and pulled Bue away from the window.

"Roxanne," this time the voice was louder, "if you don't open this window and let me in, I'm going to wake everyone here."

"Go ahead," I hissed at him through the window. I spoke louder than I meant to and Bue growled. It took me a moment to quiet him.

"Roxanne, I need to speak to you. Let me in."

I put my mouth close to the glass. "After what you did, Lymond, I don't care to speak to you. The nerve of you, sleeping in my bed and leaving such poems for me." I started back to my bed.

Lymond almost shouted through the window. "That's just it—I got your letter and don't know what you're talking about." His voice dropped. "Someone's going to hear me. Roxanne, please. This isn't funny. Exactly what happened?"

I stopped dead in my tracks. If Lymond hadn't done it, then who had? He could be trying to cozen me again—he'd done it before. I walked back to the window and opened it a crack. "You know very well what I'm talking about, Lymond. When we got here, I discovered you'd slept in my bed and had left those poems by Blake for me."

In the dark, I could see his fingers under the window. I was tempted to close the sash. "I swear to you,

80

Roxanne, that I know nothing about it. As soon as I got your letter, I hurried here to find out what's going on. What poems? Let me inside."

I thought a moment. "Let me get my dressing gown." I covered myself decently and opened the sash wide. "This is hardly the way to come visiting, Lymond."

"Hardly proper, but quite effective," he said as he climbed in and shut the window behind him. "I promise no one will know I've been here."

"I trust not—my reputation would be in shreds."

Lymond lit a candle and closed the draperies. He looked terrible. He was muddy all over and the side of his coat sleeve was covered with dirty water. "Heavens, Lymond," I said, horrified, "don't sit down until I cover the chair with a quilt. You're a mess." I got a quilt and draped it over the chair. As I did, I stood right next to him and got a good look at his sleeve. "Lymond, is that blood?"

He glanced down and grimaced. "Yes, but it's nothing."

"Nothing!" I ran my fingers along his sleeve. It was soaked. I glanced down at my fingers and saw they were stained with red. "I think it's time to tell me what happened. This is the same arm you hurt when you fell off your horse."

He sighed as he sat. "You were right, as usual. I lied, Roxanne, I didn't fall off my horse. When I came down here before, someone followed me and I was shot in the arm. It was only a graze, but it bled a great deal."

"And tonight?" I helped him take his coat off and got my scissors to cut his sleeve. It was soaked and stuck to his skin. "Did you get shot again in the same place?"

He shook his head. "No. Someone knew I was coming, though. I realized in London that I was being followed and thought I had lost them before I left. Evidently I was wrong because two ruffians got after me on the road and chased me until I was in sight of Bellerophon. I'd have to say The Bruce performed magnificently. He easily outran them."

"The blood, Lymond. How did this happen?" I had cut the sleeve away and saw the graze. It was purple on the edges and bleeding profusely. I didn't think it was infected, but if something wasn't done, it would be.

"I had trouble holding my horse and hit my arm."

I gave him a withering look. "I've heard that one before."

"This time it happens to be true. When I was close to the stables, out of their reach, one of them hazarded a shot at me. I wasn't hit, but the bullet grazed The Bruce and he shied. I managed to hold him, but crashed into the side of the stable. See." He pointed to his face. In truth, it was scratched and his eye had a fresh bruise. "The Bruce is all right."

"Good. Now sit still while I go get some basilicum powder," I ordered. "I want to hear all of this."

I was back in a moment and powdered his arm liberally. I had gotten some strips of an old sheet and bound his arm. I made no pretensions to being a nurse, although I could do tolerably well when I had to. "Now, Lymond, finish your story." I pulled up my dressing-table chair and sat down across from him. "No lies."

He looked injured. "Have I ever lied to you, Roxanne?"

"Many times, Lymond. Let's have the story."

He looked properly chagrined and smiled at me.

"That's about all. I stabled The Bruce and made sure he wasn't hurt. I thought I heard someone outside the stables, but didn't see anyone, not even one of the stable boys. When I could discover nothing, I came straight to your window."

I pondered this. "Who were they, Lymond?"

He shook his head. "I have no idea, but it must be connected to our investigation of the book collector murders. Also, I'm still making inquiries into Turner's death. So far, I haven't really turned up anything although Debenham and I are sure all the deaths are related."

"Reasonable." I paused. "How did anyone know you were coming to Brighton? Did you tell several people?"

He shook his head. "I didn't tell anyone, not even Debenham. When I got your letter, I was so worried that I decided on the spur of the moment to ride down and see for myself that you were unharmed. It had to be whoever's been deliberately following me."

I frowned. "It must, if you told no one about my letter." I pinned him with what I hoped was a disapproving look. "Ah, my letter to you, Lymond. That brings me to an unpleasant point. I do not appreciate your sense of humor in this matter. It's bad enough that you chose to come into my room and sleep in my bed, but to leave those poems . . ." I felt myself blush. "That one, in particular, was beyond the bounds of good taste to leave for a lady."

"That's what I mean." He leaned forward and touched my hand. "Roxanne, I swear this to you: I didn't do that. When I came down here, the house was closed and the holland covers on everything. I didn't even stay here—I stayed with friends of mine in the dragoons. I confess I walked through your room, but Holmwood was with me. I didn't touch a single thing.''

"You didn't sleep in my bed? You didn't leave me those suggestive poems?''

He shook his head. "No, Roxanne, I didn't. I swear it.''

I believed him. There are lies and then there are lies. I like to believe I can tell the difference. I looked at him, bewildered. "Then, Lymond, if you didn't, who did? And more importantly, why?''

He shook his head, the candlelight bringing out glints in it. "I don't know, but it worries me. I had thought Uncle Harley and Mowbridge would be safe here, but then after Boots told everyone in London about it, I began to worry.''

I felt my eyes widen. "You really think the murderer of the other book collectors may be after your uncle?''

"Perhaps.'' He avoided my eyes. "Show me the book of poems, Roxanne. I want to see exactly what was left for you and where. Did you say one was skewered to your pillow?''

I hesitated to show him, but went ahead. When he asked, I told him that the Blake was valuable, but by no means Papa's finest.

"Could I keep this?'' He fingered the page on which was written "For you, Roxanne.''

"I'd rather you didn't, Lymond. I intend to compare the handwriting to every scrap of paper that comes into the house. If this is someone's idea of a malign joke, I intend to discover the culprit.''

He looked at me. "I suppose it's futile to ask you to leave it to me.''

"It certainly is, Lymond.'' I glanced at the clock. "And now, if you don't mind, I'd like to go back to bed.''

"I could spend the night here in the chair."

I was firm. "Absolutely not. You'll go back out the window."

"There I draw the line, Roxanne—I'll go up the back stairs. I can find my way to my room."

I raised an eyebrow. "I hope no one has appropriated it. We had to insist it stay empty. The house is bulging at the seams. Your uncle brought his entire family and Boots brought a friend. Then there's also Miss Hinchley and her cat."

"God." It was a word of utter despair and I couldn't have agreed more. "I'm sorry, Roxanne." He ran his fingers through his hair and I noticed there was blood matted on the top of his head.

"Lymond, why didn't you tell me your head was hurt? Sit back down and let me sponge it."

"It's nothing. My head hit the eave of the stable as The Bruce reared. It's just a scratch." He sagged against the back of the chair and looked unbelievably weary. "Exactly who's here?"

I gave him a verbal list. "Evelyn, too?" he asked with a sigh. "Perhaps they won't stay long." He stood to leave.

"Care to wager?" I asked as Lymond left for his room.

I noted he didn't accept the bet.

Chapter 6

Between the fatigue of the journey and of Lymond's nocturnal visit, I didn't get down to breakfast until late. Lymond was at breakfast, looking wretched, trying to use his arm and blanching every time he moved it. Kenyon sat beside him, trying not to look worried every time Lymond moved. Uncle Harley was there as well, pacing and fuming. Also Boots was there with two other gentlemen, one of them George Gage. The other seemed to be running an errand of some sort and acknowledged me on his way out. I raised a quizzical eyebrow at Lymond as I poured my coffee. Lymond stood beside me and mumbled that the man was Parrott, Gage's valet. It seemed he had just arrived this morning. I paled as I wondered just where the man would sleep. The available bedrooms were taken and I hadn't really made any provision for Gage's man. I started to worry about it, then realized that it really wasn't my responsibility. Lymond, the host, could settle that one.

Parrott returned shortly to bring something to Gage and as he passed by and nodded to me, I had a nagging flash of memory that I had seen him before, but I couldn't place him at all. I couldn't imagine anyplace

I could have ever seen him. I shrugged, dropping the feeling and started to sit down to my breakfast. Uncle Harley stopped me.

"Dash it all, girl, we need to get to work! You don't have time for frivolous pursuits."

I felt myself freeze. I am hardly an old lady, but I certainly didn't wish to be called "girl" in those tones. Besides, I hardly considered breakfast to be a frivolous activity. Lymond intervened before I could say anything. "Calm yourself, Uncle Harley. I'm sure Miss Sydney needs her coffee this morning." He tried to hand me my coffee but paled visibly as he reached for the cup and had to stay his hand. Kenyon, evidently as worried about Lymond as I, handed me the cup. Although this episode lasted only a moment, George Gage seemed to be quite interested. His eyes never left Lymond. Uncle Harley, however, was oblivious to everything.

"She could bring her cup with her," Uncle Harley said, flipping the lid on his watch and frowning at it. "I've already wasted over an hour waiting." He went to the dining room door. "Mowbridge!" he bellowed. "Mowbridge, come here!"

Mowbridge came wandering in, looking sleepy. He ignored Uncle Harley's bellowing and poured himself a cup of coffee, then sat down beside me. Uncle Harley kept pacing and snapping the lid on his watch. Mowbridge paid no attention and I followed his lead.

"Sat down in the drawing room and fell asleep," Mowbridge said by way of explanation. "I stayed up half the night because I always have trouble sleeping when I'm out of my own bed."

I nodded agreement, and Mowbridge continued as Uncle Harley huffed and puffed in the background. "Tell me, Miss Sydney, do you know what's in your

87

library? Mr. Sinclair seems to think you have some extremely valuable books in there." Out of the corner of my eye, I noticed that Gage transferred his attention from Lymond to my conversation with Mowbridge.

"I don't think so," I said, buttering my toast. "Papa didn't discriminate in his collecting—he simply collected anything and everything he could find. He certainly never mentioned having any valuable books, other than the scroll, and, as I told Mr. Sinclair, I'm not sure it's valuable."

Uncle Harley could be heard behind us, gnashing his teeth. The watch lid clicked shut once, flipped open, and shut again. Mowbridge smiled at me and I realized he was playing a game to tantalize Uncle Harley. "Ah, yes, the scroll from Samarkand reputed to belong to Alexander."

"The *Iliad*," I said.

He nodded again. "I've heard Alexander had several copies but didn't need them. He had the entire poem memorized—every one of the more than fifteen thousand dactylic hexameters."

"So I've heard," I said. "I wasn't there."

"Such a scroll would be very valuable," George Gage said, looking at us over the rim of his cup. "A serious collector would pay whatever you demanded for it."

"George is a book collector, too," Boots informed us. "Buys and sells books from all over the world. Very interesting books."

Lymond looked at Boots with interest. "I didn't realize you had turned to intellectual pursuits, Boots."

Boots looked disgusted. "You know me well enough, Robert, to know that's not what I meant. There does happen to be a great deal of money in books." He looked directly at his father and I realized this was another game to bait Uncle Harley. He smiled as he continued, "Collections can be sold for a fortune. Spencer, for example, would pay almost any amount for what he wants."

"By God, you young . . ." Uncle Harley screeched, checking himself on the last word. His face became a mottled red that changed to purple. I thought he was going into apoplexy in front of my eyes. "I'll see hell freeze over before my collection is sold. Much less to that . . . that . . . *Spencer!* I'll . . . I'll *burn* it!"

Lymond and I jumped to our feet at the same time, but Lymond fell back into his chair. He had raked the side of his arm on the table and was white as the tablecloth. However, other than Kenyon and me, no one noticed it—everyone else had resumed eating breakfast. Evidently they were accustomed to this kind of behavior from Uncle Harley. Boots merely raised an eyebrow and began a conversation with Gage; Mowbridge calmly sipped his coffee. Lymond, Kenyon, and I looked at each other. Uncle Harley was still a dangerous shade of purple. "Let's begin now," I said hastily, as Lymond stood carefully and pulled Mowbridge to his feet. Kenyon propelled Uncle Harley out the door as we left Boots and Gage to their conversation.

Mowbridge turned out to be an excellent librarian. He was methodical and thorough. Uncle Harley wanted to begin ripping the books from the shelves immediately, but Mowbridge was having none of that. In the library, it appeared Mowbridge's word was law. Uncle Harley hovered around, looking but not touching. Since they couldn't assist, Kenyon and Lymond left us. I hoped Lymond was going to his room to rest. I tried to get Kenyon aside and tell him to make sure of it, but was unable to since Boots and George Gage came into the library at that point. To my surprise, Mowbridge asked them to leave and, to my greater surprise, they did.

Aunt Hen and Julia came in about noon to see if we were making progress. "Have you found the treasure yet?" Aunt Hen asked as soon as she was in the room.

"Henrietta, I told you it was probably an early version of the *Iliad*," Uncle Harley said.

Aunt Hen batted her eyes at him and simpered. "So you did, Harley. Have you found it yet?"

Julia and I stared at each other. *"Henrietta?"* I mouthed at her. *"Harley?"* she whispered back. Mowbridge appeared not to notice.

Aunt Hen did take Uncle Harley off for a cup of tea and left us alone. Mowbridge had been sneezing occasionally, and I offered him tea but he declined. "I'm a coffee drinker," he told me. "I never touch tea. Picked up the habit when I worked in Virginia."

This was another surprising side of Mowbridge. I thought briefly about striking up a conversation about it, but didn't. "You should talk to Mr. Gwynn. He lived in the colonies for several years. Or rather I mean the United States," I said instead.

Mowbridge sneezed again. Mrs. Beckford and Aunt Hen are excellent housekeepers, but the books had gotten dusty. Also, no matter how often one dusted books and scrolls, the things always kept a thin film of dust. Mowbridge was covered with smudges and dirt. I could even see the outlines of his fingers on some of the books. He kept wiping his hands to make sure he didn't get the pages dirty.

"If you have something else you need to do, I'll call you if I have a question," he said cheerfully, leaning back on his heels. "I don't want to feel I'm imposing on your day."

"You aren't." He was, and so was Uncle Harley, but I wasn't going to be impolite.

"Why don't you sit?" he suggested. He looked up and smiled at Julia. "Watch or you'll get your gown dusty."

Julia smiled at him and moved away, sitting down and taking up her embroidery. "I'll be glad to stay here and answer Mr. Mowbridge's questions, Roxanne," she said.

I sat down wearily. I had been standing beside Mowbridge since breakfast. "You don't know anything about the library, Julia. I'll have to stay here to answer what he needs to know."

She smiled again. "Then I'll just keep you company."

We sat like that for a while, then I got bored. I got up to get a book from the shelf just as Uncle Harley and Aunt Hen came back into the room. "Did you find it?" Uncle Harley yelled in my ear, so loud that I jumped and dropped my book right at Mowbridge's knees.

"No," Mowbridge said, picking up my book. "I'll let you know. Right now, I've just begun on this section of books. There are some first editions, worth some, but not extremely rare." He opened the book I had dropped. "George Chapman's Homer. A very good choice for reading, Miss Sydney." He closed the book reverently and handed it to me.

"I had one of those once," Uncle Harley said, taking it from my fingers and opening it. "Lent it to one of my relatives when he was visiting. What was his name, Mowbridge? I can't remember all those in-laws and out-laws."

"George Clarke." Mowbridge tried unsuccessfully

to suppress a smile. "He said he'd return it immediately."

Uncle Harley nodded. "That was a year ago. I'll be lucky if I ever see the damned thing again." He frowned. "Make a note, Mowbridge, for me to drop in on him and collect that book."

"Do you like Homer?" I asked.

Uncle Harley closed the book and returned it. "He's all right. I had enough of Greeks and Romans in school to last me a lifetime."

"Mr. Sinclair is not a reader," Mowbridge told us, getting to his feet and dusting off his clothes.

"Don't have to be a reader to like books," Uncle Harley growled. "An investment, that's what they are. And a damned good one." He paused and grimaced. "Sometimes." He started pacing and prowling again, picking up first one thing, then another. After an hour of this, I left Julia and Aunt Hen placidly doing their embroidery while Mowbridge carefully went through book after book and Uncle Harley paced and checked the time. I didn't see how the hinge on his watch could last much longer—he opened the lid at least once every five minutes. I shut the door behind me with relief.

George Gage strolled out of the drawing room as I stood in the hallway and looked down at my gown. I was filthy. "I trust your efforts have not been in vain," he said, smiling.

"No." I didn't mean to speak shortly, but there was something about the man that I didn't like. I didn't know him at all, but I didn't like him. I forced myself to smile at him and be pleasant. At his hint that he'd like to see the grounds, I found myself offering to show him around as soon as I washed my hands. Actually I took a little longer, taking time to dust myself off thoroughly. When I returned, he was waiting by the door, but Evelyn was there as well, smiling at him in a familiar sort of way.

Gage offered an arm to each of us. "Two lovely ladies for an outing. Was ever a man more fortunate?"

Evelyn was not at all shy about the fact that she was setting her cap for George Gage. He ignored her more forward comments. He was polite to her, but no more than he was to me. She, however, skirted the edges of propriety.

We ran into Lymond and Kenyon Gwynn at the stables. Gwynn was just dismounting, and I was glad to see that Lymond hadn't tried to ride. His color was improved and he looked better than he had at breakfast, but that wasn't saying much.

"Been out riding?" Gage asked. "I'd love to do some riding myself. I told Boots this morning that the country air gave me the urge to gallop."

Since we were right on the edge of Brighton, I hardly thought Bellerophon qualified as being in "country air," but I said nothing. After another hint or two, Lymond offered the use of his stables. All the horses were his except three of ours. "I'd love to try that one." Gage gestured towards The Bruce.

Lymond smiled. "That one is mine and no one rides him except me. We've been together for a long time."

Gage went over to pat The Bruce and Evelyn went right beside him. "I do love horses," she said, smiling up at him.

"Can you believe that?" I murmured to Kenyon and Lymond. "Not a half hour ago she was complaining about smelly animals all over the place. She seems to have taken Bucephalus in aversion."

Lymond grinned. "The feeling is probably mutual." His voice dropped slightly. "Kenyon, too, is having trouble dodging the dog." He glanced up to make sure Evelyn and Gage were out of earshot. "Kenyon's just back from Brighton. Debenham has sent word that there's been an attempt on another book collector."

I felt myself go pale. "Was anyone ki- . . . hurt?"

"Hurt, but not dead. We're hoping the man will be able to tell us something about his attacker." He began speaking about the weather as Evelyn and Gage rejoined us. Bucephalus came bounding across the grass towards us, his collar jangling. Kenyon took a step backwards, then stopped himself and forced himself to stand still although I noticed he was pale. In a flash, I realized that Kenyon wasn't simply uncomfortable around dogs, he was terrified of them. I would have to ask Lymond about this.

I stepped in front of Kenyon, Evelyn, and Gage to stop Bue, because I knew from past experience that Bucephalus had no fond feelings for strangers. To my surprise, and Lymond's, Bue dashed around me and went up to Gage. He wagged his tail and made all sorts of what Gage thought were appealing sounds. Gage reached in his pocket and got out a treat, unwrapped it, and fed it to Bue. Bue tried to lick him in thanks, but got Evelyn right on the chest instead. She screamed and said a few rather unladylike things about wayward dogs.

When Evelyn had calmed, I spoke to Gage. "I'm surprised. Bue usually doesn't like strangers. What did you feed him?"

Gage smiled. "A concoction my cook at home makes. It's rather like a hard biscuit with jerky ground up in it. Dogs love it. I usually carry one with me just to pacify any dogs around."

"Dogs should be chained," Evelyn sniffed. "I detest dogs."

De gustibus . . . I thought and let the comment drop. After Lymond saw I wasn't going to rise to Evelyn's bait, he and Kenyon went off on their own while Evelyn and Gage accompanied me into the library to see if Mowbridge had made any progress. "Enjoying yourself, my dear?" Uncle Harley asked Evelyn.

"Papa, you know I abhor the country." She sat down and looked around. "This room is certainly dark enough. You should throw out all these books and paint the walls and woodwork white. That would brighten it. A touch of gilding would help as well."

Uncle Harley looked at Gage and me. "And is this your fiancé, young lady?"

I looked around to see who was there, and discovered he was talking to me. Hastily, I corrected his error. "No, this is not my fiancé. This is a friend of your son's. George Gage. He was in the breakfast room this morning. He's a book collector."

"Ah, yes. Came up in the other carriage with Boots, didn't you?" For the first time, Uncle Harley looked interested. "Mowbridge, come here and meet Mr.— what did you say your name was?—Mr. Page. Fancy that, a wonderful name for a book collector."

Gage smiled easily at him. "It would be, but the name is Gage—George Gage." He nodded to Mowbridge as he came up. "I've been abroad for several years so I'm just discovering some of the things I've missed."

"What's that, Mr. Page? Abroad? I suppose you're aware of the collections in Italy and France."

Gage nodded. "I've heard of most, and actually seen some of them. I've been in Portugal for some years and some of the collectors there have some very old manuscripts, many of them in Arabic, of course."

"Anybody got anything worthwhile to sell that you

95

know of?'' Uncle Harley looked at him from beneath bushy eyebrows. ''Reasonably priced of course.''

''I don't know of anything, but I could write some people I know.'' Gage looked around Papa's library admiringly. ''Are you finding very much here? There seems to be a . . . uh, a variety of material here.''

''A damned mess,'' Uncle Harley said.

I couldn't stop myself. ''You certainly don't have to bother yourself with it.'' My voice was ice. Uncle Harley looked at me in surprise. He probably had no idea how insulting he had been. Mowbridge took my arm and smiled. ''Come over here, Miss Sydney, and let me show you some things.'' He drew me over to a shelf on the far side of the room. ''I apologize for Mr. Sinclair. He means well, but as you've noticed, he doesn't appreciate books for their own sake, he likes them solely for their value.''

I was slightly mollified. ''I realize that, Mowbridge, and I also realize that Papa had no system for his books. They're all thrown together. He simply purchased whatever he liked.''

''Often the best way,'' Mowbridge said. ''Look at this.'' He showed me a small book with a wooden cover that had a metal clasp on it. ''A book of hours, if I remember correctly,'' I told him.

Mowbridge nodded. ''Hand painted, of course. Valuable, as well.'' He looked at the shelves. ''I've done only these shelves. Tomorrow I'd like to do the books on these and, if possible, get to all those maps and scrolls on the bottom shelf.''

''You don't need to ask, Mowbridge. I've already given my permission.''

He looked troubled. ''I'd rather you or a member of your family stay while I examine them. Those scrolls are very old and may crumble. I want you here to tell me to stop if you believe I'm damaging anything."

I waved his objections away. "I trust you, Mowbridge. Lymond tells me you're one of the best librarians in Britain." Mowbridge blushed but I saw he was quite pleased.

Aunt Hen came in. "Have we found the treasure yet?"

Gage wheeled so sharply that I noticed it from the corner of my eye. "Oh," he said easily with a smile, "I thought I'd heard a treasure discussed. Do you have a treasure as well?"

I tried to signal Aunt Hen, but, as usual, when she was on the subject of the treasure, there was no stopping her. "Oh, yes. George left us the treasure of Agamemnon, but we haven't been able to find it. The poor dear died before he could tell us more." She looked at Uncle Harley and batted her eyes. "Harley, have you found it yet? I told you to hurry." I was horrified—my Aunt Henrietta was playing the aging coquette.

She looked back at Gage. "For a while, we thought it might be jewels or something similar, but now we've decided it's probably a very rare copy of Horace."

"Homer," Uncle Harley prompted.

Mowbridge sighed and I caught his worry. Mine was exactly the same. I could see Papa's books and artifacts being handled and discussed by anyone and everyone. "Don't worry, Mowbridge," I said to him under my breath, "I'll keep them away from you."

"I would be most grateful," he whispered back. "Do you think you could occupy Mr. Sinclair's time as well?"

It was a challenge, but I got them all out of the library and into the drawing room. Aunt Hen was still chattering to Gage about the Treasure, Uncle Harley was trying to discover if Mr. Page was a librarian, Evelyn was complaining, and I was already exhausted. I wasn't going to bear this alone—I sent a footman for Lymond.

I dragooned Livvy, Julia, Kenyon, and Lymond into helping me organize entertainment for everyone. It was quite a chore since Uncle Harley didn't wish to be entertained and Evelyn complained constantly. Boots generally didn't care for any form of entertainment that didn't involve drink and cards. Gage was always agreeable, no matter what was suggested. As the days went by, I was revising my opinion of him—at first I had decided I didn't care for him, but then he was always so charming, so mannerly, and so pleasant that I found myself liking him.

I tried to pair off Aunt Hen and Miss Hinchley, but Aunt Hen, so she said, had developed a sudden aversion to cats. She started sneezing every time Miss Hinchley and Precious came around. Personally, I thought Aunt Hen quite an actress, although I did admit life was difficult when long strands of cat hair were always floating around and landing on one's clothing. Miss Hinchley usually preferred to stay upstairs in her room anyway.

After a few days, my entire repertoire of entertainment was exhausted. I dragged myself to my room close to midnight and fell into a chair. Julia and Livvy came in behind me. "What are we doing tomorrow?" Julia asked.

"Lining the entire lot up against the nearest wall and shooting them all," I said bitterly. Being social was not my strong suit.

"How about a picnic?" Livvy asked, sitting down on the edge of my bed.

"We did that yesterday. Don't you remember how Evelyn complained about dust, ants, and grass? Besides, I got tired of listening to Bue howling all the time."

"Perhaps you can let him out."

I sighed. "I hope so. Poor Bue doesn't take kindly to being locked in the shed. He feels Bellerophon is his house, and frankly, I think he has a point."

Julia rolled her eyes. "Unfortunately, the rest of us feel the same way. Now, what about tomorrow?"

"How about sea bathing?" Livvy asked. "I'm sure Evelyn wouldn't like it, but at least it might take up some time."

"Aunt Hen would die first," I said. "You know how she feels about bathing. I don't know—we've shopped and we've looked at all the sights. There's not much else."

Livvy got up and gave me a quick kiss on the forehead. "You'll think of something, Roxanne. You always do." With that, she was off to bed and a sound sleep. I envied her.

I was, however, delighted that she had chosen to leave Julia and me alone for a few minutes. There was something delicate I wanted to discuss with Julia and, as late as it was, I wasted no time. "Julia, do you think Livvy and Kenyon Gwynn could make a match?"

Julia looked appalled. "Now you know I'd never force Livvy to marry someone she didn't care for," I added hastily, "but I have noticed that the two of them seem to rub along famously. From what Lymond tells me, Kenyon's well to grass and will inherit when his father dies." I got up to close the curtains. "What do you think?"

"Does Livvy care for him?" Her voice sounded strange and I only half heard her as I stared out the

99

window. Did I see someone moving around the garden? "I don't know," I said. "I haven't asked her. Why don't you do it? You're better at that sort of thing than I am. Then, if she's agreeable, we'll throw them together at every opportunity." I peered out the window again and saw nothing. I must have been mistaken. I turned around to look at Julia. "Will you do it?"

"I'd rather not." Why did she sound hesitant? "You're the oldest—perhaps you should see how Livvy feels." She stood and looked at me strangely. "Livvy and Kenyon. You may be right, Roxanne. It might be the perfect match." Before I could reply, she was gone, the door shutting softly behind her.

Strange behavior, I thought, then dismissed it. Julia was tired, just as all the rest of us were. And she was right—as the oldest, I should be the one to talk to Livvy. I would, I decided, do it tomorrow at the first opportunity.

I blew out one of my candles and turned back to the window. Once again, I saw a movement. I blew out my other candle, leaving my room in darkness. After a moment when my eyes adjusted, the moonlight was bright enough for me to discern someone pacing back and forth in the garden, looking around as though he was waiting for someone. I watched for a moment or two before I identified the figure—it was Mowbridge. I should have known; he was carrying a book in his hand. He waited for a few minutes as I watched, then pulled his watch from his pocket and checked it. Repocketing both watch and book, he went out of sight around the front corner of the house. "Another one off to bed for a night's sound sleep," I muttered to myself as I relit my candle and drew the curtains. I picked up my book—a copy of Horace's *Odes*—and tried to read.

100

Horace usually puts me to sleep, but not tonight. I finally had to slip down the hall to Aunt Hen's room to borrow one of her Minerva Press books. She was still up and gave me her latest.

"It was the fish course," she said, patting her chest. "I shouldn't have partaken. It gives me dyspepsia every time. Poor Mowbridge told me he suffered from it occasionally."

I nodded. "I saw him out getting some air in the garden a little while ago."

Aunt Hen nodded sagely. "I knew it. Dyspepsia again."

I agreed and went on to bed without thinking any more about it, an action I would come to regret.

Chapter 7

The next morning, before I even got to the breakfast room, I could hear Uncle Harley. "For what I pay him, he should be here! The damned . . ." Lymond nudged him as I walked into the room. "Damned slacker," Uncle Harley muttered beneath his breath.

"Uncle Harley has temporarily misplaced Mowbridge." Lymond pulled out a chair for me while Kenyon poured me some coffee. All this attention was extremely gratifying. I decided I must make Livvy start getting up to eat breakfast so she could enjoy this as well. Julia and I were usually the only ones in the family who regularly ate breakfast.

"I'm sure he's around somewhere," I said.

"That's what I told them." This was from Gage. He leaned back against his chair and surveyed the rest of the table negligently. "He's probably out for a morning walk."

"Perhaps," I replied. "I did see him out late last night. Aunt Hen thought he might have a touch of dyspepsia. He told her he had it occasionally."

Gage leaned forward. "Ah, you saw him. Where?"

"In the garden. He came back in the house after a few minutes. I suspected he only needed some fresh air." I had other problems on my mind. "Lymond, did you decide what we're to do today?"

He looked as surprised as I had thought he would be. "Livvy, Julia, and I thought you and Kenyon could furnish our entertainment today," I said with a smile. "Just let us know what you want to do. We're entirely at your disposal."

Lymond didn't get a chance to reply. Uncle Harley leaped to his feet, crashing his fist down on the table. "I pay the man a king's ransom to be here when I want him, and I want him *now!*"

Lymond looked from me to Uncle Harley and decided that Uncle Harley was the lesser of two evils. "I'll go up and rouse him," he said quickly. "Just sit down and stay calm. You don't want to go waking everyone up."

"Why not?" Uncle Harley growled to Lymond's retreating back. "Most of the day's gone as it is." He sat back down.

Kenyon, Gage, and I endeavored to engage Uncle Harley in conversation until Lymond returned, but he was in such a state that he was having none of it. He just sat there, glowering at each one of us in turn until Lymond walked back through the door. "Well?" Uncle Harley demanded.

Lymond looked at me. "Did you say you saw him come in last night after a walk?"

I nodded, and Lymond looked puzzled. "His bed is untouched. I checked with the maids and they haven't been in there this morning, so there's no possibility that he slept there."

"What?" Another roar from Uncle Harley, this one loud enough to alert Mowbridge, wherever he was. "He's gone? Absconded? Just left without a word?"

"I'm sure there's an explanation," Lymond said mildly.

"Mowbridge isn't the kind to leave in the middle of a job. I'm sure he's just gone into Brighton for something."

"He may have gone for some medicine," Kenyon said. "As for his bed being untouched, if he did have dyspepsia, he may have sat up all night in a chair. My father's done that a number of times."

Julia came in for breakfast and we caught her up on events.

"He's gone." Uncle Harley's voice rang with finality. "I know just what's happened: he found the *Iliad* and went off to sell it to Spencer. How could I have such a viper in my employ?" Uncle Harley stood, then turned and pointed a finger at me. "Which way did he go? What was he doing?"

I blinked, then stood so the man wouldn't appear so intimidating. "Mowbridge doesn't have the scroll. I found it and have it in my possession." I tried to speak in reasonable tones. "I told you that he was in the garden. He was looking at a book as he walked around. I got the impression he was waiting for someone."

"Reading a book?" Lymond broke in. "Good Lord, Roxanne, I thought you saw him after dark!"

"It was around midnight. I didn't actually see him reading, Lymond. He was only *carrying* a book and turning the pages."

"He's stolen it! The *Iliad!*" Uncle Harley moaned. "Right out of my grasp! I'd wager that Spencer is paying him a pretty penny for it right now."

"Have you looked in the library for him?" Julia asked in a small voice. "He may have come down early to begin his work."

We looked at each other, feeling foolish. Before the

others could get up, Uncle Harley sprinted out the door and down the hall. We all followed him. "Mowbridge, are you there?" he yelled, throwing the library door open. The heavy statuette of a cat that we used as a doorstop was in the way and the door banged against it hard enough to chip the paint. "Mowbridge?" Uncle Harley turned in the doorway and faced us. "See, I told you he was gone." He looked at Julia and me. "He's taken the scroll and you've lost as much as I have. You'll never see a farthing of Spencer's."

"Mowbridge would never do anything dishonest," Lymond said, trying to get by his uncle. "You know he's one of the most honest, direct men ever to live. You've told me that's what makes him so valuable— he always tells you the true worth of an item."

Uncle Harley looked deflated and sat down in a nearby chair. "All right, I grant that, but where is the man?"

I walked over by the desk and looked at the shelves. "Everything looks the same as yesterday. He's probably out for a walk." I glanced down at the desk where a book lay. It was Chapman's *Iliad*. I could have sworn I had put it back on the shelf. While Lymond calmed his uncle, I replaced it and glanced at Mowbridge's work. As a librarian, the man was a wonder. It was no surprise that he had worked in famous libraries all over the continent. Uncle Harley was fortunate to have him.

"Will you accompany us, Roxanne?" Julia asked.

I brought my attention back. "I'm sorry. What did you say?"

"I suggested that we take Uncle Harley for a ride around the grounds. We'll probably find Mowbridge walking along the shingle and we can bring him back."

Uncle Harley settled down in his chair. "I'll wait

here," he said stubbornly. No matter what we said, he would not be moved.

Lymond, Kenyon, Julia, and I decided to take our horses out for a gallop. If we were to run into Mowbridge, it wouldn't be far from the house and then we could continue our ride. With a look at Kenyon, I dashed to our apartments to see if Livvy would go with us, but she didn't want to ride. How, I wondered to myself as I donned my habit, would she ever get an offer from Kenyon if she didn't make an effort to be in his company? This project was going to take more than hints on my part. Perhaps Aunt Hen could lend a hand as well.

It was a fine morning for a ride, just the right amount of breeze to feel invigorating, and just the right amount of warmth in the air to be comfortable. The fog had all blown away by the time we went out. Kenyon and Lymond got up a race, offering to return to Julia and me. In no uncertain terms, I let them know that my Buttercup could race with the best. We took off across the field towards the sea, our destination the large mausoleum that Papa had built so he— and the rest of us—could look out forever over the wine-dark Channel. I asked Kenyon if Bue could come along and he said yes somewhat reluctantly. Now Bue bounded along joyfully beside me, barking. We hadn't done this in ages.

When we came in sight of the musoleum, Lymond suggested that we ride along the beach rather than return, and we did. Bue dashed back and forth to the mausoleum a couple of times, but finally followed us, his huge feet making puddles in the sand. Lymond and I went in front as Julia and Kenyon lagged farther and farther behind. I hoped fervently that Julia was talking about Livvy.

"Happy?" Lymond asked unexpectedly.

"Yes, very much. Why do you ask?"

He shrugged. "You're just a different person when you're at Bellerophon. You seem happy, rather as if you're . . ."

"At home?" I suggested with a smile.

He didn't smile back at me. "Yes, that's it. Do you think you could ever be happy somewhere else?"

This wasn't the time or place for this line of questioning and I brushed it away. "Perhaps, but I don't intend to live anywhere else, so the question is academic." I turned to look at Julia. She, too, looked splendid, her color high and her eyes sparkling. Bellerophon was good for her as well.

"We're almost into Brighton and haven't seen Mowbridge," Kenyon called out. "I don't think he came this way."

Lymond reined The Bruce in, and I turned Buttercup to look at Julia and Kenyon. "I'd have to agree. Perhaps we should return." I gave Lymond a smile. "Your Uncle Harley will have the whole house at sixes and sevens by now if Mowbridge hasn't returned."

"We'll be lucky if that's all," Lymond said with a sigh as we started back towards Bellerophon. Bucephalus wheeled and tried to jump in front of The Bruce, causing him to rear. Lymond kept his seat well. I think he was expecting it since it seemed to be one of Bue's favorite tricks.

"You're going to have to borrow some dog treats from Gage," Julia said with a laugh as we rode back beside them.

Lymond shook his head. "How does the man do it? I've spent months trying to become friends with that dog. Gage walks in here and in three minutes they're on speaking terms. I've done everything I know to do and the animal barely tolerates me." He paused and gave Bue a measured look. "Sometimes he doesn't even do that."

We laughed as we came out at the point where the mausoleum stood. Bue began dashing around the front, hiding behind the columns in the front, then running out to Buttercup and barking. I stopped and looked at the mausoleum closely. Because it was isolated on its windy point, it had been used as an assignation point by smugglers and thieves in the past. Everything looked just as it should have, but I still felt uneasy.

"I'm going to check the mausoleum," I said, dismounting. "Go ahead and I'll catch up with you."

"There's no point, Roxanne," Julia said, giving the place a cursory glance. "You don't even have your key. There's nothing on the outside that can be bothered."

Bue kept barking and I got a strange feeling between my shoulder blades. I shook it off; Lymond has told me I have an overactive imagination. Still, the prickling up my neck persisted. "I'm sure you're right, but I'm going to look anyway."

"You might as well talk to the wind," Lymond said to Julia as he dismounted from The Bruce. "We may as well stop until she satisfies her curiosity."

I walked briskly towards the porch of the mausoleum, while Bue barked and dashed around. Lymond tried to catch up with me, but Bue kept getting in his way. "Roxanne, will you restrain this animal?" I turned to discover Bue trying to jump on Lymond's chest. "He's trying to be affectionate," I told Lymond. "Just give him a hug and he'll stop." Bue put a muddy paw on Lymond's shirt and lapped him generously across the face. Lymond's manners lapsed and be did what he usually did when Bue was around and trying to be friendly: he began cursing under his breath, quite fluently.

"There's no reason to disparage Bue's parentage, Lymond." I was trying not to laugh. Kenyon and Julia walked up beside us and they didn't even try. Lymond failed to see the humor in the situation.

Bue dropped to his feet, grabbed Lymond's leg in his teeth, and pulled. "He's trying to play with you, Robert," Kenyon said, still laughing. I noted Kenyon was as far away from Bue as possible.

"Look at my boot." Lymond held his leg up and, true enough, there were several large scratches from Bue's teeth. Lymond looked at Bue sadly. "He hates me."

We laughed as we climbed the steps to the mausoleum porch, Bue getting more excited by the moment. At the top of the steps, I stopped and gasped. "Lymond!" I clutched his sleeve and pointed.

Mowbridge sat there against the mausoleum door, his legs straight out in front of him, his eyes staring forever at the bleak sea. Even from where we stood, we could see he was dead.

Lymond put an arm around me. "Don't faint, Roxanne."

I gave him the look that remark deserved. "Don't be ridiculous, Lymond." In truth, I did feel a bit shaky, but I certainly wouldn't admit it to anyone, much less Lymond. I turned to see about Julia. Her eyes were wide with shock, and Kenyon was holding her up. "Sit down on the steps, Julia, and put your head on your knees," I directed. Kenyon helped her sit and I sat beside her, holding her shoulders. Lymond and I exchanged a glance.

He and Kenyon went to look at the body. "I'm all right, Roxie, I really am," Julia said, taking a deep breath. She stared out at the ocean, not really seeing it. "Why would anyone harm Mowbridge? He was such a sweet, patient man."

"You're reading things into this, Julia." I tried to sound convincing. "I saw no mark on the body and no blood anywhere. Mowbridge was probably walking and overexerted himself. When he stopped to rest, he had an attack of some kind." This time, Julia gave me the look this remark deserved.

I glanced behind me as I heard the sound of Mowbridge's body being moved. Kenyon and Lymond had turned the body over and were examining the back. My curiosity overcame my squeamishness and I left Julia a moment. "Did he have an attack of some kind?" I asked, hoping that the man had at least died a quiet death.

Lymond pointed to a very small slit in the back of Mowbridge's coat. It was so tiny as to be difficult to see and there was hardly any blood staining the edges. "Yes, an attack, but not the kind you mean. He was stabbed. Probably a long, thin knife to the heart."

"A stiletto," Kenyon said as Lymond nodded in agreement.

"The poor man," I said softly with real regret.

"Yes." Lymond sounded business like, examining the body further. "But why?"

"And who?" Kenyon helped him turn the dead weight back over and lay it gently on the stones. The sightless eyes seemed to catch mine and, without realizing it, I gasped. Kenyon quickly closed the eyes and mouth. Lymond took out his handkerchief and covered the face. Bue rubbed against me and began sniffing all around the porch. He picked something up and swallowed it before we could stop him, then licked the stone.

"Blood?" Kenyon asked as I held Bue and Lymond looked.

Lymond shook his head. "No, it must just have been an insect or something." He looked at us and gave a tight smile. "Animals accept death better than we do—they acknowledge it, then go on about their routine." He walked back over to the body and glanced over at Julia. "Speaking of routine, I need to search the body and see if there's anything there. Roxanne, do you want to take Julia home? You can send for the magistrate when you get there."

I really didn't want to leave, but saw it was the logical thing for me to do. I tried to help Julia up. "I can't, Roxanne. I simply can't get back on my horse and ride away."

I looked back at the body. "We can't do anything for him now, Julia. Lymond and Kenyon will be here." I started to say more, but Lymond called to me. "Roxanne, come here and look at this." Julia was clutching my hand. I sat Bue down beside her and she put her arm around his neck. Bue responded by trying to nuzzle her. He really is the most understanding dog.

It was easier to look at Mowbridge's body since the face was covered. "Look at this," Lymond said, holding Mowbridge's hand out. He had pried the fingers open and there was a scrap of paper in his palm. The paper was crumpled and clammy so Lymond had a difficult time smoothing it out.

"The frontispiece of Chapman," I said instantly. I'd seen it a dozen times or more.

"The what?" Kenyon peered over my shoulder.

"The front page from Chapman's translation of Homer. See, here's the title and name. Here's the picture of the translator, George Chapman." I pointed,

111

but kept my finger above the paper. I couldn't bring myself to touch it.

"Could the book be around here someplace?" Lymond rose to his feet and looked around the porch. "Was it his own copy of the book or perhaps Uncle Harley's?"

I shook my head. "I don't think it was Mowbridge's and I remember your uncle said he had lent his to a George Clarke."

Lymond nodded. "A cousin." He paused. "So then you think this was—is your book?"

"Yes." I stood as well, trying to remember the last time I had seen the Chapman. It had been recently. "This morning," I said slowly.

Lymond stared at me. "What are you talking about, Roxanne?"

"The Chapman." I looked at him, frowning. "Lymond, the Chapman was in the library this morning. Don't you remember? When we went in with your uncle, the book was on the desk. I picked it up myself and reshelved it."

"Was the frontispiece torn out then?"

I shook my head. "I don't know. I didn't look at it. I just thought it odd that it was out of place and put it back on the shelf where it belonged."

"It might not have been the same book," Kenyon suggested.

"Or," said Lymond slowly, "if it was, how did it get back to the library desk?"

We all looked at each other. "We need to get back to Bellerophon immediately and look at that book," Kenyon said. He turned and put his hand on Julia's shoulder. "Do you think you can ride now? If not, I'll go bring a carriage back for you."

Julia nodded and Kenyon and I helped her mount.

I hated to leave Lymond alone there, but I was dying of curiosity to take a look at the Chapman in the library.

We set off for the house. "I'm all right now," Julia said. I thought she looked a trifle pale, but she was rallying. Our family usually has quick recuperative powers.

At the house, I took a moment to send Julia upstairs with a maid while Kenyon sent for the local constable and magistrates. I almost flew to the library, practically crashing into George Gage and Boots in the hall. "You do seem to be in a hurry, Miss Sydney," Gage said as we untangled ourselves.

"I . . . uh, I need to look something up in the library."

"We've just been there," Boots said sullenly, "and there's nothing there but Father."

"Oh." I certainly didn't want to be the one to tell Uncle Harley about Mowbridge. I looked at Boots for a moment—he wasn't the one to do it either.

Evelyn came down the stairs. "George, how are you?" She smiled effusively at Gage, ignoring the rest of us. Miss Hinchley came behind her, carrying Precious. I looked quickly behind me to see if Bucephalus had stayed outside. I didn't see him, but in a second or two, I heard him. He bounded inside and up the stairs, baying and pawing at the cat. Precious spat at him and came in a flying fur ball over Evelyn's head. Evelyn screamed and managed to give a good imitation of a swoon right into George Gage's arms.

"Oh, hell," Boots said in disgust. He walked towards the door, kicking Precious aside with one polished boot. Then he came to Bucephalus and tried the same thing. Precious had yowled and gotten out of the way. Bucephalus simply sank his teeth right into

Boots's gleaming Hessian-covered leg. Boots yowled and shook his leg, but Bue hung on.

"Precious!" Miss Hinchley screamed, jumping across Boots and chasing Precious into the drawing room. I feared for the draperies and cornices. We had just finished repairing them.

It was time for me to enter the fray. "Bue, let him go," I said, grabbing at his collar. I looked up to see Woodbury, staring at all of us with the fascination of a scientist studying a new and strange insect. He was immobilized. "Woodbury, get Holmwood! I can't do a thing with this dog."

"Shoot the damn thing," Boots said. I didn't think he was hurt—most of the damage seemed to be to his boot. "Give me my pistol."

"I certainly will not," I told him. "If you hadn't kicked him, he wouldn't have bothered you. Bue is the gentlest animal alive." Boots reached out to grab Bue's collar. Bue released his hold on the Hessian and made a lunge for Boots's hand and arm. Boots managed to stagger back on one foot and fell backwards into the drawing room. He shut the door with a slam.

Holmwood came in then. "What's all the fuss about?" He touched Bue's collar and they walked off together, Bue wagging his tail and lapping at Holmwood's hand.

Uncle Harley came out of the library. "What's that noise? Has Mowbridge come back yet?" He got a look at Evelyn, still pretending to be in a languid swoon in Gage's arms. "Evelyn, have you lost your mind? Stand up, girl!" He grabbed her by the arm and jerked her upright. "Next time she does that, just shove her to her feet. It works every time," Uncle Harley said to Gage. "I do wish you'd be a little quieter around here." With that, he turned and stomped off into the

114

library. I edged around Gage and Evelyn and followed him inside, Kenyon right behind me.

"I was seeing to Julia and missed the excitement," Kenyon murmured. "Have you told him?" He looked at Uncle Harley.

I shook my head. "No, I didn't think I should be the one to do it. Why don't you?" I went over to where I had shelved the Chapman, trying to appear nonchalant. I looked, then looked again. "It's gone!" I exclaimed without even realizing it.

In a second, Kenyon was at my side. "What!"

I pointed to the space between books. "It was right there this morning. I put it there myself." I looked at Uncle Harley. "Mr. Sinclair, did you get the Chapman from the shelf?"

He glared at us from under his shaggy brows. "No. Why would I do a fool thing like that? Mowbridge don't like to have his books touched once he puts them where they're supposed to be."

"Someone's been in here and taken it," Kenyon whispered in my ear. "Either that or Mowbridge took it for some reason." We looked at each other, wondering the same thing. If the book was gone, there had to be an explanation.

But what was it?

Chapter 8

Kenyon and I didn't have long to stare at each other. Uncle Harley came and stood between us. "Just what the deuce is going on here?" he demanded. "What about the Chapman? What about the scroll? We need to locate Mowbridge. Did you see him?"

I felt myself pale. "Yes, we found him."

Kenyon wasted no words. "He's dead. We found him out at the mausoleum. Judging from the body, he's been dead several hours."

I think both of us expected little reaction from Uncle Harley so we were surprised when he clutched his chest and sagged into a chair. It was gratifying to know he cared about the man.

"Dead! He can't be dead. Now I'll never know about that scroll! The next thing I know Spencer will have his librarian in here and he'll have it!" He stood and grabbed Kenyon by his lapels. "Tell me, sir, do you know anything about books? Could you tell the worth of that scroll?"

Kenyon tried to step back, but the desk was in his way. He next tried to move Uncle Harley, but couldn't do that either. "Nothing! I know nothing about scrolls, I swear it!"

Uncle Harley dropped his hands and pinned me with a stare. "You, this is all your fault! You've hidden the thing, haven't you? I don't know why Mowbridge wanted to look through the books first. If he'd searched those damned scrolls first and looked at the thing, then I'd know by now if it was valuable. I think he did it just to keep me on tenterhooks." He jabbed at the air with his finger. "Now all of London will know why I'm here and Spencer will be here to see you. I want to see the thing now. Get it for me."

This was too much. I felt my spine stiffen and I stood up straight in front of him. "I certainly will not! Don't you care that the man is dead? Don't you have an ounce of human compassion? You could at least *pretend* to care!"

"I care! I care! Now let me see the damned scroll!" His face was turning purple.

"No." I turned away to speak to Kenyon. "Should we go back to the mausoleum to stay with Lymond until the authorities get there?"

Kenyon looked at me and I could have sworn he was trying not to smile. "I'll go. You should perhaps stay here."

I sighed. Men always were in the forefront of things while females always had to stay home. There was no justice in the world. Kenyon took a few steps across the floor and I tried to move around Uncle Harley, but he was blocking my way. "The scroll," he said hoarsely, "don't you see that I *must* have that scroll!"

"And you will," I said, sidestepping, "but not right now. I showed it to Mowbridge yesterday and he asked me to put it away until he was ready to examine it carefully. I'll get it for you later, after we take care of Mowbridge."

Uncle Harley moved towards me and, if I had had

117

lapels, he would have seized them. As it was, he contented himself with clenching his fists in front of my face. "He saw it? Did he say anything?"

"No. He took it from its bag, glanced over it for a little while, and then told me to put it away in a safe place until he could examine it inch by inch. He wanted to get everything else finished first. I got the impression that he intended to spend quite a bit of time looking at it carefully."

Uncle Harley sagged into a chair. He looked like a broken man. "I knew it. Mowbridge always saved the best for last—rather like dessert. That means the scroll is a find of the first magnitude." He looked at me and frowned, then changed his expression to what he imagined was a pleading look. "Don't let Spencer have it. That's all I ask. If you won't give it to me, just don't let Spencer have it." His eyes narrowed and a scowl crossed his face. "Could Spencer have done this to Mowbridge? I wouldn't put it past him." He leaned back against the cushions, moved uncomfortably, then pulled a book from behind the side cushion. "What's this? The Chapman. You should take better care of your books. This one is only of piddling value—Elizabethan isn't it?" He opened the book and leafed through it. "It'll be damaged if many people sit on it."

Kenyon and I both reached for the Chapman. I was closer and quicker and had the book open to the frontispiece before Kenyon reached it. He looked over my shoulder. "It's gone," he whispered in one breath. "Torn out."

"Do you want to wager that it would be a perfect match if we put the edges together?" I asked, closing the book. "That leaves some questions: did he have the book with him and, if he did, how did it get back

118

here on the desk? Then, how did it get back off the shelf and behind a pillow?"

"If Mowbridge didn't have it with him, then how did he get the frontispiece? Also, would he desecrate a book by ripping out a page?" Kenyon asked.

Uncle Harley glared at us from under his brows. "Just what the deuce are you two talking about? The only person I've seen with that book was Boots. I made him put it down—the boy don't know a thing about books. He'd as soon use a Gutenberg for a doorstop." He paused, then gave us a wry smile. "Of course, if he *knew* it was a Gutenberg, he'd sell it in a trice. Whatever you do, don't let him have that scroll." Evidently Uncle Harley knew his children better then they thought he did.

Kenyon stayed to talk to Uncle Harley while I went to talk to Aunt Hen and Livvy as well as check on Julia. I found both Aunt Hen and Livvy in Julia's room. Julia seemed to have recovered, although she was still somewhat pale. "I should have gone with you," Livvy said in disgust. "I always miss the excitement."

"It wasn't pretty." I tried not to shudder as I remembered the condition of Mowbridge's body. "By the way, Livvy, Kenyon was so helpful. He took charge immediately. I don't think we could have managed without him. Could we have, Julia?"

"No." I grimaced as there was silence. Julia knew what I was trying to accomplish, but she wasn't being helpful at all.

"Kenyon's talking to Lymond's uncle right now," I continued. "I do own that he's good at that sort of thing. Very compassionate, very intelligent. Don't you agree, Julia?"

"Yes."

I gave her a quick, disgusted look. I was going to have to talk to her immediately. Livvy and Kenyon would be the perfect match—I knew it in my bones. It would simply take a little nudge from the rest of us. We needed to throw them together at every opportunity.

"And how is Harley?" Aunt Hen asked. "Should I go see how he's doing? I know this was a terrible shock to him."

"You can go sit with him if you wish, Aunt Hen, but I warn you that the man lacks human feelings." I proceeded to tell them of his reaction when we told him of Mowbridge's death.

Aunt Hen was unperturbed. "He was merely hiding his true feelings, Roxanne. Harley is a very sensitive man." With that, she drifted out the door, humming to herself.

"Do you two," Livvy asked, looking at the door, "get the feeling that there's something brewing in that quarter?" She thought a moment. "Aunt Hen? Surely not!"

Before we could answer, we heard the sound of the local constable riding up. He certainly didn't tarry—by the time I reached the front of the house, all I could see was a puff of dust. "Mr. Gwynn took them to the mausoleum," Woodbury told me.

I started to go back to my room when I noticed Woodbury's face. "What happened to you?"

"Miss Hinchley's cat. Again."

I looked at him and noted he was covered with long cat fur. "On the cornice again?" I asked. Woodbury nodded and I sent him to the kitchen for some salve. That cat should . . . I didn't permit myself to dwell on it. I might have been tempted to take action.

I wandered aimlessly around for a while, waiting for

120

Kenyon and Lymond to return with whatever news they had. Aunt Hen and Uncle Harley were still in the library, so I couldn't even go in there to pass the time. I started back to our apartments where my personal desk was located, thinking I might do some work on Papa's translation of Xenophon. I had certainly neglected it of late.

George Gage met me in the hall. "Well, Miss Sydney, I heard you had met up with an unfortunate experience."

"My experience wasn't as unfortunate as Mowbridge's." I smiled as I looked at him. Miss Hinchley passed us on her way upstairs. Precious was safe in her arms and she was looking all around before she took each step. "The gardener has taken the dog outside," I told her. She looked at me in gratitude, clutched Precious even more tightly, and went on up the stairs. I really felt sorry for her; her cat was all she had in the world for affection. She certainly wasn't held in any esteem by either Uncle Harley or Evelyn.

"Tell me about it." Gage returned me to our conversation. "Why don't we go for a stroll in the garden while we talk about it?" He held his arm for me. I really didn't want to take it, but it would seem quite gauche to refuse. We reached the door just as Woodbury did, a pot of salve in his hand. He had difficulty opening the door since his fingers were slick, but I didn't help him. We haven't had a steward in years, and Lymond didn't hire one when he took the house, so Woodbury takes his door-opening duties very seriously. Actually, Woodbury takes everything seriously.

"Now, Miss Sydney," Gage said smoothly as we walked along the flagstone path Holmwood had put down through the grass, "tell me what you discovered."

"That's easy," I replied, smiling at him. "Nothing."

"Oh, come now, I heard about Mowbridge. How did you know there had been foul play? Were there clues?"

I wondered briefly if we had an amateur detective on our hands. "Yes, we did discover poor Mowbridge, but there were no clues that I know of. You'll really have to ask Mr. Gwynn or Mr. Lymond when they return. As for how we knew there had been foul play, Mr. Lymond discovered a puncture wound when he looked at the body." I paused. "Do you know why anyone would want to harm Mowbridge?"

"Why would anyone want to harm anyone else at all?" he said lightly. "As for Mowbridge and a motive, it could be any one of a dozen things. I really didn't know him at all."

"Oh," I said, fishing, "I thought perhaps you'd been to the house with Boots and knew something more about Mowbridge."

Gage shook his head. "No, I've never been to the Sinclairs' country place and only been in and out of their London digs. If you recall, his father didn't know me at all. Boots and I are good friends." He paused and gave me a grin. "I suppose you've noticed that his family is not what could be termed close."

"I've noticed." I smiled back at him, thawing. There was something about Gage that I hadn't really liked, but perhaps I had been wrong. We walked on through the garden, chatting about trivialities, and I found him amusing and friendly. I was surprised—I'm usually an excellent judge of character at first meeting. Bue came bounding up to us and Gage gave him a treat from his pocket.

"I must get your recipe to give to Lymond," I said as Bue gulped down the treat and sat, wagging his tail and drooling. "He and Bue seem to have difficulty communicating."

"A wonderful dog," Gage said, giving Bue another treat and patting him on the head. "Dogs have an instinct about character, you know." He smiled. He was right—Bue was an excellent judge of character as well, although I had always thought he was a little harsh on Lymond. The man did have *some* good qualities.

It was late afternoon before Lymond, Kenyon, and a wagon carrying Mowbridge's body got back to Bellerophon. Holmwood had been overseeing the building of a coffin, so the maids were able to see to getting Mowbridge properly laid out. It seemed he had no family at all, and no home. Uncle Harley had suggested burial in Brighton, but I hated to have the man disposed of impersonally, so I had asked the girls if they minded him being buried on our property. They agreed it wouldn't be unseemly—after all, the family had the mausoleum. Two men were already digging the grave, and we planned services the first thing in the morning.

Supper was rather like a sit-down affair between the Romans and the Huns. It wasn't until after this disastrous meal and dodging Gage for conversation that I finally cornered Lymond in the drawing room. "All right, what else did you discover?" I demanded under my breath as the others set up to play cards. Aunt Hen and the other girls were trying to be social, but it wasn't working very well.

"After the fiasco that was supper, you can still ask that?" Lymond looked at me incredulously. "Good heavens, Roxanne, if we aren't all on guard, the entire assemblage may come to blows." He paused. "Actually, I thought it was going to happen in there."

I thought back to supper. It had indeed been a fiasco: Uncle Harley was moaning about Spencer and asking if *anyone* knew of a good librarian, Boots was his usual sullen self, Evelyn was flirting brazenly with Gage, and the rest of us were watching their antics. Suddenly, for no reason, Boots slammed his fist down on the table. He glared at Evelyn and said: "I would have thought you'd be overset about this latest tragedy, sister dear. After all, weren't you the one who followed Mowbridge around like a lapdog for weeks?"

"That's enough!" Uncle Harley roared.

Boots smiled a very small smile, as if he had accomplished what he wanted. "Why, Father? Don't you want it mentioned? Are you afraid someone might think our esteemed family might be responsible in some way?" He looked at Evelyn. "After all, Evelyn might have killed Mowbridge in a fit of pique. Yet another man who wasn't interested in her charms."

Evelyn stood and threw a saltcellar at him, followed by both her own glass of wine and Julia's. "Do you know what you are?" she hissed at him, leaning as far as she could towards him. "You're a son of a bitch. That's all you are and all you've ever been."

Boots brushed the salt off his arm and grinned at her. He had managed to dodge the wine. Most of it had landed on the footman behind him. "Tsk, tsk, dear sister. Castigating Mother in such terms? How could you?"

Uncle Harley smashed his fist down on the table, overturning two or three more wine glasses. "Enough, I said!" He glared at Boots. "You, sirrah, if I ever hear you speak to your sister in such a fashion, I'll have you whipped." He turned to Evelyn and glared. "And you, miss. Your mother was a saint. I want to see you in the library. Now!" He stood and stalked out the door. Evelyn paled visibly, then followed him. Boots leaned back in his chair, motioned for more wine, and smiled sunnily at all of us. "Just another family evening with the Sinclairs." He tossed off the wine, turned and picked up the bottle and went out. We heard the front door slam behind him.

There was dead silence all around as the rest of us picked at our food. Suddenly, Aunt Hen spoke up. "Cards, anyone?"

Her suggestion seemed better than sitting in the dining room, and we adjourned to the drawing room. This was my chance to speak to Lymond, but Gage came over to us. "Shocking about Mowbridge," he said to Lymond. "Did the locals come up with anything?"

Lymond shook his head. "Murder by person or persons unknown." He stopped speaking as Evelyn and Uncle Harley came in. She was white as a sheet. She looked for a place to sit and I was certainly proud of Julia: she made a space for her and engaged her in conversation until things reached a semblance of normalcy. In the meantime, Uncle Harley was quizzing Lymond just as Gage had done.

"I think you should examine Spencer's whereabouts," Uncle Harley said. "He'd do anything to stop me from acquiring something better than he has."

"I really don't think Spencer would go this far," Lymond said mildly. "I rather think that someone local may be involved."

"Perhaps." Uncle Harley dismissed the subject, looking at Kenyon and Julia getting ready to sing together while Livvy played for them. I noted that Kenyon seemed to look down at Livvy with great pleasure. She certainly appeared to advantage in the light. Julia moved to stand between them. I was really going to have to talk further to Julia—and soon. I turned my attention back to Lymond and Uncle Harley.

"What I need is a librarian," Uncle Harley was saying. "I know about books, but I need a man to validate things for me. It'll take time to replace Mowbridge."

"I doubt you can ever replace him," Lymond told him, "but I might have a temporary solution for you. A friend of mine on the continent has gone to Brazil for a few months, and his librarian is free. Better luck, the man is in London right now." He paused, giving me a look I couldn't interpret. "If you wish, I'll have him come here until you can find another librarian to replace Mowbridge."

"Can he be here tomorrow?" Uncle Harley came close to smiling.

Lymond stifled a grin. "I don't think so, but he could be here within the week." Uncle Harley nodded and turned his attention to the singers. Lymond looked at me and spoke. "The magistrates and constables want to look at the library to see if they can find a link between the page Mowbridge was clutching and your books."

"What's that?" Uncle Harley said. "My books? I don't allow the *hoi polloi* to touch my books!"

"No, the books here at Bellerophon." He started to turn back to me, but Gage stepped up from behind us. I hadn't seen him there. "A page? What's this? Have you been keeping important information from us, Mr. Lymond?" There was a pause and I could see Lymond was forming his thoughts.

"Mowbridge was holding a torn frontispiece in his fist," Lymond finally said. "It's probably nothing—probably just something he had in his pocket and clutched as he was stabbed. The magistrates just want to check. I don't expect anything to come of it."

"Then why do it?" Uncle Harley asked. "I know

126

those damned people. Poking and prying every-where."

"We need to try and cooperate," I said while Lymond searched for an answer. "After all, they may uncover something that would locate the murderer. Anything that might help is worth a try."

"Damned waste of time." Uncle Harley looked at the singers and started to say something else when Boots came in. He, too, was singing, but it was some kind of a tavern song, rather filthy if the two or three words I caught were any indication. Gage and Lymond rushed to the door and hustled him outside. The rest of us acted as if nothing had happened. Everyone, that is, except Evelyn. She smiled with satisfaction as she looked at the disgusted expression on her father's face. The rest of the evening was not any more successful than the first part had been, and we all went to bed early.

The next morning, I passed Miss Hinchley in the back hall. Her color was high and she appeared agitated, but she didn't stop. She wheeled and went upstairs. I was wondering if I should follow her when I caught Gage's man, Parrott, skulking around the library door while Uncle Harley, Kenyon, and Lymond were inside talking. As soon as he saw me, he disappeared down the hall. This wasn't the first time I had seen him where he wasn't supposed to be. I resolved to keep an eye on the man. I had altered my opinion of Gage, but I still didn't care for Parrott. I wondered why Gage kept him around.

Lymond informed me that the magistrates would be here at eleven to look through the library, and, since I had some time, I hunted up Julia so I could talk to her. As luck would have it, she was alone.

"Julia," I began, getting right to the point, "I want

to talk to you about Kenyon Gwynn." I looked behind me. I needed to talk quickly—Livvy could come in at any moment. "I think we could work up a match here and there seems to be some attraction already."

"Do you think so?" Julia blushed rosily.

"No point in denying it—I've seen it a dozen times." I thought I heard a noise and went to the door, but there was no one there. "I think the man has his eye on Livvy, and I think, with a little encouragement, she'd reciprocate."

"Livvy?"

"Yes, goose. Don't tell me you haven't noticed. Every time they're together, I've noticed a something in the air. They're made for each other, Julia, I just know it. Haven't you noticed how much their coloring is alike? Their tastes are just the same as well. And last night, did you see the way he looked at her as he sang?"

Julia dropped her embroidery and bent to pick it up. "I haven't noticed," she said. Her voice sounded oddly muffled.

"Well, I have," I said briskly. "I notice such things. I've also noticed that you're always around when they're together. Now, Julia, I have no problem with that, as long as you stay on the other side. Don't get between them. Give them an opportunity to get to know each other." I smiled at the thought. "We could have another wedding in the family."

"Livvy and Kenyon." Julia got up and looked out the window. "I know you've mentioned it before, but I thought you'd forgotten about it. I . . . I don't know, Roxanne."

"Well, I know, Julia, and I'm telling you that he has something of a *tendre* for her. It's up to us to encourage it. Lymond says Kenyon's of a good family

TO GET YOUR 3 FREE BOOKS
FILL OUT AND MAIL THE COUPON BELOW

3 F R E E B O O K S

Mail to: Zebra Regency Home Subscription Service
120 Brighton Road
P.O. Box 5214
Clifton, New Jersey 07015-5214

YES! Start my Regency Romance Home Subscription and send me my 3 FREE BOOKS as my introductory gift.
Then each month, I'll receive the 3 newest Zebra Regency Romances to preview FREE for ten days. I understand
that if I'm not satisfied, I may return them and owe nothing. Otherwise, I'll pay the low members' price of just
$9.90 for all 3 books and save over $2.00 off the publisher's price (a $11.97 value). There are no shipping, handling
or other hidden charges. I may cancel my subscription at any time and there is no minimum number to buy.
In any case, the 3 FREE books are mine to keep regardless of what I decide.

NAME

ADDRESS _____ APT NO. _____

CITY _____ STATE _____ ZIP _____
(   )

TELEPHONE

SIGNATURE _____ (if under 18 parent or guardian must sign)

Terms and prices subject to change. Orders subject to acceptance by Zebra Home Subscription Service, Inc.

RG1093

GET
3 FREE
REGENCY
ROMANCE
NOVELS—
A $11.97
VALUE!

ZEBRA HOME SUBSCRIPTION SERVICE, INC.
120 BRIGHTON ROAD
P.O. BOX 5214
CLIFTON, NEW JERSEY 07015-5214

and has prospects. With both Cassie and Livvy married off, we'd be able to spend all our money on outfitting you for the marriage mart. Wouldn't you like a season?"

To my surprise, Julia wheeled and looked at me fiercely. She looked like Papa in his worst moods. "I'll never marry! Never!"

I rose and patted her arm. "Don't be ridiculous, Julia. Of course you'll marry."

"You say you'll never marry," she said.

"That's different," I told her. "No one's ever expected me to marry and I've never seriously entertained it as an option. It's enough for me to see all of you married." I smiled at her. "Just think, I can come visit each of you for a while and look at all my nieces and nephews, then come back to Bellerophon and live quietly with Bucephalus. It'll be an ideal life for me."

"I'll be right here with you." Her mouth was set in a stubborn line I hadn't seen in years. I started to answer her, but at that moment, Livvy came in. We all sat down and I did my best to steer the conversation to the merits of Kenyon Gwynn, but Julia kept talking about when we would all be spinsters and put on our caps. I could have throttled her.

I left the two of them. If this was going to work, I had to bring Julia around to my point of view. If I couldn't do it, then I knew who could and it was time for reinforcements. I went to get Aunt Hen.

Chapter 9

I was delayed by some morning chores and didn't get to the library until almost half past eleven. I could hear the brawling before I opened the door. Inside, Lymond and Kenyon were doing their best to restrain Uncle Harley. He was screeching at the men searching the library and his face was almost purple. As I looked around, I could see why.

There were four of them. One was on the library ladder, the other three were going through the lower shelves. They were tossing books around like so much firewood. Piles and heaps of books littered the floor. Gage was going along behind them, trying his best to keep the books from falling to the floor and being damaged.

"Reprobates! Damned Philistines!" Uncle Harley was yelling.

Evidently Lymond had had enough. He got right up in his uncle's face. "Uncle Harley, if you don't keep quiet, I'm going to call the footmen and have you bound and gagged."

"You wouldn't dare." Uncle Harley glared at him. They looked much alike, glaring at each other, but Uncle Harley was the first to give way. "People shouldn't treat books that way," he said as he sat down in a chair. He transferred his glare to the magistrates.

Lymond threw me a despairing glance, then went to see if he could make the searchers treat my property with more respect. Evidently they weren't book lovers. I said as much to Gage who gave me a wry smile. "Book lovers? I doubt they even read."

We were unable to say more as the magistrate, Squire Marston, saw me and started my way, talking. He didn't notice that the heavy statue Papa always used as a doorstop had been moved to stand by the desk. He tripped over it and tried to catch himself on the edge of the desk, managing to send everything on top of it crashing to the floor in a pile at my feet. One of the other searchers dropped his armful of books on the floor and sprang to help him, but ran into the library ladder. The man on the ladder teetered for what seemed like minutes, then came crashing to the floor, right on top of Square Marston. He—or the Squire— let out a howl of agony and everyone rushed to help. They trampled books, inkwells, papers, what have you. Papa's library would never be the same. I did take a quick look at Uncle Harley, expecting him to be at least in the throes of apoplexy, but he was merely sitting there, surveying the entire fiasco with a horrified look.

It seemed the man on the ladder had broken his leg, so it took the rest of the morning to take care of that and get him safely loaded on a wagon and on his way home. I offered him a room at Bellerophon, but the Squire declined after taking a look around at the assembled company. In truth, I didn't blame him.

The search was to resume later in the afternoon. I left the men and took Livvy and Julia into the library to see if we could pick up a few things before everyone returned.

"Papa would die," Livvy said, surveying the damage. The place looked as if a whirling dervish had been through it.

There was a smooth voice behind us. "Evidently the Brighton authorities are not well versed in searches." It was Gage, a hint of laughter in his voice. "I don't mean to make light of the situation, but, in truth, it seems humor may be only way to get through this."

Livvy returned his smile. "I think you may be right, Mr. Gage."

The four of us spent some time picking up and getting the worst of the mess out of the floor. I picked up the offending statue—one of a pair of Egyptian cats that Papa had picked up in Cairo—and put it back beside the door. Papa's crystal inkwell had been chipped, and we couldn't find his gold letter opener at all. I assumed it was under a pile of books somewhere. By the time the others returned to resume their search, we had, at least, managed to make pathways through the piles of papers and books.

The searchers were almost finished when Gage picked up a book from the top of a stack. "What's this? Look at this, Miss Sydney." He handed me a book and I was horrified to see that the pages had been slashed over and over. The entire book was in ribbons. Even the paper covering the bindings had been ripped out.

"An expensive one?" Squire Marston asked.

I shook my head as I handed him the book. "No. A recent copy of Pope's translation of Homer's *Iliad*." I looked again in amazement as he thumbed through the shredded book. "Why on earth would anyone do that? It certainly wasn't a valuable book."

"Nor a very good one, either," Lymond added. We'd had this discussion before and I had discovered that Lymond was no admirer of Pope.

"There must be something." Squire Marston looked at all the things I had just put back on top of the desk and, evidently judging they were inconsequential, swept them off with his arm into the floor and spread the shreds of Pope's book across the desktop. With a sigh, I bent down to pick up Papa's inkwell again. When I stood back up, Parrott had come in the room with a letter for Gage. He glanced at it, then at Parrott. "I'll answer this later." He returned the letter to Parrott, then turned back to the desktop where the mutilated book was spread out. Parrott looked at the book and whispered something to Gage. Immediately Gage spoke to Squire Marston. "I believe my man may have some information for you," he said, motioning Parrott up to the desk as I replaced the inkwell.

"I see you've found Mowbridge's handiwork," Parrott said, looking at the shreds.

"Do you know something about this?" Squire Marston demanded, waving his hands around. I snatched the inkwell up just in time.

"I saw Mowbridge doing this yesterday," Parrott said. "I asked him what he was doing, but he just smiled at me. 'There's others that will know,' was all he said." Parrott shrugged. "It was no business of mine, so I went on my way." He paused. "There were other books in the same shape."

"Others?" Squire Marston came around the desk. "Where, man? How many did you see?"

"The better part of a dozen, I suppose. I thought it was something either Miss Sydney or Mr. Sinclair had ordered him to do. As I said, it was no business of mine."

133

I looked hard at Pope's mangled version of Homer. "I can't imagine Mowbridge doing that. He loved books."

Parrott gave me a hard look. "As I say, Miss Sydney, I saw the man doing it. Why, I don't know. All I know is I saw him with my own eyes."

"I'm sure you did, and I'm sure there was a reason for it," I said hastily. I didn't believe the man for a moment, but there was no point in antagonizing him. There had to be an explanation.

Lymond had been standing quietly, listening to all this. He frowned and joined us. "If Mowbridge did other books this way, then they must be around here somewhere. Where did you see them?"

"He burned them," Parrott said bluntly. "He had a good fire going and was throwing the pieces of books onto the fire. 'An expensive blaze,' he said with a laugh as he threw some in."

Lymond looked at him in amazement. "Good God, Parrott. If you saw him destroying Miss Sydney's property, why didn't you say something?"

Parrott shrugged. "As I said—it wasn't any of my business." He looked at Gage for permission to leave. Squire Marston asked Parrott to keep himself available for questioning, and he left us.

"Is that man trustworthy?" Lymond asked baldly.

Gage looked unperturbed. "I'd stake my life on anything he had to say. I've never caught him in any kind of falsehood."

Lymond looked around, ran his fingers through his hair, and grimaced. "Damn it all—excuse me, Miss Sydney—it just doesn't make sense. No sense at all."

The authorities turned up nothing else although they searched all afternoon. They took the ruined Pope with them and left behind a complete shambles. Lymond stood by my chair as I surveyed the damage. "Why don't you just close up the library and wait until DeWitt comes? I've already sent for him."

"DeWitt?" I could hardly work up any interest. One look around the library and I was almost defeated.

"The new librarian I'm borrowing from a friend." Lymond moved some books and sat down beside me. We were alone in the library while everyone else was dressing for supper. "Tell me, Roxanne, do you think Mowbridge shredded that book?"

I reflected a moment. I really hadn't known the man, but I could never see him hurting a book. "No." I paused. "But that raises the question of who did. And why." I turned to look at him. "Lymond, that means someone in the house did it."

"It also means that Parrott is lying."

I nodded. "But why?"

Lymond looked as baffled as I knew I did. "There's no explanation at all."

"Unless Parrott or Gage is covering up for Boots."

Lymond looked at me sharply. "Why Boots?"

"I don't know." I leaned back and sighed. "Perhaps because your uncle wants these books. He and Boots don't seem to have very much of a familial relationship."

"That's an understatement." Lymond grinned at me.

"I could see Boots trying to anger his father by destroying books," I continued.

"But there's a problem, Roxanne. That book—or those books as the case may be—didn't belong to Uncle Harley. They were yours. And, if I understand correctly, the book by Pope wasn't particularly valuable."

"It wasn't valuable at all," I replied. "That's the puzzling part. There must be a hundred books in here that are worth more, and those are just the ones I know about. The Pope is one I picked up in London some time back—just a book from a bookstore.''

"Could the connection be because it was a translation of the *Iliad?*''

I shrugged. "I just don't know, Lymond.'' I sighed. "This whole thing baffles me. There's no logic anywhere. Does this atmosphere follow your Uncle Harley wherever he goes?''

Lymond laughed, stood, and held out a hand to help me up. "I think it does.'' He smiled right into my eyes and once again I felt that strange, giddy feeling I get when he looks at me that way. "I've been bereft of your company lately, my dear Miss Sydney. Would you care for a stroll in the garden after supper?'' His fingers touched mine lightly as he moved slightly closer. "I feel sure the stars, the moon, and the sea air would refresh your state of mind.'' Those fingers were now on my wrist. To my horror, I broke out in goosebumps and stepped back quickly so Lymond wouldn't notice my reaction.

"That would be wonderful, Lymond,'' I said with my most dazzling smile. "Bucephalus hasn't had his exercise today, so I know he'd love to walk with us.''

"Damn it.'' I heard Lymond mutter under his breath as I walked towards the door. It was a good thing I was in front of him since I was grinning broadly. I turned at the door, the smile still on my face. "I'll tell Holmwood to have Bue waiting for us. What a thoughtful thing for you to suggest, Lymond.''

I dashed to my room to dress for supper. As soon as I closed my door behind me, I checked my forearms. Traces of the goosebumps were still there. I don't know why being close to Lymond does that to me occasionally.

It was cool after supper when we planned our walk. Holmwood had Bue on flagstone outside and the dog was yapping and jumping, excited about walking with us. Of course the first thing he did was leap right for Lymond. Lymond, however, was getting better—he neatly sidestepped and Bue went right by him. Bue wheeled and came again. This time Lymond took the coward's way out and stepped behind me. "Here, boy," Gage said, strolling outside and offering Bue one of the dog treats he carried. "Have this." Bue wolfed down the treat and then rubbed himself against Gage's leg, accidentally drooling on his boots in the process. Gage frowned, but said nothing. For a second, I got the distinct impression that he really didn't like dogs at all.

"Mind if I walk with you?" he asked, placing himself on the other side of me and offering his arm. "It's cool but clear tonight. The very best time for a stroll."

"Looks to me like fog rolling in," Lymond said stiffly as we rounded the corner of the house.

"Wait for me!" We heard the door slam behind us and in a trice, Evelyn was right beside us, breathing heavily. She was unaccustomed to running. "I needed some fresh air after supper," she explained as Lymond offered his arm to her. She ignored him and stepped up beside Gage, linking her arm through his. "I always enjoy a stroll after supper, don't you, George?" She smiled up at Gage and batted her eyes at him.

We walked on around the path that Holmwood was so proud of. Holmwood had his work cut out for him since the sea breeze kept a good many flowers and shrubs from thriving, but he always managed to have a beautiful garden. Gage and Evelyn dropped back behind Lymond and me as we walked on. I kept my hand lightly on Bue's collar to keep him with us. He did have an unfortunate tendency to run all over the place. Tonight he wanted to walk beside Gage, his nose in Gage's pocket. It took a firm hand to restrain him.

"Evelyn's going to be sitting in his lap in a moment," Lymond whispered, glancing behind us.

"Impossible, Lymond," I whispered back, not deigning to look at them, "he doesn't have a lap when he's walking."

"Well," he answered irritably, "if he had one, she'd be in it." He paused. "Confound it, Roxanne," he lowered his voice so that I had to strain to hear, "I don't like that man."

"Nonsense, Lymond." I lowered my voice to match his. "I'm an excellent judge of character and I think he's quite acceptable. I do admit that I had my doubts at first, but I believe he's a gentleman. Besides," I added, "Bue likes him, and you know what they always say about dogs and children."

"They're nuisances?"

I gave him a disgusted look. "No. They're always good judges of character. Bue likes him, ergo, he must be all right."

"Bue likes those treats." Lymond sighed as Bue bumped him. "I wonder if Gage would give me the recipe?"

"I've already asked for it," I assured him. "Lymond, what's that?" I gestured to a shadowy form that was silhouetted a moment on the outside of the library window. "Do you see it?"

"Where?"

I pointed, releasing my hand from Bue's collar. "By the library window. I don't see anything now, but for a moment, I thought . . ." Before I could continue, Bue wrenched free and bounded towards the back of the house with a howl. Precious, Miss Hinchley's cat, came dashing between Lymond and me like a speeding bullet, every hair on end. Bue wheeled and followed, knocking Lymond right into one of Holmwood's flower beds. I caught of glimpse of not one, but two shadowy forms breaking free from the darkness and slinking around the corner of the house. I ran to the corner and tried to follow, but I could see nothing. The back door to the kitchen was open slightly and I went inside. Outside, the noise was terrible: Lymond was cursing, Evelyn screaming, the cat yowling, and Bue barking. I closed the door behind me and looked around. The kitchen was quiet and no one appeared to be there. I stood still and listened. I heard a board creaking and picked up an earthenware pitcher to use for a weapon if need be, then followed the sound, being as quiet as possible. The noise of the din outside masked my footsteps. From inside the pantry, the sound came again, accompanied by the clink of glass. I rounded the corner of the pantry, pitcher raised, and wasn't able to stop the downward swing. I hit poor Woodbury right on the shoulder just as he was taking a quick nip from the bottle he had stashed behind the plates. Brandy, glass, and bits of pitcher flew everywhere. Woodbury was so surprised that he struck out at me, hitting me right in the face. I staggered back and sat down hard in the floor.

Woodbury was so horrified that he didn't immediately rush to my aid. Instead, he stood and stared at me, completely speechless. "Help me up, Woodbury," I said irritably. I touched my face. My nose was bleeding and felt strange. "Did anyone come in here?"

He shook his head and held out a hand for me. "Oh." He stared at me, then closed his eyes and moaned. "Oh."

"Woodbury," I said as clearly as I could, "get me

a towel. I'm ruining my gown." I held my hand under my nose to stop the bleeding. Lymond walked in the back door. "Roxanne? Are you in here? Gage took Evelyn back inside." He came into the pantry and we looked at each other. He looked only slightly better than I. He had dirt and flower petals in his hair and clinging to his face. His coat was torn and had a mix of dog and cat fur on it. "Good God!" he exclaimed as he caught sight of me. "What happened to you?"

Woodbury gestured and made an inarticulate sound. "Oh."

"It's all right, Woodbury," I said as clearly as I could. I could no longer breathe through my nose. "Lymond, will you hand me a towel?"

Lymond helped me to the table and got a bowl of water and a towel. Woodbury kept getting in the way, so Lymond finally sat him down across from us. Very gently Lymond bathed my face and felt along my nose with his fingers. I crossed my arms—I was getting those goose-bumps again from his touch. He was close to my face and I could smell the faint scent of his soap and see the stubble of his beard. Very lightly, he touched me again. "Not broken, I think, but you're going to have quite a bruise there tomorrow." He sat down, looked at me, and broke the spell with a laugh. "You look, Roxanne—if you'll pardon the expression—like hell."

"Thank you," I said as icily as I could under the circumstances, "and may I say that you don't look suitable for a portrait either."

He touched his face and pulled away a flower petal or two. "That cat landed right on my chest, so of course Bue had to follow. If Holmwood and Gage hadn't come to my aid, I'd probably have been scratched to death. I don't know where Miss Hinchley was." He looked at me. "Just exactly where were you during the melee? As I recall, you disappeared when the excitement began."

It was difficult to speak and breathe at the same time since I couldn't breathe through my nose, so I spoke slowly. "I saw someone at the library window, Lymond. Whoever was there scared the cat—that's why it ran between us. As soon as Bue took after it and distracted us, that's when he—they came in here."

"He? The person you saw? Are you sure it wasn't just Miss Hinchley? That cat's always right with her and she's always skulking around in odd corners trying to be unobtrusive."

I shook my head. "There were two of them and one was a man, I'm sure of it. Anyway, Miss Hinchley would come after Precious to make sure the cat wasn't hurt. It was either two men or a man and a boy, and they slipped around the corner of the house. The kitchen door was open so I supposed they ran in here." I glanced at Woodbury. He was sitting there with an empty glass in front of him. Lymond had deemed it necessary to fortify him with a glass of brandy. "Woodbury saw no one."

"And these persons were at the library window? Are you sure?"

"Of course I'm sure, Lymond," I snapped. My nose hurt abominably and my head was beginning to pound. I felt as if my whole face was the size of a washtub. I touched it and it felt puffy.

"It's beginning to turn purple," Lymond said cheerfully as he helped me to my feet. "You'd better go to bed. You're going to feel like the very devil tomorrow."

I wanted to tell him I felt that way now, but it was too much trouble. Instead, I just went to bed, leaving Lymond to make up a suitable story to tell the girls and Aunt Hen.

The next morning, the day of Mowbridge's funeral service, I woke and my face felt strange. One look in the mirror told me Lymond was correct—I looked like hell. A quick assessment of my condition confirmed Lymond's diagnosis as well—I felt like the devil. My face hurt, my head hurt, even my teeth hurt. I thought about crying off from the service, but knew there'd be few there to mourn him. I dragged myself to the bell pull and rang for breakfast and a bath. Neither helped very much.

Aunt Hen bustled in with Julia as I was trying to dress. "What a terrible thing to happen to you, Roxanne," Aunt Hen cried. "To think that Holmwood would be so careless as to leave loose stones on the path! I'm so glad Robert was there to rescue you."

"Rescue me?" I said, my voice muffled.

"Yes," Aunt Hen said, "he told us all about it." She smiled. "You need someone like Robert around to take care of you, Roxanne. Tell me, wasn't it an experience to have him rescue you?"

"Rescue me?" I repeated.

Julia looked at me and tried to suppress a grin, but was not successful. She then tried to look sympathetic, but that didn't work either. "Lymond told Aunt Hen how you fell and he carried you into the kitchen and bandaged your wounds. If it hadn't been for him, you might have been prostrate in the grass and mud all night." Her voice broke on a gurgle of laughter.

"Robert's such a dear man. So kind, so caring," Aunt Hen said, leading me to the window where she could see me better. "Roxanne! You look terrible!"

"Thank you, Aunt Hen," I managed to say. Speaking seemed more difficult today. I fervently hoped we didn't have to sing any hymns at the funeral service.

I did my best, but nothing helped. I finally gave up and searched for a heavy veil to wear to the service.

No one was going to see me for days if I could help it. I borrowed another veil from Aunt Hen just to make sure. Julia had to help guide me to the front to join the others. Looking through those veils was somewhat like trying to look through a wall of pitch. My only consolation, I thought as Julia propelled me into the front hall, was that if I couldn't see out, then conversely, no one could see in.

"Are we ready?" I asked as soon as Julia stopped me. I did rather wish I could see who was there.

"Lord, Roxanne," Lymond said. He was standing next to me. "I had no idea you were going in full mourning. How are you this morning?" Before I knew what was happening, he flipped my veils back over my hat and peered into my face.

"Oh," Woodbury said, sheer horror on his face. Lymond turned and gave the others a smile. They seemed as shocked as Woodbury. "Miss Sydney fell on the flagstones last night," Lymond explained. "I told her how treacherous it can be walking on heavy dew and stones, but she didn't listen to me." He looked at me and shook his head sagely. It was one of those times when I wished I were a man so I could plant him a facer.

Instead, I was all manners. I smiled at everyone and nodded at their sympathy. "Shall we go?" I asked politely. "Woodbury, the door." Woodbury was standing stock still, quite in shock.

He hurried to the door and flung it open. I pulled my veils down as everyone went out and then I couldn't see a thing. I glanced around for Julia to assist me out and down the steps, but she wasn't there. I tried to locate the door opening, but bumped right into the door facing. It hurt terribly.

"Here, Roxanne," Lymond said irritably, "let me take those things off or you're going to crack your head on something." He lifted the veils and handed them to Woodbury. "Now. Believe me, you look just fine."

"Of course I do. Everyone's accustomed to seeing me with a bulbous blue nose."

He grinned at me and offered me his arm. "I think it's somewhat attractive. It gives you, shall we say, a rakish air."

"We shall not say that, Lymond," I said firmly. I did, however, take his arm and permit him to escort me to Mowbridge's services.

Mowbridge was as unnoticed in death as he had been in life. No one was in attendance at the service except our group and the minister. The service, I thought, was excellent considering that the minister had absolutely no knowledge about the qualities or background of the man he was eulogizing. After the service was over and we were returning to the house, I reflected to Lymond that not a single tear had been shed.

"Somewhere, sometime, Lymond, I know someone must have cared for Mowbridge. I wish that person could have been here."

"One person was here who had an interest in Mowbridge," Lymond said under his breath so only I could hear. We were walking further back than the others.

"What do you mean?"

"I don't think Mowbridge was killed by a passing stranger." He paused and looked at the company walking ahead of us. "I think we have a murderer in our midst, Roxanne."

Chapter 10

We walked the rest of the way to the house in silence. I couldn't believe Lymond's premise that there was a murderer at Bellerophon. The only people I found likely to fit this description were Evelyn, who was too frivolous to do anything that might get her gown dirty, Boots, who didn't care to do anything that would interfere with his drinking, or Parrott. I gasped and almost stopped right on the path. "Parrott," I said to myself.

Lymond stopped alongside me. We were almost at the door, so he looked at me curiously. "Parrott," I repeated to him softly. "He must be the one. He's a sinister man, Lymond."

"Why do you say that? Do you know something you're not telling me?"

"No." I thought a moment. "Intuition, Lymond. Mine's never wrong. You know what a judge of character I am."

He made a noise that sounded somewhat like a snort and took my arm. I wasn't ready to go up the steps so he almost dragged me. I glared at him as we went inside. "Perhaps I should have left those veils on," he said with a grin. "If glares were daggers . . ."

145

I smiled at him sweetly. "If intentions were acts, Lymond, you'd have been dead years ago." It was as good an exit line as any, so I walked away as regally as possible and joined Gage. We had arranged a cold collation—the funeral baked meats as it were—and I sat between Gage and Evelyn. Lymond was stuck with Boots and Uncle Harley and glanced my way several times. He was not enjoying himself. I made sure to be smiling continuously, although I did frown when I saw Julia sitting between Kenyon and Livvy. She glanced at me, then at Livvy, and gave me a strange look. I nodded back that I understood—occasionally circumstances prevent even the best of plans from being carried out. I was sure Julia would do her part to promote the match between Livvy and Kenyon.

I went into the library later in the afternoon. It seemed strangely quiet. I wanted to check as many books as I could, to see if any of the others had been mutilated. My only reward for my efforts was a rather thick coating of dust. How, I wondered, did those books get so dirty—I knew Mrs. Beckford was a fanatical housekeeper. As I started to shelve the last ones I had checked—a leather-bound set of Francis Bacon— Gage came in. He walked to the middle of the room as though he owned it, and started looking through the books and papers on top of the desk. I was so amazed that I dropped the *Novum Organum*. Gage wheeled around, his hands in a position to fight. He saw me, took a deep breath, and smiled.

"You frightened me, Miss Sydney." He walked over and picked up the volume. "Heavy. Let me have those others and I'll put them back for you." He took them, stepped up on the stool, and replaced them as though he knew exactly where they should go.

"Thank you." My voice was cool. I decided the best

approach was the direct one. "I'm surprised to see you in here, Mr. Gage."

"You forget—I'm a book lover, too." He laughed as he stepped down and turned to me. "You have dust on your nose," he said with a laugh, touching the tip of my nose. "I must say that it's most charming." He pulled a handkerchief from his pocket. "May I? I'll be careful." Before I could tell him that he was being overly familiar, he was dabbing at my face with the handkerchief. He was very close to me—I could feel the warmth from his body and the mix of scents. He smelled of soap and shaving lotion, a mix I found extremely pleasant.

When he stopped, he looked down into my eyes and smiled. I felt slightly giddy. No wonder Evelyn was enchanted with the man. He could be more than charming. I forced myself to step back. "Thank you, but I'm hardly in fine form today." I touched my nose and felt it still swollen badly.

"No matter. You're still lovely, Miss Sydney."

I fought down a blush and turned away. "As I said, I'm surprised to see you in here." I touched the top of the desk. "Were you looking for something in particular?"

He smiled and replaced the handkerchief in his pocket, the same pocket where he kept the dog treats. His clothes fit superbly, so I wondered how he kept all those things in his pockets. He took my arm and interrupted my train of thought. "Come over here out of the dust and sit down." He led me to the sofa and sat next to me. "I lost one of the fobs on my watch chain when we were in here yesterday and thought someone might have found it and put it on the desk. Have you seen it? It's gold with my initials on one side and tiny rubies on the other. It's not extremely valuable, but a dear cousin gave it to me, so I would hate to lose it."

"No, I haven't seen it." I frowned. I had never seen it. I recalled him wearing a fob with diamonds on it, but that was the one he had on now. Still, the explanation was reasonable. I was letting Lymond's aspersions color my judgement. "I'm sorry if I frightened you," Gage went on. "I should have announced myself when I first came in, but I had no idea anyone was in here." He smiled at me, a very engaging smile. "Am I forgiven?"

"Of course." I smiled back, possibly more enthusiastically than I had intended. It occurred to me that I might take this opportunity to discover something about Parrott. I was becoming convinced that he was the one responsible for some of our catastrophes. I really didn't know what, but as sinister as the man acted, he had to be responsible for something.

A firm believer in the direct approach, I got right to the point. Almost, at any rate. Livvy came in and I asked her to join us and we sat to talk a while. We spent five minutes or so idly talking about the weather and the general deplorable state of the government before I deemed the time right to change the subject.

"And how long has Parrott been with you?" I asked.

He looked surprised and raised an eyebrow. "Quite a while. Why do you ask?"

I fumbled. "He's an interesting person. I've noticed him several times and wondered. He seems rather . . ." I paused. I wanted to say "out of place," but that didn't seem quite the thing to say, so I cast around for a substitute. "Rather . . ." I gave it up while Gage sat there and smiled at me. I could have sworn he was highly amused.

Livvy came to my rescue. "He seems very taken

with Miss Hinchley's cat. I'm delighted he's spending some time with Miss Hinchley. The poor dear seems so in need of a friend.''

"Yes, she does, doesn't she? Tell me, where did your father acquire most of his books, Miss Sydney?" Gage included both of us in his question. "Did he have someone purchase them for him?"

"Sometimes," I said. "Sometimes he bought them himself here and there." I tried to return to my subject. "Is Parrott married?"

"No. His position with me rather precludes marriage since I do so much traveling." He gestured towards a shelf of very old leather-bound manuscripts. "I'd wager your father found those on the continent. Southern France?"

"Austria." I stopped, trying to think of a way to introduce Parrott back into the conversation and couldn't. Gage, in the meantime, started to discuss books with Livvy, but hadn't said more than three sentences before Evelyn came wandering in.

"There you are, Miss Sydney and Miss Sydney," she said, sitting down right beside Gage. She was almost in his lap. "I wondered if you'd care to go into Brighton with me. I need some . . . some ribbon."

"I don't think we should shop today," I said. "After all, we've just had a funeral service."

"It was just Mowbridge," she said, turning to Gage. "Tell me, George, will you go with me? I really do *have* to go, and don't want to go all by myself." She pouted, batted her eyelashes and leaned right into George's chest. "I need someone along to protect me."

Livvy declined as well and got up to leave. I certainly wasn't going to stay with Evelyn and Gage, so I did the same. "I definitely think you should accompany Evelyn, Mr. Gage," I said briskly, heading for the door right behind Livvy. I'd had all I could stand of Evelyn. Most days I could manage five minutes, but she was worse than usual today. "Heaven knows Brighton is full of brigands and everyone needs protection there."

I risked a look at Gage as I went out the door. He was trying to move Evelyn over without actually touching her. I didn't think he was going to be successful. "Go get your pelisse and I'll meet you in half an hour," I heard him say as I went out. Out of the corner of my eye, I saw him stand quickly and dash behind the sofa, putting it between Evelyn and himself. I chuckled as I closed the door. I supposed he agreed to go in self-defense.

I had just settled myself at my desk to work on the household bills when Evelyn walked in, her pelisse over her arm and her bonnet already on. She was, I noted, smirking. "How long will your face be disfigured?" she asked.

"Probably a few days." I made an effort to try to be civil.

The smirk didn't leave. "It'll probably be longer. I want to warn you again to stay away from George. He's mine and I want that made perfectly clear. You couldn't attract him in a hundred years."

I bit my tongue to keep from being uncivil as she wheeled and left the room. I could hold it no longer. I leaped to my feet and threw a book—Caesar's *Gallic Wars*—against the wall. The nerve of the chit! "I'll show her," I said aloud. "We'll see just how attractive he might find someone else."

Lymond walked in and looked around. "Are you practicing for a bad play or just getting ready for a future argument?"

I sat back down at the desk. "Don't start with me,

Lymond." I touched my nose and it felt rather the size of a loaf of bread. I had looked at it as I passed the mirror and noted that it was changing from blue to a deep purple. My whole face hurt and my head was beginning to throb abominably.

"I wouldn't dream of it." He sat down in the nearest chair and stretched his feet out. Bucephalus came up from behind the sofa and headed for him. "Roxanne, stop that animal. He's after me again." He held out his hand to Bue in a conciliatory gesture. Bue stopped, sniffed his hand, growled, and plopped down between the two of us. Lymond sat back down in his chair.

"Bue is seeing to it that I'm not disturbed," I told him. "What do you want?"

Lymond sighed. "I want to ask you about last night. I think there must be a link between the figures you saw silhouetted against the window and whoever killed Mowbridge. Nothing else makes sense." He leaned forward. "Could you identify whoever it was?"

"I already told you, Lymond, that it was dark. I have no idea who it could have been. I thought it was Parrott, but Gage says it wasn't. It could have been anyone."

Lymond learned warily across Bue and reached for my hand. He couldn't quite touch me, and I didn't move forward. He leaned further until he had his hand on mine. He was dangling precariously on the edge of his chair, right above Bue. "Roxanne, I want you to be careful. Let me handle this. You know that I have the men and resources to take care of this and I don't want you interfering."

I raised an eyebrow. "Interfering, Lymond?"

He grimaced. "That's not what I meant." He looked at my quizzical stare. "I know that's what I

151

said, but it isn't what I meant. I just don't want you to get hurt, Roxanne. I'm . . . I'm terrified that something might happen to you."

My head felt as if someone were beating drums inside it. I stood up, suddenly very hot all over and slightly ill. "Don't worry, Lymond," I said shortly. "I can take care of myself." That was the last thing I remembered other than a terrific din somewhere in the background. When I opened my eyes, Lymond was holding me and he looked worse for the wear. His face was scratched and his clothes were torn. He was in the process of putting me down on my bed, more of a job than it seems. While I am not fat at all, I am, as Chaucer and I are fond of saying, by no means undergrown.

"What happened?" My voice sounded far away to my own ears.

"She's alive!" Aunt Hen shrieked. "She's alive!" Lymond flinched as she yelled in his ear.

I tried to sit up, but Lymond was holding me down. I thought at first that he was confining me, but when I jerked, I discovered that my hair was caught in one of his buttons. I was still groggy and my head and face felt strange. "What happened?" I asked.

"You fainted," Lymond said shortly.

"Oh." I thought about this for a moment. "That can't be true, Lymond. I've never fainted in my life. Well, maybe once." I remembered that I had fainted when Papa was killed, a circumstance I didn't care to discuss. I regarded Lymond. "What happened to you?"

"That damned dog. You fell right on the thing and I tried to catch you. I wound up stepping on him and he almost tore my clothes off."

"If I hadn't rescued dear Robert, who knows what injuries Bue might have inflicted," Aunt Hen said, fussing over him. I might as well not have been in the room. "Robert, dear, do let me bathe those scratches. I have just the thing for them." She bustled out.

"Did I really faint, Lymond?"

He sat down on the edge of the bed and nodded. "Yes." He peered at my face intently. "Did that blow to your face hurt you more than you've told me, Roxanne? Are you sure you remember everything that happened?"

"I'm fine," I said again. We couldn't talk further since Aunt Hen returned with her salve as well as Livvy and Julia in tow. Lymond escaped only moments after Aunt Hen insisted he go straight to bed. I was left as the only patient she had. My head hurt and I didn't want to be bothered, so I pretended to roll over and go to sleep. To my surprise, I did sleep, waking up long after dark.

Also to my surprise, my head felt much better and I was hungry. I lit a candle and checked my little watch. It was almost one o'clock in the morning. I got out of bed and checked my face and head in the mirror. Purple bruises were under both my eyes now, but otherwise I couldn't see any difference. I smoothed the wrinkles from my dress, patted my hair, and headed for the kitchen to find something to eat. Bue was sprawled on the rug outside my door. He stretched hugely, lapped at my hand, and walked beside me to the kitchen. Bue is always hungry.

As I neared the kitchen, carrying my single candle and keeping as quiet as I could, I heard voices. I stopped and quickly snuffed my candle. There was a light in the kitchen that I could see as I went towards the door. I put a hand behind me to restrain Bue, but it was no use. He bounded right by me and on into the kitchen, coming to a screeching halt right beside

George Gage's pocket—the one where the treats were kept. I walked in to discover Gage and Boots deep in conversation, a bottle of blue ruin between them. Gage appeared as sober as a judge, while Boots had gone round the bend some time ago.

"Good evening, Miss Sydney," Gage said, handing Bue a dog treat, "or I suppose I should say good morning." He smiled. "Your sisters and aunt told us you were ill. Are you feeling better?"

"Yes." I looked around and sat down. "What are the two of you doing in the kitchen at this hour?" It was too early—or too late—for tact.

Gage smiled at me, then looked at Boots. "Boots wanted some company. We felt the kitchen was far enough away so that we wouldn't wake anyone else. I hope we didn't wake you."

"No." I couldn't think of anything else to say. It was a reasonable explanation that I couldn't fault. I got up to hunt something to eat. Bue kept snuffling at Gage's pocket. "Bue, stop that," I said sharply. Bue glared at me and collapsed on the floor, crossing his paws. I found some cold ham and fruit to eat, then started to sit, but didn't want to eat with the two of them sitting there watching me. "I hope I didn't interrupt," I said, packing up my supper to take to my room. "Good night."

Gage rose, pulling Boots to his feet. "Wait a moment, Miss Sydney, and I'll walk you to your room. You need someone to light the way." He glanced at Boots. "I think it's time for us to go to bed as well." He smiled at me. Boots frowned and picked up the bottle, looking at the half glassful or so left in the bottom. On second look, he didn't seem to be any more inebriated than usual. He looked at me slyly and grinned as he poured the last of the blue ruin into a glass and downed it. "Don't worry about lighting my way; I always could see in the dark." He got up and walked out of the kitchen in front of us. He lurched a little, but seemed steady enough. He went up the stairs and I heard him round the corner, whistling tunelessly in the dark.

Gage walked me to my door, wished me good night, then left. I let Bue in my room, spread his rug for him, then sat down and shared my ham with him. Why would the two of them be talking in the kitchen at this time of night, I wondered. The explanation had seemed reasonable enough on the face of it, but somehow didn't ring right. Gage was convincing enough, but Boots was clearly up to something. I decided to mention it to Kenyon and Lymond in the morning.

There was a new face among us when I got up the next morning. I rose late, after midmorning, checked my face, only to see that it was still purple, although turning green around the edges. Then I went to find Lymond or Kenyon. Both of them were in the drawing room talking to the newcomer. He was much the same age as Lymond, although stockier and very cheerful. He had brown hair and eyes and rather reminded me of someone who should be a parish priest.

"Good morning," Lymond said, looking at me anxiously. "How are you feeling this morning?"

"Fine." I waited for an introduction. Lymond usually has to be reminded of the amenities.

"This is Edward DeWitt," he said in an offhand manner.

"The best librarian in all England other than Mowbridge," Kenyon added. "You're fortunate to get him."

"Or rather, your uncle is," I corrected. I certainly had no need for a librarian. I smiled a welcome at

155

DeWitt. "Is this just a visit, or have you come to stay?"

DeWitt laughed. He even laughed like a parish priest. "I'm here as long as you need me," he said. "I've been trying to get Lymond and Gwynn to let me into the library, but they wanted you to do the honors."

I lifted an eyebrow. That wasn't particularly like Lymond—he'd ridden roughshod over my sensibilities more than once. "Go right ahead," I told DeWitt. "Someone seems to have mutilated several of our books, so don't be shocked."

"Not to mention the constables throwing everything on the floor," Kenyon added with a grin. "It's a good thing you weren't here, DeWitt, or we'd have had to restrain you. There were books all over the place, just tossed here and there."

DeWitt smiled at him, then looked at me and hesitated. "One thing first, Miss Sydney," he said slowly. "I understand you have a rather valuable scroll here. I'd very much like to see it and also discover if there are other valuable scrolls in your father's collection. I, of course, wouldn't discuss this with Mr. Sinclair unless I had your permission."

"Uncle Harley's been going into apoplexy over that scroll," Lymond said. "I rather hope it turns out to be worthless."

I sighed. "I don't think it's worthless, Lymond. Mowbridge glanced over it and told me to put it away carefully, so I think it must have some value. He wanted to devote considerable time to examining it thoroughly."

"Would you mind if I looked at it now?" DeWitt asked. "You'd be welcome to stay when I examined it, of course."

"I'll get it," I said. "Lymond, could I have a word with you?" I smiled at DeWitt as I left. I didn't want him to think I planned to discuss him with Lymond, but that was exactly what I had in mind. I thought about hinting to Lymond, but I was on my way to my room to get the scroll, so I really didn't have time. "Tell me about DeWitt," I said. "Do you know him well? Can he be trusted with the scroll if it proves to be valuable?"

Lymond stopped and chuckled. "Do you want those answers in order, Roxanne, or do you prefer that I give you DeWitt's resume?"

"Don't be snide, Lymond," I said, ignoring him and walking towards our apartments at the back of the house. "Before I entrust Papa's books and scrolls to the man, I want to discover something about him. Heaven knows I know little enough about most of the visitors in this house." I opened the door to our apartments and waited until Lymond caught up.

"You could have let me get the door." His tone was aggrieved. He waited until I went in, then followed me. "All right, I admit that the house is full of strangers, but *I* know them—except Gage and his man, that is." He paused and looked at me. "You should know all about *him*, Roxanne. It seems that every time I look out the window or into a room, you're smiling and talking to Gage."

I hated to let this go without argument, but I needed to tell him about Boots and Gage in the kitchen in the middle of the night. Lymond frowned as I finished. "And you have no idea what they were discussing or if they were merely sitting there drinking?"

I shook my head as I opened the drawer where I stored the scroll. "No, I don't know. I really couldn't tell if Boots was drunk or not. I thought he was, but then he seemed to be merely acting that way."

Lymond grimaced. "It's difficult to tell, especially when the man is pickled most of the time. I'll try to talk to him and discover if he knows anything. If they were planning something, it was probably just something he wants to do to make life miserable for his father. He hates Uncle Harley."

"I've noticed he doesn't seem overly filial." I turned and looked Lymond in the eye. "Now what about DeWitt? You were going to tell me about his background."

"I've known DeWitt for years and can vouch for him."

"Another of your old school friends?"

He looked annoyed. "No, of course not. I knew him in another capacity, but I'd stake my reputation on his honesty and integrity."

Lymond had walked into that one. "Your reputation, Lymond?" I raised my eyebrows. "I'm not exactly sure about that recommendation. Do I dare give DeWitt Papa's scroll?"

"To quote someone I know—don't be snide." He glared at me. "You know very well what I mean. As for my reputation, even you would have to admit that there's nothing at all to blemish it."

"If you say so, Lymond." Actually, I didn't know of any blots on his reputation, but baiting Lymond was one of life's little pleasures. This time he seemed annoyed out of measure.

"I'm going out for a ride," he said shortly. "If you need me, I'll be back later." He turned on his heel to leave.

I sighed. I really hadn't meant to anger him. Usually Lymond took my comments in the same spirit I gave them and answered with some of his own. He must be either more tired or more overset than I had thought. "Don't be such a goose, Lymond," I said with a smile. "You know I meant nothing by it. As a matter of fact, I'd be the first to say that your reputation is . . . is . . ."

"Spotless?" he suggested with a touch of a grin.

"I don't think I can go that far." I laughed and pulled the scroll from the drawer. "If you'll wait a few minutes, I'll go with you. I could use a ride—as long as I don't have to face anyone."

He smiled. "Done."

I gathered up the scroll in its leather bag, opened it to make sure everything was in order, and started back to the library, cradling the copy of the *Iliad* in my arms like a swaddled child.

I was back in the library handing the scroll to DeWitt before I realized that Lymond hadn't really told me a single thing about our new librarian.

Chapter 11

I own that DeWitt seemed to know what he was doing. He treated the scroll lovingly, and began examining it carefully from beginning to end. First he examined the leather pouch, taking his time. "The covering dates from late fifteenth century, I would say." He extracted the scroll and looked at it all over before he ever began unrolling it. His long fingers were quick, but sure. He ran them over the ends, the scroll itself, the edges, the remnants of a seal, and everything else available.

"Well?" Lymond asked impatiently.

DeWitt laughed. "It'll be days before I know for sure, hours before I can even begin to tell you anything. Why don't you come back later and perhaps I'll know enough then to give you an opinion."

I tried to catch Lymond's eye. I know I had promised to ride with him, but I really didn't want to leave DeWitt alone in the library with the scroll. If it was valuable, as Mowbridge had indicated to me, then he could be halfway across the Channel with it before anyone missed him. "Roxanne," Lymond said, turning to me, "are you ready for our ride?"

"Lymond, I have the beginnings of a headache." It

was the first thing I could think of. I put my hand to my head for emphasis.

"Then you need to go to bed," he said sympathetically. "I certainly don't want you to hurt yourself. Does your face hurt?" He looked so concerned that I stumbled for words.

The door opened as he was speaking and Livvy and Julia came in. "You two are just in time," Lymond said. "Roxanne has a headache and I'm afraid she needs attention. Could one of you get her to bed?" He smiled at me and I saw that he wasn't fooled at all by my protestation of a headache—the corner of his mouth was twitching. Lymond was attempting to teach me another lesson. "After you get her into bed, would you two ladies like to go riding with me?"

"Oh, Roxie," Julia said, coming over to put her hand on my head.

"I'm fine, Julia." I might as well have been talking to Bue.

"You come to bed right now, Roxanne, and I'll have Aunt Hen fix you a tisane. That always seems to help your headaches."

Julia didn't know that I always poured Aunt Hen's concoctions out the window. That was what helped my headaches. "I'm fine," I said again, but it was no use. "I'll stay and read to you," Julia said, picking up a copy of one of Mrs. Radcliffe's silly novels. I would really have a headache if I had to listen to that.

"Go on and I promise I'll lie down until I feel better."

It took little more urging to get them out to ride. Julia and Livvy went to put on their habits and I nabbed Lymond just as he went out the door. "Take Kenyon with you," I told him in a low voice, "and make sure he rides with Livvy."

Lymond looked at me in surprise, then broke into laughter. "Matchmaking again, Roxanne?" I didn't deign to reply to this.

I felt forced to leave the library since I had claimed a headache, so I went in search of Woodbury. He was in his pantry off the kitchen, standing there, gazing longingly at something on the shelf. I suspected it was a bottle. Woodbury seemed to be nipping more than usual lately. He started when I appeared at the door. "Oh!"

"Woodbury, stop that this instant. I know you didn't mean to strike me. It was my own fault for surprising you."

Woodbury stood at his best parade stance—he's very proud of being a veteran. "I'll be resigning my position and I don't expect a reference."

I waved that away. "Woodbury, I have no intention of letting you go or accepting your resignation. I want to hear no more about it. Now . . ." I stopped in amazement as Woodbury gave me a hug. He recovered himself in a second and stood at attention again. "I beg your pardon."

"Quite all right, Woodbury." Was that a tear in the corner of his eye? I should have been in earlier to reassure him, but I had no idea he was worried about being thrown out on his ear. "Woodbury, I want you to do something for me."

"Anything," he said fervently.

"DeWitt is in the library and I'd like for you and Mrs. Beckford to arrange for either one of you or else one of the maids to be in and out constantly. He's checking the scroll."

"I understand perfectly." Woodbury gave me a slight bow. "I'll take care of it. Do you wish me to report periodically?"

I hadn't even thought of that. Woodbury must have been in intelligence in the army. I had thought he was in the infantry. "That would be very good, Woodbury. I'll be at my desk." As I went out, I could hear him humming to himself.

Woodbury reported every hour until I told him it was no longer necessary. On his last trip, he did report that Uncle Harley had discovered DeWitt with the scroll and was hovering over him like an avenging angel. "Mr. Sinclair keeps telling him to be careful," Woodbury reported. "I rather think Mr. Dewitt is at the end of his patience. Mr. Sinclair's head keeps getting between his magnifying glass and the scroll."

I told Woodbury he could end his surveillance since Uncle Harley seemed to be on the job now, then I ventured out. It was almost noon and staying cooped up at my desk was giving me a real headache. I stuck my head in the library to see how things were going. Aunt Hen had joined them and poor DeWitt seemed barely functional. I smiled, closed the door, and left him to cope as best he could.

George Gage and Boots came down the stairs just as I reached the hall. They were dressed for riding. "Good morning," Gage said. Evelyn darted from the drawing-room door. Evidently she had been waiting for him there. "George," she said, smiling and almost knocking me down in her haste to reach him. "Would you like to take me into Brighton today?"

He smiled at her and, to my surprise, said, "I'd be delighted. Miss Sydney, would you like to go with us?"

I declined, much to Evelyn's satisfaction, and the three of them set off, Evelyn sitting much too close to Gage in the carriage. Boots regarded the two of them with a jaded eye and turned up his flask as they rolled away.

I was thinking of taking a quick look at DeWitt's room—just to see what the man's character was, of course. One can discover a great deal about a person just by standing in the middle of a room and seeing, for instance, how that person arranges his hairbrushes. Before I could do anything, however, Livvy came strolling in with Kenyon, followed by Lymond and Julia. I smiled approvingly. Things looked quite satisfactory. Livvy and Kenyon were having a deep discussion.

"How are you feeling?" Lymond asked.

"Fine. Why shouldn't I?" I was busy watching Livvy and Kenyon together. They made a splendid-looking couple. I felt sure that Papa would have approved my machinations in that quarter.

"I thought you had a headache, Roxie," Julia said, putting her hand on my head. "Isn't that what you said?"

"It's gone," I assured her, then hastened to change the subject. "Did you pass Gage, Boots, and Evelyn on their way to Brighton?"

"No, we were in a hurry," Julia told me. "One of those army men was looking for Lymond. They talked a few minutes, then we came directly back here." I lifted an eyebrow at this information. Evidently something was happening. I looked at Lymond.

"Yes," he answered as he interpreted my look. He was already on the stairs. "I'm afraid I'm going to have to leave immediately for London."

"Why?" I asked, but he pretended not to hear. He had heard me, I knew it.

He was up the stairs and around the corner before I could ask him again, so I asked the others. "Really, Roxanne," Livvy said, "the conversation was private, and we didn't ask. Lymond merely said that he had to

164

leave immediately, so we came back here." She turned to Kenyon. "I believe I promised to show you the stream and the path to Jervyne House this afternoon. Roxanne, Julia, do you want to accompany us?"

"No," I said quickly and gave Julia a sharp look. She must have been taking lessons from Lymond—she pretended not to see. "I'd love to," she said. "I haven't been to Jervyne House in an age."

They agreed to meet later in the afternoon and dispersed. I was of two minds—on one hand, I wanted to find Julia and have a few more words with her about leaving Livvy and Kenyon alone so they could become acquainted, but on the other hand, I wanted to stay at the foot of the steps and find out what had been urgent enough to make Lymond head out for London so quickly. I decided to stay by the stairs.

Lymond came rushing down with only his saddlebags in his hand. "I doubt you're waiting here to wish me well," he said with a grin. "I'll talk to you when I get back. Right now I have to leave."

"Why, Lymond?" I asked, chasing along behind him. "What's happened?"

"Debenham wants to see me. He's found an informant. That's all I can say, and, for God's sake, don't repeat it to anyone. I'll tell you more as soon as I get back." With that, he was out the door and off to the stables. In just a moment, he was on The Bruce and riding out of sight. I sighed and came back inside. I know Mr. Milton pointed out that they also serve who only stand and wait, but I was almost of the opinion that standing and waiting were more difficult than actually doing something. Besides, I didn't relish the idea of Lymond leaving me more or less in charge of the assortment of characters at Bellerophon. Any one of them could murder any other in the blink of an eye, except perhaps for Gage.

Actually, over the next several days, no one did much of anything. Livvy and Kenyon were together more or less constantly, even though Julia was with them at all times. Perhaps, I decided, it was a good thing for Livvy to have a chaperon—I certainly didn't want to risk a breach of propriety. Aunt Hen had taken to sitting in the library with a book in her lap—usually something totally unsuitable, such as Isaac Newton or Horace. Aunt Hen actually preferred Mrs. Radcliffe. Uncle Harley was annoying poor DeWitt beyond endurance. DeWitt had decided the scroll wasn't from the time of Alexander the Great, but it was very old, and probably quite valuable. Some of the more intelligible markings indicated that the scroll had originated in the ancient city of Samarkand, and had traveled more than the rest of us put together. DeWitt did seem to know what he was about, and he pointed out to me several different markings in the margin and over the words that indicated the many owners throughout the centuries. He wanted to look through Papa's other scrolls before undertaking an exhaustive study of the Samarkand scroll, as we had come to call it. I agreed to this, over Uncle Harley's very strenuous objections. Only after DeWitt mentioned that there might be other valuable items lurking in the scrolls and on the shelves, did Uncle Harley agree.

As it was, Uncle Harley refused to leave the scroll alone. He even slept in the library for two nights. We tried to get him to go to bed, but he refused. Finally, because the man looked so haggard, we talked him into going to bed with the scroll under his pillow, right where he could keep his hand on it.

This didn't work either—the poor man was so worried that he was unable to sleep. He sat up in the bed with the scroll, now wrapped up like a babe, cradled in his arms. He looked wretched.

"Roxanne, you must do something," Aunt Hen said to me. "Poor Harley is going to collapse from lack of sleep. Besides, he's a completely at sixes and sevens from staying in the library all day on tenterhooks. He thinks everything DeWitt picks up is going to be the one thing that Spencer can never have."

I sighed. "I can't do anything about that except suggest that DeWitt banish him from the library, but I will have Woodbury take charge of the scroll."

So it happened. Uncle Harley was not at all happy with the arrangement, but I was firm. Woodbury took the scroll, wrapped in a white cloth bag, and promised to keep it safe. DeWitt established certain hours for Uncle Harley to be in the library—he couldn't stay at other times. We thought this would help, but the upshot was that Uncle Harley paced the halls constantly when he wasn't in the library. He muttered to himself constantly as well—I was afraid to ask what he was saying. I didn't feel it would be complimentary.

DeWitt and I finally relented enough to allow him to sleep with the scroll, but we were firm about the daylight hours. Woodbury was to be in charge then. After all, I asked DeWitt, what could possibly happen to the thing in broad daylight?

Lymond had been gone for days. Gage left us as well for a few days, explaining that he had to make a very short business trip. Parrott stayed with us. Evelyn moped around, made a few sheep's eyes at Kenyon, then concentrated on bothering DeWitt. Boots disappeared for a day and a night, but then was back. I had expected him to return roaring drunk, but he was quite sober. Not only that, he drank tea and coffee for the next few days until Gage returned. I was surprised.

The day after Gage returned, I got a note from Lymond telling me to watch the scroll. That was all. No "How are you," no "I miss you," nothing but "Roxanne, watch the scroll. I'll return soon." He hadn't even signed his name, just the initial *L*.

The days passed slowly and I had dozens of things to do but didn't want to do any of them, so I was wandering aimlessly around the house when Gage came in and asked if I would consider showing him around the grounds. Since the day was balmy and beautiful, we elected to walk to the mausoleum and back by the woods that bordered the boundary to Jervyne House. I stuck my head into the library to see if DeWitt needed anything, explaining that Gage and I were going walking. DeWitt was in the middle of a whole box of very dry scrolls and was not having an easy time of it. The things tended to crumble unless handled very carefully. Often they crumbled even when handled carefully. They had not had very good care over the centuries.

DeWitt, in the library alone for a change, looked up from his work. He was wearing a kind of white smock that protected his clothes, but he was still grimy. I asked him if he wished to go with us just to get out of the library dust, but he said he would be busy for hours and, no, he didn't need a thing. I left word for Aunt Hen and got my bonnet.

The day was beautiful, Gage was an entertaining companion, and I was very glad I had decided to get out. Bue went along with us, bounding over the grass and rocks, chasing butterflies and assorted bugs. It was a picture fit for a watercolor.

We walked close to the shore next to the mausoleum, enjoying the view of the Channel. "Do you ever have a problem with vandals or smugglers?'' Gage asked, tossing a stick for Bue to retrieve.

"We've had a problem or two in the past," I admitted, thinking of the picture thieves who had been in Brighton, "but that's over. Brighton is a very dull place to live except for the times when the Prince Regent comes to visit. However, I seldom get involved in that kind of froth.''

Gage started to say something else, but was interrupted by a long wail, followed by shrieks for help. The sound was behind us, right on the edge of the cliff, where the cliff broke off going down to the sea. In just a second, we heard a splash and a scream. We dashed for the spot, just as DeWitt came running up from behind us. He had replaced his smock with a dark coat, I noticed.

"It's Miss Sinclair," he said, peeling off his coat and looking over the edge. "I saw her fall.''

I dropped to my knees and peered over the edge. I could see Evelyn in the water. She was thrashing about, so I knew she was still alive, but I didn't know if she could swim. I rather doubted it. "Be still, Evelyn," I shouted, trying to calm her. "Take hold of a rock and we'll rescue you.''

I don't know whether she couldn't hear me over the waves or if she was terrified or if she merely wanted Gage to come get her, but she kept on shrieking. "She's going to get water in her mouth from all that yelling," I said to DeWitt. He was starting down the cliff edge. Gage had also removed his coat and was preparing to descend. Both the men were having a rough time of it. At the rate they were descending, Evelyn could take on enough water to drown.

"What's going on?" I jumped at the voice behind

me, then recognized it. "Lymond," I asked, standing, "what are you doing here? Evelyn's drowning."

"Good God!" Without any more talk, he too peeled off his coat and started down the cliff. The three men would probably all fall together and wind up pushing poor Evelyn out to sea. I quickly ran back to where the cliff smoothed out and there was a path down to the water. I ran down the path, picking up a stray branch from the shore as I ran. I got to where Evelyn was and extended the branch to her. "Grab this, Evelyn," I called out. The men were only about two-thirds of the way down. As I had suspected she would, Evelyn ignored me. She flailed about in the water, getting farther away from the branch. "George, help me! I'm drowning!" she wailed. I gave her a disgusted look as Bue streaked by me and went into the water. He must have thought Evelyn's flailings were meant as play, as he immediately started rolling her under the water.

I looked at the men and gave up on them—none of them were at the bottom yet—then waded out into the water. I hated to get my slippers wet and my gown would never be the same. With one hand, I shooed Bue away and tried to hold him. He was thoroughly enjoying himself. With the other, I grabbed Evelyn by the hair and pulled. She tried to scream, but only managed to take on another mouthful of water. By the time she had spit it out, I had dragged her up on the shore. DeWitt reached the bottom at that moment and helped me pull Evelyn to safety. He held her sideways until she stopped choking on the seawater. She sat up, put her arms around his neck, and smiled at him. "You saved me! How can I ever thank you! My life is yours!" The whole performance was utterly disgusting.

Gage and DeWitt took turns carrying Evelyn back

to Bellerophon while Lymond and I walked behind. Bue danced around us, still thinking Evelyn wanted to play with him. I made Lymond carry all the coats.

"How could you let Evelyn fall?" he asked me as we trailed behind the others.

"What do you mean, how could I? I didn't even know she was back there until she started screaming. By then, she had already fallen." I paused. "What I want to know is why she was there."

"Why were you there?"

I glanced at him but he didn't look at me. "Gage and I were out for a stroll. I was showing him around. Evelyn wasn't invited to go with us."

"So she followed you?"

"Evidently. And so did DeWitt—after he told me he would be busy all afternoon."

He shrugged at that and ignored my implication. "Was that all Gage wanted—to have you show him around?"

I looked at Lymond sharply. "What are you saying, Lymond? Are you implying that I would allow liberties? Are you saying that I don't know enough to observe the social proprieties?" I felt anger rising along with my voice.

"Quiet," Lymond said, looking ahead to see if Gage and DeWitt were looking at us. "No, you know I don't think those things of you, Roxanne. I merely wondered why Gage would want you to show him around."

"Perhaps he likes the country," I said shortly. "By the way, Lymond, why were you there? I didn't know you were coming back. Just what was the important business that called you to London? I believe you promised to tell me about it."

"That's what I wanted to discuss with you. Roxanne, it seems . . . ." He stopped speaking and walking.

171

I had walked a few steps and turned to look at him. "Good Heavens, Lymond, get on with it."

Instead of speaking, he pointed to the house. "Fire." That was the only word he said, but it struck fear through me. I followed his gaze and saw the smoke rising. I broke into a run, screaming for Lymond to follow me. I ran by Gage, DeWitt, and Evelyn, shoving them off the path. "Fire!" I screamed back at them. I heard Lymond running behind me. "It looks like the stables, Roxanne,' he gasped. "I just left The Bruce in there."

I didn't answer him. I couldn't.

Chapter 12

I ran, gasping, up to the back of the house. Everything looked normal. I hesitated a split second, wondering if I needed to go in the back way to get help, but instead, I veered off to the side and ran around the side of the house. Lymond had passed me by and was ahead of me now, rounding the corner of the house. "It is the stable," he called back over his shoulder as he ran out of sight.

I slowed down as I went around the corner of the house, completely out of breath. I took in several deep lungfuls of air and stumbled to the front where everyone was piling out of the house. Woodbury was there, calling everyone possible to line up with buckets. He sent some footmen to the duck pond as well. He was barking out orders as if he were still in the army.

"Are you all right, Roxie?" Livvy asked me. She and Kenyon had come out together and he had run towards the stables to help.

I nodded and kept walking towards the stables.

"Don't go," Livvy said, holding my arm. "You're white as a ghost. There isn't a thing you can do there."

I pulled away from her. "I'm going. If nothing else, I can hold the horses." As I started for the stables, I heard Evelyn moaning behind me, begging Gage and DeWitt to stay with her because she felt faint. It was one of the few times in my life that I really wished I could slap someone.

At the stables, Lymond was leading The Bruce out. The horse was pitching and rearing so much that Lymond had blindfolded him. Lymond and Kenyon were covered with grime and smoke. Lymond coughed as he handed the reins to Kenyon, then wiped his watering eyes with a sooty hand. "Someone set this, Roxanne," he said, "but we've got it under control. You can thank Woodbury for that."

We turned to look at the blaze, contained now in just one corner of the stables. All the horses were out, but they were skittish and hard to hold. The Bruce appeared to have a burn on his flanks. I pointed this out to Lymond.

"I noticed," he said grimly. "The blaze appears to have started in the stall across from The Bruce's and spread from there."

"Why do you think it was deliberate?" I kept my voice low.

He looked at me, shook his head slightly, then went over to talk to Woodbury. Seeing that everything was under control, he walked back to me. At that moment, grimy and disheveled as he was, I thought he looked quite splendid. I caught myself thinking all sorts of strange thoughts as I watched him walk towards me in the sunshine, his shirt open and torn, bits of hay clinging to his hair, and soot smudging his face. He came over to me, leaned over so that only I could hear him, and murmured, "I want to talk to you in a few minutes." Then he turned to Kenyon. "Take a look at this burn on The Bruce, Kenyon. I don't think it's deep, but it needs salve."

I moved away, backing right into Julia. "I didn't know you were here," I said, looking at her. She was white and her eyes were enormous. "Everything's going to be all right, Julia," I told her. "The horses are fine and the fire's under control. Let's go back to the house. Livvy's gone back inside."

"Was anyone hurt?"

I shook my head. "Everyone's fine. All the stable hands seem to be accounted for."

"Kenyon?" She paused. "Lymond?"

I took her arm, assuring her they were all right, and we went back to the house. Inside, Livvy was hovering over Aunt Hen while Evelyn was prostrate on a sofa, hanging on to DeWitt with one hand and Gage with the other. I checked on Aunt Hen and left Evelyn to be comforted by her erstwhile rescuers, then dragged Julia with me to the library to get some brandy. I knew I needed it, and she looked as if she did.

"Why are you so upset, Julia?" I asked after she had taken a sip or two and some color had come back into her face.

She didn't meet my eyes. "I was just worried. I thought someone had been hurt."

I smiled and hugged her. "You're overly sensitive, Julia, but I think that's a good trait." She returned my hug and stood up. "By the way," I continued, "I want to thank you for bringing Kenyon and Livvy together so much. I've noticed during the past few days that you've managed to throw them together every day. It's very good of you to be chaperoning them."

"There's something I really want to discuss with you about that, Roxanne," she began, but I heard a noise at the door. Lymond walked in, looking as splendid as he had before and I caught my breath. I couldn't understand why I seldom gave the man a second glance

175

when he was dressed to the nines, but every time he was completely disheveled and dirty, he struck me as quite handsome, or even, I admitted to myself, much more than handsome.

Kenyon came in behind him. "Livvy's in the drawing room attending Aunt Hen," I said with a smile, knowing that Lymond wished to talk to me alone. "Julia, why don't you and Kenyon see how they're doing?"

"With pleasure," Kenyon said with a smile at Julia as he offered her his arm. In the meantime, I poured Lymond a rather stiff measure of brandy and handed it to him. He sat down in a chair and downed it in two or three gulps, then smiled up at me. "I'd have to say, Roxanne, that you always know just what a man needs."

"Hardly," I said, more dryly than I had intended, as I sat down in the chair next to his. "What did you want to discuss with me, Lymond? What was the cause of the fire? Will the damage be very much? Also, what did you do in London?"

"I didn't go to London." He drained the last of his brandy and put the glass down.

"You didn't? Then where did you go? I thought you'd gone to London to confer with Debenham. That's what you told me."

"I know. I did that for a reason. Actually, I went to Bristol to check on something for Debenham, then we met in Lyme to discuss it." He stopped speaking and smiled at me. I waited patiently.

Patience isn't exactly my strong suit, so I finally gave in as he just sat there. "Well, Lymond? What then? Why must you force me to drag every single detail out of you? It's maddening."

He laughed. "I love to see you when you're angry."

"I'm merely perturbed, Lymond. If I were angry, I think you'd know it."

He laughed again and stretched in his chair, revealing an alarming amount of bare chest under the rip in his shirt. I tried to avert my eyes. "There's been another murder, Roxanne," he said seriously. "This time it was a man who has been known to fence. Do you know what I mean?"

I frowned. "I've heard the term. A man who buys and resells stolen goods?"

Lymond nodded. "In this case, the goods were stolen books." He paused. "A poem—'Whoso List to Hunt'—was torn from a book and pinned to his chest, almost like a clue or a taunt. I can't decide which and neither can Debenham."

"Whoso list to hunt, I know where is an hind," I quoted. "Lymond, that doesn't make sense."

"Unless the thief knows we're hunting him, and he probably does. We can't figure out how the rest of the poem fits in, if it does at all. I told Debenham that it may simply be a false scent. At any rate, right now we're going on the premise that only the first line or the title of the poem is relevant." He sighed and stretched again. "I don't feel as if I've slept in days."

"You don't look as if you have either," I said absently. I was still thinking about the poem. "Lymond, do you remember when I wrote you when we first got here and I found those poems in my room? They were strange selections as well."

He sat up suddenly, all attention. "I had forgotten. Tell me again." His voice was quiet and cold, not like the Lymond I knew.

I glanced at him, startled. "Why? Do you think there's a connection?"

He shook his head. "Probably not, but I want to

refresh my memory. I believe you accused me of sleeping in your bed and leaving poems? What poems were they?"

"The poems? 'The Angel' and 'The Bait' by Blake. 'The Angel' was the one that angered me so." I paused and looked at him. "In spite of your denials, I did think it was you, Lymond." I spoke slowly. "What could be the connection?"

He laughed, very much himself again. "Blake rather than Wyatt? In that case, probably none at all. When I'm baffled, I often try to see connections where none exist." He looked down at his hands, grimy with soot.

It was the first time I had noticed his hands. "Lymond, you've burned yourself!" The back of his hand was almost charred.

"I hit a flaming post while I was trying to get The Bruce out." He touched it gingerly. "It hurts like the devil."

"Of course it does. Let me have Woodbury bring some water and some salve." Without waiting for him to tell me not to, I pulled the bell rope. In seconds, I had dispatched a footman to bring the necessary items. I held his hand and looked at it carefully. "I want no complaints, Lymond. If you don't bandage that and take care of it, it could get putrid."

"Roxanne, the ministering angel," he said with a grin. "I'm not sure about this new role."

"Fine. Let your hand drop off." I dropped his hand and returned his gaze. "Was there much damage to the stables?"

He shook his head. "No. The worst was to the corner where The Bruce was stabled. I think it can be repaired without too much effort or expense. The only injuries were burns to The Bruce and to me." He

178

paused and looked at me. "Roxanne, I'm almost sure that fire was set."

I felt myself freeze. "And by whom, Lymond?"

"I don't know. Gage was with you."

I looked at him sharply, but saw nothing in his face. "As was DeWitt. What about Boots?"

He grimaced. "I just can't imagine Boots doing a thing like that. Gage, yes, but not Boots."

"I don't understand why you don't like George Gage. He's a very well-mannered gentleman. The past few days, I've come to know him quite well, and, as you said about DeWitt, I'd be willing to vouch for him." I gave him a telling look. "After all, any man Bue likes can't be bad. You know the old saying about dogs and children."

"That they haven't got the sense God gave a goose?"

I started to retort, but Woodbury came in with a footman carrying salve and water. I began cleaning and dressing Lymond's hand while Woodbury fussed over my shoulder, telling me about various burns and wounds he had witnessed in the army. As soon as I began, Lymond detained Woodbury but dismissed the footman.

"How are you enjoying your guardianship of the scroll, Woodbury?" Lymond asked with a grin. "I'm told you're the only person trustworthy enough to watch it."

A pained expression crossed Woodbury's face. "Indeed. No, that is, I don't mean I'm the only trustworthy person. I do watch the scroll constantly. Except at night, of course. Mr. Sinclair sleeps with it then."

Lymond laughed to cover a grimace as I swabbed at the grime and some skin came with it. His voice seemed a little shaky as he continued. "Tell me, Woodbury, did you see anything suspicious around the stables before the fire?''

Woodbury's eyes grew huge. "Nothing. I did see Mr. DeWitt go dashing out of the house and down by the stables a short while before the cry went up about the fire. I wasn't sure, but I didn't think he stopped at the stables. Then you came in." He almost held his breath. "Is something wrong?''

Lymond frowned and looked down at the clean bandage I had just finished putting on his hand. "Probably not, Woodbury. I do, however, want you to let me know if you see anything at all unusual.''

"Yes, sir," Woodbury said smartly in his best army voice. I thought for a moment he was going to salute, but he restrained himself.

"You know," I said to Lymond as Woodbury went out, "that this will be all over the kitchen in seconds.''

Lymond grinned at me. "I hope so. Perhaps one of the servants will remember something." He stood and held out his good hand to me. "Let's go find something to eat. I hurried here and didn't take time to stop, so I'm starving. We'll ask Kenyon and Julia to join us. I'd like to find out if anything has happened since I've been away.''

"Kenyon and Livvy," I corrected. "Julia's chaperoning them.''

Lymond laughed. "Still matchmaking, Roxanne? I predict a disaster.''

"Mark my words, Lymond, you'll be wrong. This time, it's going to work out. I feel it in my bones.''

We found Kenyon, Livvy, and Julia together and they joined us in the dining room while Lymond ate some cold meats. It took all of five minutes to bring Lymond up to date on what had happened at Bellerophon in his absence. "It seems, Robert," Kenyon said with a grin, "that little happens unless you're here. The moment you returned, Evelyn almost drowned and the stables caught on fire."

"How is Evelyn?" Julia asked politely. "I saw Gage and DeWitt carrying her in."

"She's fine," I said shortly. "She can't decide to which rescuer she should cling—DeWitt or Gage—so she's in her bed, calling for each in turn." I glanced at Lymond. "She's left you out, Lymond. You did as much to save her as the others."

He laughed. "I doubt Evelyn will ever call for me. I thought, however, that you were the one who saved her. Has she called for you?" I gave that remark the look it deserved and we all went to our rooms. Lymond said he needed some rest and, to tell the truth, he looked it.

The evening was quiet. Evelyn came down to join us after supper, sitting to her best advantage draped over a striped chair, looking appropriately pale and wan. She was in her element as Gage and DeWitt hovered over her. The rest of us played cards, with the exception of Aunt Hen and Uncle Harley. They sat in a corner and discussed books. Rather, Uncle Harley discussed books and Aunt Hen nodded every now and then. I could see that she didn't understand a word he was saying, but that didn't deter them. Boots didn't join the rest of us, either. He sat in a corner, drinking quietly, dividing his glowering looks among Evelyn, Gage, and his father.

At bedtime, Uncle Harley rang for Woodbury as had become his custom. Woodbury brought the scroll in, still wrapped carefully, and presented it to Uncle Harley. As usual, Uncle Harley clutched it close to his chest and went off to bed.

Our party was just breaking up and the rest of us

were getting ready to drift off to our rooms when we were startled by Uncle Harley running into the drawing room. He was screaming at the top of his lungs and we couldn't understand a single word. His face was a purple color and he was having difficulty breathing.

"He's having an attack!" Aunt Hen threw herself at him. "Harley, speak to me!" Uncle Harley stood stone still in the middle of the floor and stopped yelling. He tried to take a breath, but couldn't. Then he tried to speak, but couldn't. Instead, he made a few inarticulate noises and began pointing to the scroll he still held in his arm.

"It's been opened," I said, trying to take the scroll from Uncle Harley. I couldn't move it. "Lymond, help me."

"DeWitt, come over here," Lymond said, helping Uncle Harley to a chair and taking the scroll from him. "Take a look at this. What's happened?"

DeWitt took one quick glance. "This is not the Samarkand scroll. It's been taken. The outside wrapping is the same, but this is not the scroll of the *Iliad*. This is something else." In the complete quiet he unrolled a portion of the scroll and looked at it. "Household accounts, looks like," he said. "Worth a little bit as a curiosity, but not really valuable. Not like the Samarkand scroll." He looked at Lymond. "I think, Robert, that the book thief has struck."

I looked at the scroll carefully. Papa had dozens of the things around in various stages of decay and disrepair, but I thought I remembered this one. I had seen DeWitt looking at it one day and we had both commented on what excellent condition it was in. DeWitt even said the condition was unusual for a scroll that appeared to be merely a listing of accounts. Usually those scrolls were cleaned and reused after a period of time. I started to say something about it, but decided to wait. After all, if I suspected DeWitt of either thievery or collusion, it might not be wise to mention it to Lymond. After all, the man was a friend of Lymond's.

While I was hesitating—someone—Kenyon, I thought—had the presence of mind to send for Woodbury. When Woodbury came in, I planted myself close by him. I was not going to allow him to be badgered by questions. Woodbury had been with us so long he was almost like family.

"Where is it, you scoundrel!" Uncle Harley roared, taking that inopportune moment to regain his speech. He leaped to his feet and grabbed Woodbury by the lapels. "Going to retire on the proceeds, are you? Newgate is the only place you'll be spending time!"

I took Uncle Harley's arm, but couldn't budge him. Lymond and Kenyon moved forward to get him while I propped up poor Woodbury. "Do you need something to drink?" I asked Woodbury under my breath. The poor man was as white as his cravat. "Pay no attention to Mr. Sinclair."

Woodbury swallowed hard and nodded to me as Lymond and Kenyon turned back to him. Lymond was smiling. "The scroll seems to have disappeared, Woodbury," he said calmly, pouring a stiff brandy and handing it to Uncle Harley. Boots picked up the brandy bottle, looked at it carefully, and poured one for himself.

"Impossible," Woodbury said. He had turned even paler, a condition I had thought impossible. "I handed it over myself to Mr. Sinclair."

Kenyon picked up the scroll and its wrappings. "Is this what you gave him?"

Woodbury nodded again. "Not above a half hour

ago. I went to the pantry where I keep it locked, took it out, and gave it to him."

"Did you examine it before you handed it to him?" Lymond asked. "Did it look the same as always?"

"Exactly the same, so I didn't look at it. Actually, I've never looked at the thing except for when it was given to me. It felt the same and looked the same."

"Evidently, Woodbury," I said, "someone has substituted a valueless scroll in place of the Samarkand scroll."

Woodbury staggered slightly and reached for the back of the chair to steady himself. "While it was in my care?"

Kenyon and Lymond nodded together. "Who else knew where you kept the scroll?" Kenyon asked kindly.

"I don't know." Woodbury appeared broken. "I just don't know. I kept it with me most of the time, but there were some times when I just couldn't be walking around carrying the thing. It got in my way. On those times, I locked it up with the silver."

Aunt Hen gasped. "Oh, Woodbury, don't tell me someone's helped himself to our silver!"

Woodbury's eyes widened and a slow look of horror crossed his face. "I haven't checked," he said in a strangled voice.

"Go check, Woodbury," I said quickly, before he became more distressed, "and I'll be there shortly. Be sure to look carefully."

The poor men fled while Aunt Hen collapsed into a chair. "The silver, all gone! What will we do?"

"I doubt the person looking for the scroll would be after silver," Kenyon said.

"It was probably Spencer," Uncle Harley said with venom in his voice. "I knew he was going to try something, but I didn't know he'd stoop to this." He crashed his fist onto the chair arm. "I should bring him before the magistrates and force him to confess."

Lymond rolled his eyes heavenward and looked to Evelyn and Boots for assistance, but got none. "Better yet," Uncle Harley roared, working himself up into a fine state, "I should thrash the scoundrel myself. It would be just retribution."

I left Lymond, Kenyon, and Aunt Hen to do something with Uncle Harley and went to find Woodbury. He was still ashen and was throwing things all around the closet where we kept the silver locked.

"I think it's all here," he said shakily, "but I won't know until I count everything."

"Do that tomorrow, Woodbury." I looked around at the mess. "I really don't think any of the silver has been touched."

"I agree. The person was after only one thing—the scroll." Lymond spoke behind us. He walked in where Woodbury and I were, pulling the door shut behind him.

"Did you get your uncle settled?" I asked.

Lymond shook his head. "He's never been settled, so he isn't going to start now. I did leave Kenyon and Julia trying to soothe him. Olivia is calming down your aunt. They're better than I am at that sort of thing."

I chuckled. "Don't lie to me, Lymond. You simply didn't want to have to cope with the man."

"True, you're right as usual, Roxanne." He sighed. "I know the man too well." He smiled at us and clapped Woodbury on the shoulder. "I didn't come to chastise you at all, Woodbury, but I would like to ask you some questions if you don't mind."

"Yes, sir." Woodbury stood at parade stance. "Whatever you say, sir."

"Relax, Woodbury," I said, going to the sideboard

185

and pouring him a glass of Papa's best brandy. I wondered how many this made today. "Drink this. No one is blaming you in any way. I know you watched that scroll as if it were your own child."

"That I did. I never let it out of my sight, except for once in a while." He gulped the brandy and looked as if he wished for more, but I ignored the look. One glassful was enough for him right now. I knew he'd get his own bottle as soon as Lymond and I left him.

Lymond frowned. "You never left it unattended at all?"

Woodbury shook his head. "Never. If there was a time when I had to do something else, I locked it up and kept the key in my pocket."

"So it was locked up, then?" I puzzled over this. "Then someone must have your keys, Woodbury. That's the only explanation."

Lymond looked at him sharply. "Think back over the day, Woodbury. We know the thing disappeared sometime during the day. Was there any time—any time at all—when you might have turned your back on the scroll long enough for someone to substitute one and take the original?"

Woodbury thought, his face screwed up in concentration, then he looked up in amazement. "The fire. When the fire broke out, I was in such a hurry that I put the thing down on the sideboard and ran outside. It hadn't been touched, though. I looked at it when I came back inside and remembered that I hadn't locked it up. I locked it up right away."

"How long had it been on the sideboard, Woodbury?" I asked.

He thought. "Not above a half an hour, I'm sure. Everybody was outside to help with the fire, anyway. I'm sure no one touched it."

Lymond and I looked at each other and the same thought hit both of us at the same time. Lymond had said the fire had been set deliberately, and that could mean only one thing: whoever set the fire did it so that the scroll could be stolen during the hubbub that accompanied the blaze.

Although neither of us said it aloud, we both knew the same thing: it was also probable that the person who set the fire and took the scroll was someone in our midst.

Chapter 13

Lymond and I went back to the others in the drawing room, only to discover that the news of the scroll's theft had effectively broken up the evening. Everyone was drifting off to bed, and Lymond suggested that I do likewise. I took his suggestion, thinking he planned to retire as well.

However, I found I couldn't sleep at all. Bucephalus came to sleep on his rug beside my bed, but even he seemed restless, tossing and making dog noises in his sleep. I got up and thought about working at my desk, but decided to get a book from the library instead and read myself to sleep. As I got to the library door, I heard voices inside. I hesitated, then did what I suppose is the natural thing in such circumstances: I put my ear to the door panel and listened. It was difficult to hear very much.

Kenyon and Lymond were talking, evidently while they were having a glass—or several glasses—of something to drink. I distinctly heard the clink of glass on glass more than once. ". . . thought DeWitt might have known," Lymond was saying.

"I doubt that," Kenyon answered. "You know DeWitt's reputation from past times."

I felt my eyes widen at that. Had Lymond brought someone into my house who was suspect? It would be just like him to do that, probably on the theory that the suspect could be watched more closely. I *knew* there had been something suspicious about DeWitt.

"By the way," Kenyon continued, "why DeWitt? I'm afraid I've really lost touch with what everyone has been doing while I've been away."

"DeWitt was responsible for that job at Stowecroft. I told you about that, I believe. The one where Lady Amaray's jewels were stolen." Lymond said something else, but I couldn't catch it. I pressed closer to the door.

". . . but you recovered the jewels," Kenyon was saying.

"Yes." I heard Lymond say. Then he said something I couldn't catch, then, ". . . DeWitt did that." There was the clink of glass again. "It's late and I'm tired, Kenyon," Lymond said. "I need to get up early tomorrow and check with Colonel Broadhurst in Brighton around eleven. I'm off to bed."

I jumped back from the door and looked around quickly, but saw no one. I hurried around the corner where I couldn't be seen, and I hid there until I heard Kenyon and Lymond go up the stairs, talking and laughing in low tones. The hall darkened as they snuffed the lights behind them. I slid down the wall and sat on the floor in the dark to think about what I had heard.

So DeWitt was a thief who had stolen jewels before and Lymond knew it. That was why he dodged my questions about the man. He knew I'd turn him out the second I knew. Lymond had brought the man into Bellerophon, knowing full well that he would probably steal again. And worse, he hadn't even warned me

189

about it. I could almost forgive him for bringing DeWitt into the house, but I couldn't forgive him for not telling me. I could have been watching DeWitt. If I had known, I wouldn't have left his side. Now, with the scroll gone, there wasn't much point in watching him.

I was startled from my reverie by a stealthy noise on the steps. Someone was coming downstairs slowly, without the benefit of a candle. I listened intently for a moment, then crawled on all fours to the corner where I could peer around. I really couldn't see, so I stretched to try to see better. The person was just coming to a patch of moonlight, walking as quietly as a cat.

It was a man, that was all I could be sure of. I looked again at the black figure silhouetted against the feeble light from the moon shining in the front hall window, but couldn't really discern who it might be. I stretched further, trying to see the face as the man stopped at the bottom of the stairs.

Then the worst happened. My palm slipped on the polished wooden floor and I went crashing down on my stomach. The figure wheeled and pounced on me, grabbing me by the shoulders and pinning me to the floor. I struggled and bit as one of his hands landed on my breast. The man jumped back as though he had been hit.

"A thousand apologies," he said, and I recognized the voice as Gage's. "I thought I had an intruder. Is that you, Evelyn?"

"No, it isn't Evelyn," I said, trying to scramble to my feet. "It's Roxanne Sydney. Would you please get a candle, Mr. Gage?" I stood and tried to muster as much dignity as possible while Gage went to the front and got a candle.

"Again, I apologize, Miss Sydney," he said as he

came back to me, the candlelight making huge shadows on the wall. "I couldn't sleep, so I thought I'd come down for something to drink." He nodded towards the library door. "I had noticed some particularly fine brandy in there."

"Papa's private stock," I told him. "Very well, Mr. Gage, I think I might use something myself." I led the way to the library door and went inside. The room smelled of cigars. Lymond and Kenyon, it seemed, had smoked several. I noticed Gage went to the desk and noted the ashes, even going so far as to put his finger to them to see if they were warm.

"Evidently someone else couldn't sleep," he said conversationally, taking the glass from me. "Those ashes are still warm."

"Really?" I looked at him coolly.

He smiled. "I noticed you called me Mr. Gage, Miss Sydney. I would like it very much if you would use my Christian name. I had hoped that our acquaintance had proceeded to such footing. Please call me George."

I looked at him as I finished my wine. "Very well, Mr.—George." There was a pause and I felt terribly awkward. "I believe I'll get my book and go to bed," I said, making a show of looking at the shelves.

"Try this one," he said, selecting a book and handing it to me.

"Ovid? Really, Mr. Gage—George—Ovid is hardly the reading material I'd choose to put me to sleep."

He laughed. "No, but no one is better than Ovid at love."

I felt myself blush. "Mr. Gage—George, this is really a most improper conversation." I put the Ovid back on the shelf and pulled out St. Augustine. "This should be dull enough."

Gage took the book from my fingers and turned me

191

around to face him. "I'm sure St. Augustine is guaranteed to put anyone to sleep in record time," he said with a gentle smile, "and I really didn't mean to be forward." He let his hands rest lightly on my shoulders. "Miss Sydney, you must know that I find you quite enchanting."

I tried to move, but he slid his hands to my arms. I wanted to step back, but I was against the bookshelves. "I repeat, George, this is a most improper conversation."

"Is the truth improper? If it is, I stand accused. I find you, Miss Sydney, to be not only enchanting, but intelligent, witty, and frank. You're a rare woman, Miss Sydney." He leaned forward, and for a moment, I held my breath, not moving. He kissed me, very lightly, on the lips.

"I would like to pursue this acquaintance, Miss Sydney," he murmured, lifting his head to look into my eyes before he kissed me again. This was a much better kiss and I own I found it quite satisfying. Gage put his arms around me and I reciprocated, putting my arms around his neck.

There was a crash as the door slammed against the wall. "My sincerest apologies," Lymond said, his voice unapologetic and sounding like cold steel. "Am I interrupting a midnight tryst?" He walked across the floor towards the desk. I had never seen him so rigid and controlled. "Pray don't let me disturb you. I'll just get my papers and be on my way. You'll be able to pick up right where I've interrupted you." He jerked up a sheaf of papers from the desktop and wheeled to leave. It would have been an effective exit, but he managed to drop most of them, then had to get down on his knees to pick them up.

My face flaming, I moved away from George and bent to help him.

"I can manage," he said, his face stiff. I couldn't remember ever seeing him so angry. "Do get back to what you were doing."

"What I was doing, Lymond, was searching for a book to read."

"Obviously." He snatched up the last of the papers. I caught a glimpse of Debenham's scrawl on the page and reached for it, but Lymond was faster. He tucked the papers together and stood.

"Please don't blame Miss Sydney for what you saw," George said graciously. "The fault was all mine."

Lymond raised an eyebrow. "Don't worry, Gage. I don't intend to tell anyone about this. Not because of you, of course, but I would hate to hear a single word about Miss Sydney's reputation being sullied. I think I might have to call out the man who would do such a thing." He and Gage looked at each other and Lymond's threat was clear.

"But of course," George said smoothly. "Now, if you'll excuse me, I need to get to bed." He left and closed the door behind him, leaving Lymond and me alone. The silence was thick enough to cut. I picked up the book of Augustine's sermons and started to leave.

"That's all?" Lymond asked bitterly. "I find you all over another man and you simply think you can pick up your book and go to bed?"

I wheeled around to face him. "What do you mean, Lymond? I was *not*, as you so graciously put it, all over another man. He kissed me, that's all, and I certainly don't have to account to you."

"Good God, Roxanne," he shouted at me. I looked

193

around to make sure the door was closed and he lowered his voice. "Good God, Roxanne, what am I supposed to think? I walk in here, completely unsuspecting, and see you and Gage in an embrace." He paused. "It certainly seemed that you were enjoying yourself."

"I was, Lymond." I stared at him and said nothing else.

He poured himself a glass of brandy. "I've had too much of this tonight already." He drank it down and poured another. "Just answer one question for me, Roxanne: did you plan to meet him here or was it accidental?"

I paused, glaring at him. "It's really none of your business, Lymond, but I'll tell you. I couldn't sleep and came to get myself a book to read. I was outside when you and Kenyon were in here discussing DeWitt and I didn't want to come in then, so I waited outside. Gage came down shortly after you went up."

Lymond regarded me and put down his glass. "What was his excuse? Did he say why he was wandering around after midnight?"

"He said he needed something to drink," I said coldly, moving past him. I saw no reason to describe the scene where Gage had pinned me to the floor.

"And you believed him?" Lymond reached out and grasped my arm, stopping me.

"Of course I believed him. I also believed you when you said DeWitt was a reliable person to have in the library." I stared straight at him and challenged him. "You can't deny it, Lymond. I overheard you and Kenyon talking tonight. You knew DeWitt had done underhanded things before—I heard you discussing it."

"Underhanded?" He looked puzzled. "Roxanne, it really . . ."

194

"There's no use to deny it, Lymond. I heard you." I wrenched myself from his grasp. "Besides, I was going to tell you that I had seen DeWitt looking at the scroll that had been substituted for the *Iliad*. He was at this very desk looking at it. He even commented on the fact that it contained household accounts."

"A good reason not to use it then, wouldn't you say?" Lymond reached for me again but I went behind the desk. I wanted some space between us. He looked at me strangely, turned his back to me and took a deep breath. Then he turned to face me again and took a moment to light another candle. I noticed the knuckles of his hands were white and rigid. "Damn it, Roxanne," he said in a flat voice, "just think about it. That scroll was substituted while Woodbury was outside during the fire at the stables. That fire was set to draw everyone out. DeWitt wasn't even in the house at the time."

"It could have been a ruse." I stared hard at him. "Why are you defending DeWitt so, Lymond? Could it be that you have a guilty conscience?"

He laughed shortly. "I thought we were agreed, Roxanne, that I had no conscience at all."

"That's true, Lymond." I picked up my book and walked to the door. "I expect DeWitt out of this house immediately, Lymond."

"I can't do that, Roxanne. He's filling a valuable position." He paused. "The man is in my employ."

I realized I had no say in whether DeWitt stayed or left. Lymond had also, as far as I was concerned, made his position clear. "Very well, Lymond, if that's the way you feel about it. The books in the library are mine, however, and I want DeWitt to stay away from them. I can't afford any more thefts." I turned on my heel and went out.

I had gone part of the way down the dark hall to our apartments when I decided to turn back and see if Lymond had gone to warn DeWitt. I stood at the corner for what seemed a long time, smelling the cigar smoke drift out of the library and hearing the clink of the glass as Lymond drank more brandy. At the rate he was drinking, I thought, he'd be in bed the entire day tomorrow.

Finally he came out, carrying a candle with him and went up the stairs. I waited until he was at the top, and then I slipped up the steps behind him. I fully expected him to go to DeWitt's room or to Kenyon's, but he merely went into his own room and shut the door. I waited for a while, but the door stayed shut and the house stayed quiet.

It was two o'clock before I returned to my room and went to bed.

The next morning, I hoped Lymond felt as bad as I did. He wasn't at breakfast and no one had seen him, so I really didn't know. Kenyon thought he was still in bed.

I went to the library and discovered no one there. Perhaps Lymond had gotten word to DeWitt. I looked at some of the piles of scrolls DeWitt had been going through. They were stacked on a small table. Actually, I admitted to myself, anyone passing through the library could have picked up any one of them. Perhaps I had been hasty about DeWitt. Still, there was the matter of what I had overheard Lymond and Kenyon discussing.

The more I looked, the more the theft of the *Iliad* scroll rankled. While the scroll certainly wasn't Papa's treasure, I could have gotten a respectable sum out of it. Enough, at any rate, to pay for Livvy's wedding to

Kenyon. Besides, I simply didn't like the idea of someone taking my possessions.

Kenyon came into the library while I was sitting at the desk, thinking. "There you are," he said, smiling. "Julia, Olivia, and I were planning a picnic and wondered if you wanted to go with us."

I smiled to hear this. Julia was doing a superb job of getting Livvy and Kenyon together. "I don't really think so, Kenyon, although thank you for asking. I . . ." I paused, searching for a reasonable excuse. "I have some things to do here."

He raised an eyebrow as he looked at me questioningly. "It would do you good to get away for a few hours. Besides, I'm warning you right now that Lymond's uncle and your aunt plan to spend the day here in the library. I heard them discussing it."

"Then *I* definitely won't be here," I said with a laugh.

"Would anyone?" Kenyon smiled, and I noticed how very nice he looked when his eyes crinkled. He would make Livvy a wonderful husband although I still needed to discover how he had acquired that scar before I could sanction the match. I thought about asking right then, but he suddenly turned serious on me. "Tell me," he asked, "do you know what Gage's man Parrott was doing during the fire? No one seems to have remarked him." Kenyon was still smiling, but the smile was gone from his eyes.

I was jolted. "I have no idea," I said slowly, remembering the dark figure I had seen at the window. For that fleeting moment, I had thought it was Parrott, but I wasn't sure. "Like you, I don't recall anyone mentioning him at all."

"Boots hinted of it to me." Kenyon picked up a book and stared at it, seemingly concentrating on the

197

title. "Boots seemed to think the answer to everything might lie with Parrott." He put the book down and grinned at me. "Of course, one needs to take into account the fact that Boots was roaring drunk when he said that."

"Out of the mouths of babes and drunkards?"

Kenyon laughed. "I merely thought I'd ask. There's probably nothing at all to it. Parrott was probably upstairs seeing to Gage's cravats or else going into Brighton for him. Those, along with keeping Miss Hinchley company, seem to be his main occupations." He looked at me again. "Are you sure you won't join us for a picnic? We plan to drive along the Steine afterwards. There's a rumor the Prince is coming to town."

I shuddered. "Not for Prinny's weight in gold."

"Do you realize what you're saying?" Kenyon said with a laugh. "You'd bankrupt the country."

I laughed with him and we walked out of the library and into the drawing room, right into a scene from a Minerva Press novel: Evelyn was clinging to DeWitt, kissing him, and begging him to take her away from this cruel life. As Kenyon and I came in, DeWitt jumped and tried to remove Evelyn from his person, but she clung like a leech. "I'm afraid Miss Sinclair's harrowing experience is still proving distressing," he said, trying to hold her wrists as Evelyn began to cry. DeWitt looked from Evelyn to me. "Do you have a moment to help her?" His face was flushed and he was sweating.

"You'd never have to work again," Evelyn sobbed. "My father would see to that." She stood and looked at us. Her face was blotched and her nose was dripping. "Father's going to cut Boots off with no money. He told me so."

"Does Boots know this?" My question was rather inappropriate in such a scene, but I was curious.

Evelyn nodded. "Father told Boots the same thing. Boots owes everybody. He even owes George Gage. Why do you think George is here? He wants to make sure that Boots doesn't run to France or somewhere until he gets his money."

I stared at her with wide eyes. "Do you mean Gage is a gamester? Or do you mean he's a cent per center?"

Evelyn wiped her nose and eyes on her sleeve. "He isn't really either one. All I know is that he has piles of money and Boots has hinted that most of it wasn't gotten honestly. George doesn't mind lending it to people like Boots—men in London who have huge gambling debts and might be useful to him."

Kenyon and I looked at each other. I wasn't sure whether to believe Evelyn or not. "How do you know this?" I demanded.

She shrugged. "I just know it. Boots says things sometimes; I hear and see things sometimes." She turned back to DeWitt. "Think about what I've said. It wouldn't be a bad life, you know. I wouldn't make demands on you and you'd never have to work again." She mopped at her face again.

To my surprise—and Kenyon's—DeWitt looked at her strangely. "Work doesn't bother me and I wouldn't consider taking your father's money. I've always planned to support my own wife and family."

Evelyn reached out and touched his hand. "I think that's wonderful. I wouldn't touch Father's money if you didn't want me to. I could live on whatever I had to."

DeWitt looked at Kenyon and me, then back to Evelyn. "Perhaps, Miss Sinclair, you should allow Miss

199

Sydney to take you to your room so you could lie down."

"I can manage by myself." She started for the door and then turned. "We can talk later." With that, she left the room. DeWitt sat down heavily on the sofa and wiped at his face with his handkerchief. He looked down at it. "Drat. I really should have offered her this. I completely forgot my manners."

"No wonder," Kenyon said dryly. "What was that all about?"

DeWitt shook his head. "Miss Sinclair is really a charming, sweet woman." He looked up at Kenyon. "She hates her father. Do you know why?"

"All I know comes from Lymond," Kenyon answered. "Other than the fact that Mr. Sinclair hardly acknowledges the existence of his children, no. He doesn't beat them or anything of that sort."

"He doesn't seem to care very much for them either," I observed.

Kenyon offered DeWitt a cigar. "Evelyn seems to have taken quite a liking to you since her rescue. Does she view you as her knight in shining armor?"

DeWitt nodded and looked hungrily at the cigar. "Go ahead," I told him. He and Kenyon both lit up and DeWitt inhaled deeply on the cigar, then blew a cloud. "I'm afraid she does see me in a better light than I really am," he said. "She's a beautiful woman, you know."

Kenyon looked at him sharply. "DeWitt . . ." he began, then paused. There was an awkward silence. "She is beautiful," I said, "but you need to consider her reputation. Evelyn seems to get slightly carried away."

DeWitt nodded. "I wonder if she would accept me if she . . . if . . ."

"If she knew you were in Lymond's employ?" I couldn't resist.

Kenyon headed me off neatly. "Miss Sydney is right, DeWitt. You need to consider Miss Sinclair's reputation." He put his hand on DeWitt's shoulder. "You'd better have someone with you as much as possible. I know you'd never want a compromising situation."

DeWitt looked at him. "I would never do anything to compromise her reputation. You know me better than that."

I seized my chance. "Perhaps you should get away for a short while. It would also given Evelyn time to think."

DeWitt glanced at me and I reddened. The man knew exactly what I was planning. "I can't leave just yet—Lymond still needs me."

"He needs you? Why?"

Kenyon stepped smoothly into the breach. "We all need you, DeWitt. Without your expertise, no one will ever know what's in the library here." He turned to me with a smile. "Did you know, Miss Sydney, that DeWitt is considered one of the foremost librarians in the country?"

I regarded him coolly. "No, I didn't know that. What else is he considered?"

A flash of anger crossed DeWitt's face and I had a twinge of guilt. "Lymond told me of your suspicions, Miss Sydney, and I want you to know that I had absolutely nothing to do with the theft of your scroll. Those scrolls were on the library table, and anyone could have taken one and used it for a substitute."

Kenyon again came to the rescue. "DeWitt, how could you think such a thing of Miss Sydney? I'm sure she, like the rest of us, is completely assured of your innocence." Kenyon rose and took DeWitt by the arm.

"You look as if you could use a drink. Why don't you go into the library and have something stimulating, then lose yourself in your work?" He propelled DeWitt towards the door. "And by the way, DeWitt," he said with a chuckle as DeWitt disappeared from sight, "lock the door behind you."

I bit my tongue. The last place in the world I wanted DeWitt was in my library, but Kenyon was insistent. Here I was trying to get Kenyon into the family so I certainly couldn't say anything to him. Still, was it worth it to have DeWitt, a known wrongdoer, loose in my library? That settled it: the picnic would have to be made without me—I silently vowed to stay home and keep DeWitt under surveillance.

Besides, I had another fish to fry. A thought had struck me when Kenyon said that one of Parrott's main occupations was to keep Miss Hinchley company. I had seen them speaking once or twice but hadn't remarked it. Also, I had thought she was one of the shadowy figures I had seen at the window that night. It was certain that it was her cat that had come bounding out of the shrubbery, causing the commotion. I resolved to see Miss Hinchley as soon as possible and discover whatever I could about Parrott.

Chapter 14

The house was quiet after Kenyon, Livvy, and Julia left. I went to find Miss Hinchley, but couldn't. Woodbury informed me that he had seen Miss Hinchley, the cat, and Parrott out back. I went there, but didn't see anyone. I made a mental note to see Miss Hinchley at the earliest possible moment.

In the meantime, I returned to my surveillance of DeWitt and placed myself where I could watch the library door. I was about to decide my efforts were in vain when Lymond came to the door, knocked softly, called out DeWitt's name, and was let inside. Lymond had a man with him, a man I thought I had seen around Brighton. He was, to say the least, a rather unsavory-looking character.

As soon as the door closed, I dashed across the hall and put my ear to it. I had been there for only a moment when Woodbury came walking by. He stopped and lifted a brow in my direction as I put my finger to my lips.

"Drat, Woodbury," I whispered, leading him away from the door. "Lymond's in there with DeWitt and some ruffian, and I can't hear a thing." I had erred in telling Lymond that I had overheard his previous conversation—now they were speaking in low tones. "I don't even know the identity of the visitor."

"That's Mr. Lynch," Woodbury said solemnly. "He's visiting Mr. Lymond."

I turned on him. We were out of earshot now. "How do you know, Woodbury? I've seen that ruffian around Brighton, and I know you'd never consort with the lower sort such as he. How do you know him?"

Woodbury shook his head and gave me his imperturbable look. "Mr. Lymond told me." He was almost at parade stance again. "He's with the Runners, I think. Mr. Lynch, that is, not Mr. Lymond."

"What!" I almost clapped my hand over my own mouth. "What, Woodbury," I said in a more reasonable tone after looking at the door to see if I had been overheard. "Did you say he was a Runner?"

Woodbury nodded again. "That is what I understood, yes. Mr. Lynch of the Bow Street Runners, he said."

I dragged Woodbury off to the pantry and shut the door so we would not be heard. "All right, Woodbury, I want to know what's going on. Has Lymond brought in a Runner to arrest DeWitt? I just knew the man was a scoundrel."

"Mr. Lymond?"

"No, Woodbury. DeWitt. I knew it in my bones. What are the charges against him, do you know?"

Woodbury looked at me strangely. "None that I know of. Mr. Lynch requested Mr. Lymond's assistance. Then they went together to talk to Mr. DeWitt." Woodbury looked confused, then brightened. "Have they some inkling of the whereabouts of the scroll?"

I shook my head and his face fell. I patted him on the arm in encouragement. "Don't worry about it,

Woodbury. It'll turn up somewhere. Besides, you're not responsible. The fire was set to distract you."

Woodbury looked relieved for a moment, then alarmed. "What if the thief sets fire to the house next? Perhaps I should set a footman to watch at night."

"Not a bad idea, Woodbury," I said absently. My mind wasn't on what he was saying; I needed to discover what a Bow Street Runner wanted with Lymond. "Woodbury, could you go into the library under the pretense of taking refreshment and open a window? I'll go stand outside where I can hear." We agreed on this and Woodbury trotted off, a tray in hand. I dashed around to the outside and went around the corner of the building, keeping close to the side of the wall. I didn't see the form crouching between a bush and the wall and crashed into it before I could stop myself.

"And just what are you doing, Parrott?" I asked coldly, keeping my voice low so I couldn't be heard in the library.

The man stood at the side of the window and met my gaze levelly. He didn't seem at all embarrassed to be caught on all fours with his ear at the bottom of the library window. "Merely looking for shirt studs," he said. There was no expression on his face, but his eyes were mocking. I noted he was speaking in tones as low as mine—he evidently didn't wish to be discovered either.

"Shirt studs in the shrubbery?" I couldn't hide my sarcasm.

He pointed to the upstairs window. "My room is there and I was checking the shirt studs next to the window where the light was good. I dropped some of them."

I didn't believe him for a second, but there was no way to disprove his story. That *was* his window, so the story was plausible. "Have you managed to find any of them?" I asked pleasantly. "I'd be glad to help you look."

Before he could answer me, Woodbury flung open the window of the library, catching Parrott square on the back of his head. He crashed like a felled tree right at my feet. Woodbury looked in horror out the window, but I shook my head and put my finger to my lips. I certainly didn't want DeWitt, Lynch, or Lymond to think I was spying. I motioned for Woodbury to come outside.

Woodbury was beside me in a trice and started to speak, but I quieted him. The library window was still open. I couldn't understand the words since the men were speaking in low tones. The fragment or two of conversation I did hear seemed to concern books since Lymond spoke of leaves. He also mentioned Uncle Harley's name.

"Why didn't you shut the window?" I whispered to Woodbury, glancing up at the opening. "We can't move Parrott without alerting the men."

Woodbury drew himself up again to attention. He always gets that way when he knows he's in the wrong. "You told me to open the window," he whispered back, "and I did. You didn't say a thing about closing it."

I glanced at the window and now I could hear every word Lymond spoke. He was discussing, of all things, cigars. "The leaf must be wound just so," I heard him saying. His voice got louder and louder and I realized he was walking to the window. Quickly I shoved Woodbury back against the wall, rolled Parrott under a bush and dived in on top of him. Thank God I was wearing a green dress, I thought. Parrott stirred slightly under me, and I briefly wondered how I would explain this if either he woke or we were caught. This was one explanation Lymond would relish.

Lymond seemed to be standing at the window, smoking his cigar while he made appropriate comments on it. Finally I heard him move. "I'll send some of these with you, Lynch. I think you'll enjoy them. There's nothing better than a good cigar."

"Except mebbe a good woman," Lynch said with an evil chuckle. I felt myself blush. Parrott chose this time to move again and moan slightly. His head was bleeding.

"Did you hear something?" Lynch asked. There was a pause while I held my breath. "No, nothing," Lymond answered. I heard them move away from the window.

Every bone in my body was almost jelly. I backed out from under the bush, leaving Parrott there. I stood and grabbed Woodbury by the hand. He was chalky white and his eyes were huge. In my heart I knew he was going to head straight for the brandy and I had half a mind to join him. "Come on, Woodbury," I hissed between rigid lips, "let's get out of here." We ran around the corner of the house just as I heard Lynch saying again that he heard something outside. I peered around the corner in time to see Lymond stick his head out the window and look around. Parrott's foot was clearly visible. Lymond looked at it, then glanced in my direction. I jerked back around the corner, but not soon enough. I knew he had seen me for that brief second when our eyes met. "Nothing at all out there," he told Lynch. I heard the window close.

Woodbury and I staggered in the front door. "I feel faint," Woodbury said, propping himself against the door as he mopped at his face. Woodbury was not cut out for a life of intrigue.

"Go get yourself some water," I said. "I've got to get out of this dress." I glanced down and saw dirt, leaves, and some of Parrott's blood on my dress.

"Water?" Woodbury croaked. "Water?"

I propelled him towards the kitchen. "It'll be good for you." With that, I left him and scurried for the hall and the door to our apartments just as DeWitt, Lymond, and Lynch came out of the library. They didn't see me and I certainly didn't want to be seen. I ran to my room, stripped off my dress, and stuffed it under my bed. I had just enough time to jerk on another dress, splash my face to make sure it was clean, and pat down my hair before the knock came at my door. I had known it was coming.

Quickly I snatched up a book and sat down, pretending to read. "Who is it?" I called out, knowing full well who it was.

"Robert Lymond." He didn't even wait to be invited inside, he simply opened the door and came in. "What have you been doing?"

I opened my eyes wide. "Whatever do you mean, Lymond? You can see I'm sitting right here reading a book."

He lifted a brow. "Kenyon just returned from his outing with your sisters and I sent him outside to investigate. It looked like Parrott under that bush. He came back inside and confirmed it." He moved to look straight at me. "Tell me, Roxanne, what were you doing?"

"I really don't know what you mean, Lymond." That was true to a point. "Did you have company? I thought Woodbury told me you were closeted with a Bow Street Runner."

He had the grace to look surprised. He paused, as though judging what to say next. "Just an acquaintance," he said. "Back to Parrott. He took quite a blow to the head. Did you do that?" I didn't answer him and he continued. "I saw you peering around the corner, so there's no use denying it. I'm sure there must be some explanation."

I lifted an eyebrow. "Really, Lymond! Are you quizzing me as though I were a common criminal? Even though you do have a lease, I wasn't aware that I couldn't come and go as necessary."

"Roxanne, stop dancing around my question." He looked stern and his voice was icy. "Do you know who bashed in Parrott's head?"

"Bashed in his head?" I was horrified. "Heavens, no! All I know about is the lick he took from the edge of the window. He isn't really hurt, is he?"

"He's dead," Lymond said shortly. "Someone hit him on the head, but we don't think that's the cause of death. Kenyon seems to think he's been stabbed in the same way Mowbridge was. We'll know for sure in a short while."

I went all to pieces. "Stop trying to bait me, Lymond. Parrott isn't dead. I was right on top of him, right under the bush. He certainly wasn't dead then. He even moaned a little."

"On top of him? He moaned?" It was Lymond's turn to be horrified.

I tried my best to explain to Lymond exactly what had happened. "You can ask Woodbury," I finally said, ending my story. "He was right there and he can tell you that Parrott was just fine when we left him, other than being unconscious, of course." I paused. "Lymond, he—Parrott, that is—couldn't have been left alone for over a few minutes. Woodbury and I came straight into the house. I was going to send some-

209

one out to get Parrott as soon as possible. You said you sent Kenyon out to check on him then."

"I did." Lymond paused. "It couldn't have been over five minutes." He looked at me. "Did you know that Parrott had plans to marry Miss Hinchley?"

This was almost as astounding as the murder. "No!"

Lymond nodded. "I understand he had given notice to Gage that he would be leaving Gage's employ. According to Miss Hinchley, she and Parrott planned to marry and move to America."

I was dumbfounded. "Miss Hinchley! Who would have thought it?" I glanced at Lymond. "The poor woman. She'll be distraught."

Lymond nodded and we went into the main room where my desk was located. I sent Meggie to tell Aunt Hen to go stay with Miss Hinchley. Kenyon Gwynn came in just as Lymond asked me to go over the entire episode with Parrott once again. Kenyon glanced at Lymond and then at me, raised an eyebrow, but said nothing. Lymond ignored his look. "What else have you found, Kenyon?" he asked.

Kenyon handed him a piece of paper. "He was stabbed, just as I thought, and evidently it had just occurred when you found him. This was stuffed into the front of his shirt."

Lymond looked carefully at the paper while I craned my neck to see it. It was a page from a book. Lymond handed it to me and I took it by the corner. There was a large drop of blood staining it and the page had been torn in half, leaving only the top half of the poem intact. It was "Though I am Young and Cannot Tell" by Ben Jonson. I read it silently once, then once aloud. "Though I am young, and cannot tell/Either what Death or Love is well,/Yet I have heard they both bear

210

darts,/And both do aim at human hearts.'' I looked up at Lymond and Kenyon. "What does this mean?"

"I wish I knew." Lymond took the page from my fingers. He looked tired. "I talked to Parrott this morning, and he said he had something important to tell me. I put him off until Lynch left because I wanted to talk to him undisturbed. That's when he told me that he and Miss Hinchley were planning to marry and emigrate."

"Would Miss Hinchley be in any danger now?" I asked.

Kenyon and Lymond both started, then Lymond jumped to his feet. "I hadn't thought of it," he said, heading for the door. Then he turned back. "We need to discover what she knows, if anything." He looked at me pleadingly.

"No, Lymond," I said. I hardly knew Miss Hinchley. She and her cat had stayed out of view as much as possible. I had thought it was because of Bucephalus; I had no idea it was because she was staying around Parrott and that a marriage was in the offing.

"Your Aunt Hen?" Lymond sounded hopeful. "She's rather good at ferreting out secrets."

I nodded and went to Miss Hinchley's room and called out Aunt Hen. "The poor dear," Aunt Hen said, tears streaming down her face. Aunt Hen cried easily. "To think that happiness was snatched from her in such a manner. I'll certainly do what I can."

"Whatever you do, Mrs. Vellory," Kenyon warned, "don't let Miss Hinchley out of your sight. She'll need someone to stay with her around the clock for several days."

Aunt Hen nodded in agreement. "The poor thing may never have another offer. She may even think of doing away with herself."

211

"Exactly," Lymond said, glancing over Aunt Hen's head and exchanging a glance with Kenyon. They left it at that.

The entire house was at sixes and sevens for the rest of the day and the death cast a pall over the house. Aunt Hen never left Miss Hinchley's side. Even Evelyn was concerned for her. Underneath her selfish exterior, I saw that Evelyn did have some good qualities. It was a pity she hadn't had a mother to guide her.

Kenyon stayed close to Livvy and Julia, as usual, chaperoned. They had been together so much that I expected an offer from that quarter at any time. I still hadn't discovered the cause of his scar, but surely it couldn't be anything that would render him ineligible. If he were unsuitable, Lymond would have told me.

Livvy and Kenyon would be a perfect pair and I was already looking forward to having him in the family. I said as much to Julia as Kenyon and Livvy were talking quietly in the drawing room. "Look at them," I said, gesturing to the pair of them. "They look made for each other." I gave a sigh of satisfaction. "It's the perfect match and I've accomplished it." I turned to Julia. "I want to thank you for investing so much of your time and effort, Julia. I know it's been onerous for you to be at Livvy's side continuously, and I think it's been a truly unselfish thing for you to do. After Livvy and Kenyon are married, I'll do the same for you."

Julia gave me a stricken look and started to speak, but I stopped her and gave her a pat on the hand. "Don't say a word, Julia. You are unselfish and caring, even though you blush at compliments. I know Kenyon and Livvy thank you, and I thank you." I stood up and looked around. "Do you mind staying here chaperoning these two for a while longer? Lymond's gone into Brighton to notify the authorities, and I want to look up George Gage. I don't think anyone's given the man more than a cursory account of what happened, and I know he must be distraught. Parrott had been with him for a good while, so he must be overset." Julia looked as overset as I imagined Gage to be, so I patted her hand once again before I went in search of Gage. I found him sitting alone on a bench in the garden, smoking.

"I'm sorry about Parrott," I said, sitting down beside him. "It must be a terrible blow for you."

"It is." He ground his cigar out on the gravel and tossed it away. Bue bounded up and ran after it. "Your dog seems to have some retriever in him," he said with a slight smile as Bue returned with the remains of the cigar. Gage gave him a treat and tossed the tobacco away again. Bue flopped down at our feet.

"He likes you very much," I told him as I bent to pat Bue on the head. "He doesn't really like or trust many people." I frowned. "I don't know why he didn't alert us to Parrott's murderer. Usually Bue sets up a howl every time a stranger comes on the place."

Gage looked at me, stood, and held out his hand to me. "He was with me, so I don't suppose he saw any strangers. Would you like to walk with me a few minutes? I feel the need to get away from here for a while."

I understood his need perfectly, so we wandered down by the stables and out towards the sea, Bucephalus bounding along beside us. The day was lovely, not at all a day for dying. Gage seemed so preoccupied that I hesitated to mention Parrott, but I did anyway. "Did you know Parrott had reached an understanding with Miss Hinchley?"

Gage nodded. "I knew there was some interest, but had no idea things had progressed to the point of an

213

offer of marriage. Parrott gave me his notice last night. Had you known of it for long?''

I shook my head. ''I discovered it only when Lymond told me today. They were most discreet. I didn't have an inkling that they were attached, although Kenyon had hinted at it.''

We walked on for a moment and Gage didn't say anything. I really didn't know what to say to relieve his pain, so we walked in silence. Finally Gage spoke, looking out to sea. ''Have you seen Boots today?'' he asked almost absently. ''He and Parrott didn't get along, you know.''

I was shocked. ''No, I didn't know that. But then, Boots really doesn't get along with anyone.'' I paused. ''Are you saying that you suspect Boots of Parrott's murder?''

''Oh, no,'' Gage said hastily. ''I was merely wondering where Boots might be. I haven't seen him all day.'' He then changed the subject, turning to admire the sea and scenery, and to quiz me about Papa's motives in building at that particular spot. We walked back to the house then, and he excused himself to retire to his room. I knew he must be heavy of heart.

Supper was a subdued affair and we talked about everything possible, to keep from talking about Parrott and Miss Hinchley. Poor Miss Hinchley was not doing well at all. Aunt Hen actually feared for the poor soul's life and dared not leave her alone. Her only comfort was her cat. Precious, however, was creating problems since he didn't wish at all to comfort anyone, much less Miss Hinchley.

After supper, Kenyon and Livvy, with Julia along again, went to the drawing room to play cards just to pass the time. They tried to dragoon me to make a fourth, but I really didn't care for cards, so they drafted

Lymond. I had wanted to talk to Lymond and see if he had discovered anything else, but didn't have the opportunity. Instead, George and I sat and talked quietly until he asked me to take a turn around the garden with him in the moonlight. I thought it might be difficult for him since Parrott had been murdered right at the edge of Holmwood's boxwoods, but he didn't seem to mind.

The night was clear, the breeze from the sea was warm and tangy, and the gardens looked lovely in the moonlight. Gage, Bue, and I walked for the better part of half an hour, talking about trivialities. I finally got an opening and asked him the question that had been bothering me all afternoon: "Do you think DeWitt had anything to do with Parrott's murder or with the theft of the *Iliad*?" I had intended a little more finesse, but the garden was getting chilly and I wanted to ask before we went back inside.

I could see his face in the moonlight and a surprised expression flitted across it. "DeWitt?" Then his expression was as usual. "It's a possibility. I had considered him suspect, but I have no proof at all. How did you conclude he was involved?"

I told him about the conversation I had overheard and added my own observations about DeWitt's peculiar behavior. "What alerted me at first," I told him, "was DeWitt following us when Evelyn fell from the cliff. Not minutes before, I had left DeWitt in the library where he was declaring he had a full afternoon's work. He had to have been deliberately following us."

Gage lifted an eyebrow. "It's possible. Definitely possible."

I paused and frowned, drawing my shawl closer around me. It was really chilly. "The only thing that really puzzles me is why DeWitt hasn't left. If he has

215

the *Iliad*, what's the point in staying here? I fail to see the connection between Mowbridge and Parrott.''

''Perhaps the man is criminally insane,'' Gage offered. ''I've heard that those people look perfectly normal.''

''I don't know.'' I sighed. ''Would you mind helping me watch him? I can keep him under surveillance in the house, but it's difficult for me to keep up with him when he goes out.''

''I'd be delighted to help you. It'll be our secret.'' He stopped me in a patch of light from the window. ''There's another secret that I'd like to mention: I have something very important to discuss with you and I've wondered and wondered just how to say it in the right way.'' He turned and gazed into my eyes. ''I've concluded that I'll make a botch of it no matter what approach I use.''

I waited for a moment, then prompted him to go on.

''You're a beautiful woman,'' he said, touching my face with his fingertip. ''One of the most beautiful women I've ever seen.''

Flattering as this was, I didn't really believe it, but how I wanted to! ''Thank you, George.'' I wanted to appear calm and collected, but the words were stammered. I felt rather giddy as well. I was almost afraid of what would come next.

Instead of continuing with flatteries of my face and person which would culminate in an offer, Gage swept me into a kiss. The kiss in the library, with all its attendant feelings, was only child's play compared to this kiss. I was swept away, transported, and breathless. He stopped and looked down into my eyes. ''Roxanne,'' he whispered roughly before kissing me again. I caught myself responding and again I heard my name called. It took me a moment to realize that George could not possibly be calling my name since his lips were firmly pressed to mine. I leaped back.

"Roxanne." The voice was thick with disapproval and it belonged to Lymond. "Your aunt wants you." I took one look at his scowling, dark face and tried, not too successfully, to compose myself. "Thank you, Lymond." I turned to George. "I must be going. Perhaps we can continue this tomorrow."

"I'd love to continue this tomorrow," George said with laughter in his voice.

I felt myself go red. "I meant, of course, continue our conversation."

"Of course."

I didn't try to repair the damage this time—I fled to Miss Hinchley's room where Aunt Hen was waiting. There, I discovered that Aunt Hen had requested my presence so I could locate her vinaigrette and send for the doctor to prescribe some laudanum. I had some drops of my own and gave them to her. It took a while for Miss Hinchley to fall into a troubled sleep. There was no talking to her at all—she was beyond speaking.

After I left Aunt Hen and Miss Hinchley, I thought about going into the drawing room with everyone else, but decided I really didn't wish to face Lymond again tonight. Instead, I went to my room, taking Bue with me. He flopped down on his rug immediately and looked at me. In just a moment, he wandered over to the chair where I had thrown my dress earlier. It was the one I had been wearing when I had landed on top of Parrott. Bue started scratching at the dress and whining. I looked at him keenly since this behavior wasn't in character for him. I picked up the dress and looked at it carefully while Bue pranced around eagerly. There was only a tear where the boxwoods had snagged it and the dirt and dust I had picked up when

I landed on Parrott. Then I saw what Bue wanted. Stuck to the bottom, on the side, was one of the dog treats George always carried. I pulled it from the dress, puzzled.

This would mean that George had been nearby, since the dog treat had been unwrapped and damp enough to cause it to stick. It had no dust or dirt on it at all. I wondered briefly if Parrott carried the treats, then discarded that theory. Only George carried them, and he kept them in his pocket. This had to place him at the scene, but where had he been? I certainly hadn't seen him anywhere. Remembering Parrott's excuse, I certainly hadn't seen any studs on the ground either. Something wasn't quite right.

Still, I didn't want to implicate George Gage in any way. I went over to my dressing table and sat down to look at myself in the mirror, remembering George's kisses and felt myself blush. I turned away and looked out the window instead.

Outside, I saw a couple walking. It was, I thought, Kenyon and another person, a woman I couldn't see well in the shadowy darkness outside. Kenyon bent down and kissed her in the moonlight and I sighed with satisfaction. It had to be Livvy, and if that was any indication, an offer would be shortly forthcoming.

I turned away from the window since I really didn't wish to intrude on their privacy and thought further about Parrott, the dog treat, and the poems. I sat for a long time, thinking. The house quieted and I was still in a quandary. Much as I hated to face him, I decided to go in search of Lymond. Perhaps something he had discovered in Brighton or in his talk with the authorities could help me solve this puzzle. I even had a good idea where I could find him—he usually stayed in the library smoking after everyone else had gone to bed, so I could talk to him there uninterrupted.

There was a hint of rain and fog in the air, and the house held more than the usual night chill. I wrapped my shawl around me and headed for the library.

Chapter 15

Lymond was sitting in the dark in front of a very small fire. I stood for a moment by the door in the quiet, watching him in the glow from the fire, smelling his cigar smoke mixed with the smell of burning wood. I went in, lit a single candle and put it on the table between us, removed my shawl, and sat down in the chair opposite him.

He regarded me without expression and put the cigar into a dish. "Where's Gage?"

"In bed, I suppose. I really don't know." There was an awkward pause. "The fire feels good tonight. I thought it was chilly."

"I noticed you did."

I let this pass, although with difficulty. "Lymond, did you discover anything about Parrott?"

"The same type of knife that dispatched Mowbridge, Kenyon tells me. Also, the bit of poetry follows the same pattern as in some other deaths."

I held out the dog treat. "This was stuck to my dress—the one I had on when I fell on top of Parrott. I wasn't completely on top of him, so this must have been on the ground. There was dirt on my gown all around it."

Lymond peered at it and looked puzzled, so I identified it for him. "It's a dog treat." Lymond still looked puzzled. "And what is the significance of that?" he asked.

I shook my head. "I don't know. I was hoping you might tell me. It seems significant to me, but I can't figure out the connection. Parrott never carried the things. Woodbury certainly didn't have them. The only person besides George who's used those treats is Kenyon and he certainly wouldn't harm Parrott."

Lymond shook his head. "No, he's merely trying to protect himself from your pet. He's really terrified of dogs, you know."

"I thought as much. He seems nervous when Bue's around. He seems to be forcing himself to stand his ground in front of Bue."

Lymond looked at the fire instead of me. "That's how he got his scars. He never mentions it, but he was mauled rather savagely when he was younger. The dog was a mastiff, much the size of yours and he almost killed Kenyon." Lymond paused. "Don't tell him I told you; he considers it something of a weakness."

"I've wondered and meant to ask you. Thank you for telling me." There was an awkward silence as we both sat there. "Lymond, has it occurred to you that Bue hasn't been his usual self?"

Lymond raised an eyebrow. "I thought he was as obnoxious as usual, at least to me. I certainly haven't seen a difference."

It took perseverance to continue, but I was groping my way to the solution of this puzzle. "No, Lymond, what I mean is that Bue hasn't alerted us to a stranger when all these things have happened. Holmwood said he didn't bark whenever someone slept in my bed and left those poems; he didn't bark whenever the scroll

221

was taken; he didn't bark when Parrott was murdered."

"The only person he seems to get along with is Gage." Lymond gave me a cynical sneer. "Are you accusing your paramour?"

"He isn't my paramour." I couldn't keep the anger out of my voice. "Perhaps there isn't any kind of connection. Perhaps Bue's just getting old. I don't know." I stood and began to pace the room. It was suddenly very hot.

Lymond relit his cigar and ignored my questions about Bue. "Gage certainly looked like your paramour. The two of you looked quite friendly. One might even say, more than friends." He looked at me and his eyes almost drilled into mine. "Your reputation will be in shreds at this rate, Roxanne."

I drew myself up and glared at him. "There is nothing sullied about my reputation, I assure you, Lymond. George gave me a brief kiss, that's all. You wouldn't even have known about it if you hadn't been spying on us."

His laugh was short. "I have better things to do than spy on you. If you're foolish enough to jump over windmills for George Gage, then so be it. I just hate to see you act the goose, Roxanne, especially over someone like Gage."

This was too much. I turned on him. "Acting the goose? Foolish? At least, Lymond, I'm trying to get to the bottom of the things that have been happening around here. If you weren't so wrapped up in DeWitt, you might help me a little. Between us, we might be able to solve the murders before another one happens. But you can't do that, can you? You're too afraid you'll have to admit to a mistake, that's all it is." It was as good an exit line as any, so I stomped out the door, slamming it behind me.

My exit line done, there was nothing for me to do in the hall. I looked around and discovered Woodbury still up and looking at me curiously. I glared at him and went back to my room.

Woodbury came banging on my door early the next morning. Boots had been discovered lying outside the front door. As best as we could piece together, he had been some distance from the house when he had been hit hard on the head and left by the side of the road for dead. He had managed to crawl up to the front door, but couldn't reach the knocker. When one of the maids opened the door to sweep, she shrieked to high heaven until Woodbury discovered that Boots, although battered and bloody, was still very much alive. He kept trying to say something, Woodbury reported to all of us.

"What was it, Woodbury?" I asked. "If he tried that hard to speak, it must be important. Did he give you a name?"

"That he did." Woodbury paused, waiting until he had everyone's undivided attention. "I really couldn't understand him proper, but I thought he was saying 'George . . . Iliad, George . . . Iliad.'" He looked around at us, puzzled. "I've never heard of George Iliad."

"It isn't a person, Woodbury. At least the *Iliad* part isn't." I thought about it. "He must be talking about the Samarkand scroll, which is a translation of the *Iliad*, and has it all confused with the scrap we found on Mowbridge. That was from George Chapman's translation of the *Iliad*." I went with Woodbury to Boots's room and looked at him anxiously as we waited for the doctor. He had completely lost consciousness. Kenyon and Lymond were there and Woodbury told them what he had relayed to me. "Do you suppose," I asked

223

Kenyon, since I didn't wish to speak to Lymond, "that Boots knows where the Samarkand scroll might be?"

Kenyon and Lymond gave each other a quick look. Before I could quiz either of them, Gage came in and I quickly told him what I thought had happened. He and I went downstairs as Lymond and Kenyon took their leave. Woodbury volunteered to sit with Boots until the doctor arrived. As George and I went downstairs, I looked around for DeWitt and didn't see him anywhere. I thought about mentioning this very conspicuous absence to Lymond and Kenyon, but decided they were so biased they wouldn't listen. Instead, I shared my worries with George, beginning with my original suspicion that DeWitt might have substituted the scroll, and ending with my question about his whereabouts.

George looked at me solemnly. "It does seem, pardon the expression, somewhat damning. DeWitt should have been in the house with the rest of us when Boots was discovered unless he was outside. If he was outside, that means he could have . . ." His voice trailed off.

"Exactly." I caught his meaning perfectly. "Also, Boots kept saying 'George . . . *Iliad*' over and over. As a librarian, DeWitt would likely know where Papa's copy of George Chapman's translation was kept. He could very well be planning to use a bit of it again in another murder." I wheeled and went in the library. "I'm going to see if the Chapman's there now. If it isn't, I'm sending some men out to search for DeWitt. I don't care what Lymond says."

George stood beside me. "So Lymond thinks DeWitt's innocent."

"Innocent! He tells me that DeWitt is in his employ! Can you believe that?" George didn't answer me but

I didn't notice. I couldn't find the Chapman and couldn't remember exactly where I had last seen it. "Did Boots have a bit of a poem on his person?" George asked casually.

I was startled. "I really didn't think to ask, in all the excitement. I'll go ask Woodbury as soon as I look here." I saw the Chapman wedged in between two other books and, to my surprise, felt a keen sense of disappointment. "Here it is." I pulled the book from the shelves and it looked the same—everything intact except the frontispiece. "If the book is here, why did Boots mention it?"

George shrugged. "Perhaps he had seen DeWitt with it. Perhaps he was trying to implicate DeWitt in Mowbridge's murder."

"That's the flaw in this solution—DeWitt wasn't here when Mowbridge was murdered."

Gage lifted an eyebrow and took the Chapman from my fingers. "He hadn't been introduced into the household, but who's to say whether or not he was in the area."

I was shocked. "I hadn't considered that, George." I frowned. "But the bits of poetry. Those on my pillow, the one in Mowbridge's pocket, the scrap Parrott had." I looked up at him, since I thought searching his face would give me a clue. "Did Boots have . . . oh, you already asked that question. No, I don't know if Boots had a scrap of poetry on his person. That could be important." I ran towards the door before George could stop me. "I'll go ask Woodbury right now. You wait here."

Woodbury was in the pantry, fortifying himself with a liquid. "It's rather early for that, Woodbury," I said, trying not to chide. Woodbury had, I thought, had his share of anxieties lately. Quickly I asked if there had been a bit of poem on Boots's person, and to my surprise, Woodbury reached into his pocket and handed me a scrap. "That was in his hand."

I looked at it carefully. It was apparently a bit of a scroll, although I couldn't make out any of the faded lettering. Had DeWitt, I wondered, bashed him with a scroll? Only one person would know. "When will Boots be able to speak, Woodbury? Has the doctor told us anything?"

Woodbury shook his head. "Oh, he can speak now."

This was news. "I thought he was unconscious. When might I talk to him? Has he told Lymond or the doctor who hit him?"

"There'll be no information from Boots—young Mr. Sinclair. The doctor said the blow to the head erased his memory and he has no recollection at all."

"Is there any chance he'll regain his memory in a day or two?"

Woodbury shrugged. "The doctor didn't say, but I wouldn't think his memory will come back." Woodbury looked at me sagely. "I've seen too many war wounds like that. The men are never the same. Some of them never even remember their names."

When I went back to speak to George, he was sitting quietly, the Chapman still in his hand. Quickly I told him about the bit of scroll. "We'll never know," I finished up bitterly. "According to the doctor, Boots has completely lost his memory and no one knows if he'll be able to remember anything for days, or even weeks."

"I'm sure it'll come to him soon." George put the Chapman down on the edge of the desk and smiled at me. "I've got to go into Brighton for an appointment right now, but perhaps we could talk further this evening?" He took my hand and pulled me up. "I think perhaps the two of us need to get together to discover some things." He ran his fingers across my wrist and I knew immediately that whatever he wished to discover had absolutely nothing to do with either Boots, Parrott, or Mowbridge. I felt myself begin to blush. George laughed lightly and left. "Until tonight," he said with a grin as he went out the door.

I was at loose ends for a while. I went upstairs and discovered that Kenyon and Lymond had stationed a footman to stand guard at Boots's door. Downstairs Aunt Hen was consoling Uncle Harley. "Almost lost," he kept saying over and over. "Almost lost." Aunt Hen was bracing him up with tea and spirits. No one seemed to have seen Lymond.

In the library, DeWitt was sitting at Papa's desk, working hard. Evelyn, of course, was there, gazing at him adoringly. DeWitt kept glancing up at her, returning her gaze. They were quite oblivious to anything else. I felt in my pocket for the scrap of paper and ran my fingers over it. I decided to show it to DeWitt and see if his face betrayed any expression.

I tossed the scrap on the desk. "Do you recognize this?" I asked, being careful not to show any expression. I didn't want to give him a hint.

He took up the scrap and looked at it, then reached inside his pocket and took out a magnifying glass. Carefully he looked at the scrap, then turned it over to look at the other side. "Where did you get this?" he asked quietly in a tone that wasn't at all subservient. He sounded rather in command of things.

"It was given to me," I replied. That was perfectly true.

DeWitt handed it back to me. "It looks very much like a piece of the scroll your father bought in Samarkand. I couldn't really say, but the writing is definitely

227

Greek. There's also something on the back of it—some kind of sticky material. I don't think it's glue. It seems to be something else altogether.''

I nodded and ran my fingers over the spot he pointed out. The sticky stuff came off on my fingertip and I looked at it. It was brown and reminded me of something I had seen recently. I placed the scrap back in my pocket and left, having learned absolutely nothing from DeWitt—other than the fact that he would probably offer for Evelyn soon. I wondered what Uncle Harley would think of that and concluded that he'd probably be delighted to have his own librarian in the family—if DeWitt were indeed a librarian. At any rate, Lymond needed to be informed about how things stood in that quarter.

For lack of anything else to do, I went to my desk and began working on Papa's translation of Xenophon again. I wasn't really making much headway on it. I had worked for an hour or so when Julia came in with Aunt Hen. After a question or two about Uncle Harley, I congratulated Julia on what she had done with Kenyon. "You've done a wonderful job bringing Kenyon up to scratch," I told her. "It wouldn't have happened without you."

"Roxanne, what a goose you are," Aunt Hen said. "Of course nothing would have happened without Julia." She patted Julia's hand as Julia blushed furiously.

"I didn't know you knew, Roxanne," she said with a shy smile. "From what you said, I thought . . . I thought . . .''

"Say no more, Julia," I said warmly, getting up. "Of course I knew about your efforts. I'm very pleased." To my surprise, she flung her arms around me and broke into tears.

228

"I was afraid you'd be angry with me."

I patted her on the back. "Silly girl, how could I be angry with you?" I gave her a handkerchief and changed the subject. "Has either of you seen Lymond? I can't seem to locate him."

"Kenyon said Lymond had gone into Brighton on business," Julia said, mopping at her eyes.

I tapped the edge of the desk. "Strange. George went in as well. I wonder what's going on."

I didn't get to see Lymond until suppertime and then he wasn't really speaking to me. I managed to corner him in the drawing room afterwards while Livvy, Julia, and Kenyon sang for the others.

"What was your business in Brighton?" I asked quietly. There wasn't time for the amenities.

He raised an eyebrow at me. "Nothing that might concern you."

It was my turn to raise an eyebrow. "There's no point in being rude, Lymond. I expected at least a civil answer."

"Gage was in Brighton as well. Why don't you ask him about his business?" Lymond's voice was icy. "You two seem to be the best of friends lately."

I looked at him a moment. "I'll just do that." With that, I got up and went to sit beside George. I regretted it, since I was sure I could have convinced Lymond to tell me his business had I stayed. I had, as Aunt Hen always said, cut off my nose to spite my face. Still, once in a while it had to be done.

The rest of the evening was a total loss. I think we all felt strange to be singing, even if the songs were sad, while Boots lay upstairs, unable to remember even his name. The evening ended early with Uncle Harley going heavily upstairs to sit with Boots for a while before he went to bed.

"He seems to really care about his children," I told Aunt Hen. "In the beginning, I didn't think so."

"He does," she answered, walking back to our apartments with me. "He simply doesn't know how to let them know it. There's so much ill feeling in that family, Roxanne, and it's so unnecessary. They care a great deal for each other, but none of them can communicate it with any of the others." She paused. "I finally took it on myself to tell Evelyn that her father cared for her."

Thinking of my own loving father, I found this sad. "What did she say? Did it matter to her?"

Aunt Hen looked amazed. "Of course it did, Roxanne. She even cried." We had reached the door of my room and Aunt Hen turned to me and smiled. "I'm glad you reacted to Julia's news so well. She had been so afraid that you'd be angry because it wasn't what you really wanted. I told her it would be fine. After all, Kenyon is a fine young man and has excellent prospects."

I nodded. "I'm delighted he might be a part of our family."

"Might? Oh, my dear, it's a sure thing. Kenyon offered this afternoon."

I felt a smile all over my face. "He did? How wonderful, Aunt Hen! And of course she said yes."

"Pending your approval, of course. I suppose we might need to get Edward's approval just as a matter of formality."

Edward, our half brother, is hardly beloved by any of us. To tell the truth, Papa didn't care much for him either and had made me guardian of the girls, so Edward's approval wasn't necessary. "I don't think we need to notify him, Aunt Hen. The less we have to do with Edward, the better off we always are."

"I know." Aunt Hen sighed. "The last time he was here, I recall that he wanted you to get married immediately."

"To anyone who would offer for me." It had been humiliating and I had vowed never to be put through that again. I was going to stay on the shelf.

"Yes." Aunt Hen had a significant pause. "There's always Robert." She paused again. "He's quite a catch, you know."

"You make him sound rather like a trout, Aunt Hen." With that, I bade her good night and went into my room to write some letters.

Shortly after midnight, I was still awake, curled up in my favorite spot in my pillows, reading, when I heard a terrific crash on the upper floor. I thought for a moment that the top half of the house had fallen in and I just sat there, my mouth open, staring at the ceiling as though waiting for the roof to fall through. Then I tossed down my book, grabbed my shoes and ran for the stairs.

At the foot of the stairs, I saw part of a pedestal and bust that had been sitting in the top hall. The stairs and railing had been damaged. I dashed around the fragments and hurried up. At the top, the hall was full of people in various stages of nightdress. Beside Boots's door, the footman was sprawled on the carpet with Kenyon attending to him. "Is he . . . ?" I asked.

Kenyon glanced up at me briefly and I was glad Livvy wasn't with me. He looked handsome beyond belief in the flickering candlelight, his scar giving him a rakish, almost piratical look. "No, he isn't dead." He motioned for Woodbury to help him. "I think he's been drugged."

Woodbury stopped short and stared. "Drugged?"

231

Woodbury had put his wig on askew in the excitement. "Are you sure?"

"No, but I think that's the case." Kenyon stood and he and Woodbury dragged the footman away from the door. "We'll put him to bed. I think he'll be all right."

George came up to us. He was dressed in a dressing gown over his shirt. Evidently he hadn't been able to go to sleep immediately either. "You can put him in my room," he told them. "I haven't gone to bed yet."

Kenyon gave him a strange look. "Thank you. We may wait and let the doctor look at him first." He turned back to look at the footman. "I think he'll be all right once he sleeps it off."

"Why would anyone do this?" I asked. Boots's door was still closed, and everything looked normal except for a gouge in the wall and on the stairs where the bust and pedestal had fallen.

Kenyon nodded towards Boots's door. "Lymond's in there with him. Whoever tried to murder Boots didn't count on that."

I felt the blood drain from my face. "Murder! Right here in the house? That's impossible."

Lymond stood in the open door. He had taken a blow on his head, and there was a bruise forming. A thin trickle of blood ran into his eyebrow. "It may be impossible, but it's true." He looked around at all of us. "I think the excitement is over for the night and there's been no harm done." He glanced at the sleeping footman and a ghost of a smile played around his lips. "Unless, of course, John wakes up with a crashing headache, which I think he will. I don't think anything else will happen."

"And Boots?" Evelyn asked faintly. "How is Boots?" DeWitt was standing with his arm around her shoulders.

Lymond smiled at her. "Good news: Boots is doing much better than expected. He's regained consciousness and is speaking. We hope to question him when the doctor returns tomorrow. I think his memory is going to be fine."

"Thank God!" Evelyn leaned into DeWitt's shoulder.

After a few more reassurances, we all started back to bed. Lymond let it be known that Boots would be under guard throughout the night and that seemed to satisfy everyone. John, the footman, was carried down to his own cot, but seemed to be fine, other than quite sound asleep. I paused on the stairs to assess the damage as Lymond stood at the top, watching me.

"You're hurt," I said.

He touched the blood on his forehead. "Only a scratch. Whoever came in to finish off Boots didn't know I was there."

"Who was it and what happened?" I asked, looking up at him. I had to keep myself from reaching out to touch him.

"I don't know who, although I wish I did." He sat down wearily on the top step where he could still keep an eye on Boots's door. "As to what, evidently John was drugged and when he was asleep, someone tried to come into Boots's room to finish the job he bungled earlier. Whoever it was didn't know I was in there." He paused. "Kenyon and I thought something like this might be attempted."

"And you fought him? Or her?"

"Him. Yes, I had hoped to sit quietly and nab him, but he got a glimpse of me. I did see a stiletto in his hand and he made a lunge for me. I dodged, but his blow glanced off my head." He paused as George joined us on the stairs. "Our murderer feels retreat is

233

the better part of valor. After I resisted, he fled, evidently running into the pedestal and bust in his flight."

"Too bad," George said, joining me to look at the damage. "He must have jumped over all this and fled out the front door."

Lymond said nothing for a moment, then his tone was noncommittal. "Perhaps." He stood. "Perhaps we should also get ourselves to bed. I have a feeling that tomorrow will be a long day." He looked down at the two of us.

"I'm going to get some chocolate," I said. "Would you two like to join me? Lymond, you look as though you need something."

Lymond glanced at Boots's door and shook his head, but George joined me. I usually went to the kitchen and made my own chocolate when I couldn't sleep, but tonight, since half the staff was up anyway, I sent for chocolate and went on into the drawing room. Woodbury, his wig firmly in place by now, sent a footman in to light a very small fire for us. It was foggy outside and the chill in the house was just enough to make a very small blaze necessary.

In the library, I drew the curtains and we sat in front of the fire, making idle talk until the room warmed and the chocolate was brought. I had been so tense that my neck hurt, and it felt good just to sit back in my chair and sip warm chocolate. My tenseness subsided and I began to feel relaxed and drowsy.

"You look lovely sitting here in the firelight." George smiled and put his cup on the table in front of us. "You seem very contented."

I smiled back at him and put my cup next to his. "Not really contented, and I won't be until the culprit is caught, but I do feel relaxed for the first time in days."

He touched the back of my hand. "I would like to

hope my presence has something to do with that." He paused. "I've admired you since I saw you in London for your sister's wedding."

I looked up sharply. "The wedding? Good heavens, George! I don't remember meeting you there. My first glimpse of you was, I thought, when you were at the theater with Boots."

"It was." He laughed, his face dark in the firelight. For an instant, he looked almost devilish. I shook the thought off as he continued. "That was the first time we met, even though we weren't introduced, but I had been with Boots in London and had seen you from a distance. Boots told me all about you and that's when I insisted he invite me here." His fingers moved up to my wrist. I glanced down but seemed powerless to stop him. "We rub along together quite well, don't you think?"

Things were going along entirely too fast. I stood up by the mantel where I would be close to the branch of candles there and looked down at George. Once again, the firelight flickering on his face cast strange shadows. A chill ran up my spine. "Yes, we do seem to be quite good friends," I said lightly.

He stood beside me and put both hands on my shoulders. "There's more than friendship here, Roxanne. You know that." Before I could protest, he bent to kiss me, his hands still holding my shoulders firmly. "Roxanne," he whispered, moving his lips across mine, nibbling at the corner of my mouth. " 'Love love begets, then never be/Unsoft to him who's smooth to thee.' " He paused and touched my lip with the tip of his tongue. I shuddered as he kept whispering. " 'Affection will affection move:/Then you must like, because I love.' "

Something stirred inside my brain, a fuzzy thought. I really couldn't concentrate with George holding me. His

235

body felt hard and firm against mine and I was having trouble breathing. "Poems," I mumbled. "Poems."

George moved his mouth from mine and kissed my neck. "Poems for you. I'll quote you a love poem every day, Roxanne."

I tried to push him away. "No, George, no." I was drowning in my feelings and losing control of myself. I needed some room to breathe and make sense of the swirling thoughts in my head.

"No, my Roxanne, don't fight it," George whispered. "I'll write poems to you; I'll sing poems to you."

"Let me go, George. This isn't proper." I pushed him but he held me fast. I am not a small person, but he was able to hold me firmly. He was much stronger than he appeared. I pushed again, just as ineffectually. "Let me go!"

"No, no, no." His voice attempted to be soothing. "Let me quote love poems to you, Roxanne. Let me say the things that express my feelings." I shoved him again, but it was futile.

Lymond's voice cut through the room, his tone dripping ice. "How about 'Sing, O muse, of the wrath of Achilles,' Gage. That expresses my feelings nicely. Miss Sydney wants you to let her go, now unhand her."

I felt George stiffen, but his grip, rather than loosening, intensified to the point that his fingers were digging into my flesh. He turned and a strange look crossed his face. It took me a moment to recognize it for what it was: pure hatred. "I'm glad you're here, Lymond," he said with a harsh laugh. "It's time for us to end this."

Chapter 16

There was a long moment of silence. Lymond said nothing, but his expression was murderous. I felt George's grip loosen and heard him take a deep breath. I turned my head to see him; he smiled, but his eyes were dark. "I see you're familiar with the *Iliad*, Lymond."

Lymond came further into the room. "Yes, and I believe you are as well." I looked from him to George. There was an undercurrent there I couldn't decipher.

George's grip on my arm relaxed and I moved away so I could see both of them. I was still close to George beside the mantel. I knew Lymond was still groggy from the blow he had taken to his head. "Lymond, George, stop this," I said. "If the two of you have something to settle, at least do it in a civilized manner."

Lymond's eyes flickered from the two chocolate cups to George and me and he shook his head. "I don't believe I'm here to be civil. You wanted to finish it, Gage, and I'm ready." Lymond walked past the two of us and helped himself to some brandy. "Are you all right, Roxanne? I thought the two of you might have come up with a solution to the happenings here.

There's nothing like late-night conversation to offer insights." He sipped and looked at us coolly over the rim of his glass. I knew him well enough to know he was seething.

George shrugged. "Why ask either of us? Perhaps Boots will be able to enlighten you shortly."

"Perhaps." Lymond put his glass down, leaned back against a library table, and crossed his arms across his chest. He didn't make another move and we all stared at each other in silence.

Nature abhors a vacuum and, unfortunately, I seem to be the same way. I did the thing I always do when conversation is at a standstill—I began chattering just to fill up the silence. "Really, Lymond, you're such an ogre. You need to pitch in and help us figure this thing out." I paused and again there was silence, so I continued chattering. "After all, what are our clues? Just think of all that poetry that's been left around. There's got to be some pattern there. After all, someone who's that literate must have enough of a devious mind to establish a pattern."

"Mm." That was all I got out of Lymond. He continued to stare at me. I continued to chatter.

"Think about it, Lymond. What are the poems? Each and every murder victim—and Boots as well, but then he was supposed to be murdered as well, wasn't he?—has had a bit of a poem stuck somewhere on his person."

"Mm."

I waited a moment but the silence was as thick as glue. "Then there were those poems I thought you had left in my chamber. There's a puzzle, Lymond. You said you didn't do that, but then who did? And why didn't Bucephalus tear the person limb from limb? You know how protective he is of me and my things."

"Mm." He was staring right at me and his blue eyes looked almost obsidian in the flickering firelight. There was no expression at all on the taut skin of his face.

I frowned, thinking of the puzzle I had posed. "Those have to be the keys: the poems and Bue's behavior. I don't understand it. Holmwood is the only person who can handle Bue when I'm not around, but someone was able to walk right in past him, sleep in my bed, and leave poetry for me."

There wasn't even "mm" this time. I waited, then plunged ahead. I could feel George moving closer to me, a fraction of an inch at a time. I didn't want him that close to me again, but I was afraid to move away for fear Lymond would get violent. Instead, I kept talking. "As far as the poems—there has to be a pattern. After all, each and every one of the people murdered has had a single piece of poetry except Mowbridge had two. No, one wasn't poetry . . ." I paused and frowned. "Mowbridge." An idea was forming but I hadn't grasped it fully and I fumbled for words. "Mowbridge had two pieces on his person, Lymond. He had a piece of poetry and the frontispiece of the Chapman as well. Could one of them have been a red herring?" I paused, trying to think this through. At the back of my mind I seemed to register that the tension was increasing in the room, but I was too busy to do anything about it.

"Lymond, if one of those pieces of paper wasn't to distract us, could it have been a clue? Could Mowbridge have chosen that way to try to tell us something?" I started to walk back and forth in front of George and the fire. I have to move when I'm trying to puzzle out something. "Think about it, Lymond. As a librarian, it would be logical for him to use a piece of a book, wouldn't it?"

"Mm." Lymond hadn't taken his eyes from George and me and now I sensed a certain wariness in his stance.

I bit the bottom of my lip. "That must be it, Lymond, but what was he trying to tell us?" I stopped and looked from Lymond to George. "He had the poetry and the frontispiece of George Chapman's *Iliad*." The words Lymond had spoken when he came into the library jumped right into my mind but I couldn't get them into the proper order. It was the opening of the *Iliad* and then he had said George was familiar with the *Iliad*. I tried to think aloud. "George Chapman . . . the *Iliad* . . . George . . . George . . . the *Iliad*." In horror I looked straight at George Gage as Mowbridge spoke to me from the grave. "You! Oh, good God, George, you! You killed Mowbridge . . . the others as well. And took the *Iliad*—the scroll!"

Out of the corner of my eye, I saw Lymond move, but he wasn't quick enough. George grabbed me around the neck and I felt warm metal against my throat. "Don't move, Lymond," George said. He might have been talking about the weather. Lymond stepped back and held out his hands, palms up, so George could see there was nothing there. "Just don't hurt her," Lymond said.

"That depends on you—and on her." George moved squarely behind me and got a better grip on my neck. The edge of the blade stuck into my skin and I felt a trickle down my throat. It took me a moment to realize that it was my blood.

"I'll kill you if you hurt her," Lymond said, his voice hoarse with emotion.

George moved the knife slightly and laughed. "Try it and she'll be dead before you can touch me."

Lymond took a deep breath and stood rock still.

"Don't move, Roxanne. He's got that knife right at your throat and he's right—you'd be dead before either of us could move."

He didn't need to worry: *I* certainly wasn't going anywhere. The point of the knife was pressed right against my throat and I could almost feel it slicing my skin. The thin trickle of blood was running down my throat and into the front of my dress. I looked at Lymond and made an inarticulate sound to let him know I understood.

"You can't get away, Gage," Lymond said, his voice level again. "Let her go. If you wish, I'll promise not to follow you."

George laughed. "Do you take me for an idiot? I'd be caught and my heels dangling in the air before morning. No," he paused and laughed again, "this is my insurance. I don't think you'll bother me as long as I keep her right here."

"You can't keep her there and get away." Lymond's expression was blank. "We'll be after her."

"Not if you're dead, you won't."

I felt my eyes widen and tried to speak. "Lymond." I said, choking, "save yourself."

"How very noble." George moved towards Lymond, shoving me in front of him. "Out to the stables, Lymond, right in front of us. If you so much as move one step out of the way, she's gone."

Lymond looked at me. "I won't." He picked up a candle and shielded it as we edged towards the door. I tried to drag my feet, but George squeezed my neck harder and pricked me slightly with the knife. "Do as he says, Roxanne," Lymond said to me. "He has nothing to lose." His eyes told me that he was going to try to rescue us at the very first opportunity.

We walked quietly out the front door and down the

steps. Lymond shielded the candle to light the way. George kept telling him over and over not to make a single false move or I would be killed. Once when Lymond turned to look at us, George jabbed my neck and I cried out. Lymond froze.

"You know I'll do it, don't you?" George asked.

Lymond nodded in the darkness. "Yes, I know it. Let's go to the stables."

When we were almost to the stables, Bucephalus came bounding up to us. "Speak to the dog," George told me. "Make sure he doesn't bark."

We stopped as I spoke to Bue and stretched my fingers to pat him on the head. It was difficult to do since George was holding me so tightly around the neck. Bue didn't bark at all, he merely reached up and lapped George's hand once or twice, looking for dog treats. I realized then why Bue hadn't sounded an alarm when a stranger slept in my room or when the murderer walked in the garden. He had been bribed with treats.

We moved on towards the stables, Lymond trying to walk straight in front of us, while Bue tried to nudge him off the path. Every minute or two Bue ran back to sniff at George's pocket, looking for another treat. "Speak to him," George murmured in my ear. "If he jumps on either of us, the results might be disastrous." I tried, but Bue ignored me. He was thinking of nothing except treats.

At last we reached the stables where Lymond lit a lantern and hung it from a nail. The shadows cast on the walls seemed to be playing out the last act of a Greek tragedy, the figures larger than life, moving slowly. A chill went down my spine that had nothing to do with George. There was an air of expectancy, an air of tension. I had to force myself to look away from the shadows and back to Lymond. I knew in my heart that he would make some move against George, and I wanted to be ready when he did.

George demanded that Lymond saddle The Bruce. Lymond made no move other than to stare at George with eyes that looked like coals in the darkness. "He won't let you ride him."

"Saddle him. I can ride anything that moves and he's the best horse here." He paused and I felt his grip on my neck lighten slightly. "Besides, if he's gone, everyone will think you're gone as well. They won't even look for your body until tomorrow."

Lymond shrugged and reached for The Bruce's saddle and blanket. He slid the saddle to the stall floor and shook the blanket so that the smell of sweat, horse, and hay filled the air. I knew what he was thinking. So did George.

"One false move with that and she's dead. I can move this knife faster than you can move that blanket."

We were crowded into the stall. Bucephalus stood beside me, occasionally nudging George's pocket, still looking for dog treats. George shoved him with his knee, but Bue didn't move. He whined and rubbed his nose along George's pocket, right into my back, and George kicked at him. "Get away from here," George snarled. "Go!" Bue whimpered and out of the corner of my eye I could see him move to the edge of the stall, looking puzzled.

"Hurry up, Lymond." George relaxed his hold on my neck for a moment. "We don't have all night. I have things to do before I leave." His chuckle was not pleasant. He shifted his weight to lean against the stall gate and moved the knife. The edge dropped to my collarbone and there was no pressure from the point against my throat. I decided to take a chance.

I twisted away from George, as the sharp edge of the knife raked across my collarbone and a spurt of blood ran down the front of my dress. "Lymond!" I yelled as I flung myself out of the way. Lymond threw the saddle at George.

George nimbly stepped aside and the saddle crashed into the wall, one of the stirrups striking a glancing blow to my cheek as it went by. The pain was intense and I fought to keep from shutting my eyes. The whole side of my head felt crushed. Lymond leaped on George and tried to wrestle him to the ground. They were banging into the walls of the stall and into the horse. I kept seeing the flash of the knife in George's hand and realized he had more advantage than that. Lymond was already weak from the blow to his head. I was afraid he was either going to be stabbed or trampled to death beneath The Bruce's hooves.

I tried to move, but I was trapped between the horse and the stall wall. The Bruce was excited now and was trying to rear and crash against the walls. His hooves barely missed me as he lunged and I tried to edge along the wall towards where the men were fighting. I heard The Bruce squeal in pain as the knife blade slashed his flank. Lymond glanced at his horse and, in that split second of distraction, George caught him a hard blow to the head. Lymond staggered back as George followed with another blow and a slashing swing of his knife. Lymond ducked, stumbled, and fell onto the floor.

George laughed. "You can't imagine how long I've waited to beat you," he said. "Parrott and I almost had you once or twice before and you always managed to give us the slip."

"So you were the ones who attacked me." Lymond was gasping and I thought he was playing for time.

"Yes." George smiled broadly, savoring this moment. "Once or twice I thought you were on to me and every time you came close, I knew I'd enjoy this moment even more." He looked at me on the other side of Lymond. I was holding The Bruce's halter in an attempt to try and quiet him. "Roxanne, come here." There was a triumphant note in George's voice.

"I will not." I stood as defiantly as I dared. The knife was right over Lymond.

"I said come here. If you don't, I'll kill him right now."

"Run away, Roxanne," Lymond said hoarsely. "Run. Scream. He's just going to kill both of us anyway. If he tries to get me, you'll have time to run."

George laughed shortly. "You're half right, Lymond: you now, but not Roxanne. It depends on how amenable she is to suggestion."

Lymond gave a weak laugh. "You can't do it, Gage. Not both of us at once. Run, Roxanne." He didn't look at me; he was concentrating on George. "It's your only chance."

I looked around. There was no place for me to run out of the stall except right into George's arms, and I certainly didn't want to do that. I took the next best course and screamed. I could have sworn that I screamed loud enough to wake the dead. George just laughed as The Bruce shied and moved away, then he reached out and grabbed me by the arm, dragging me across Lymond. I fought back as best I could, kicking at him and trying to scream.

"Don't try that with me." George shook me violently and slapped me across the face with his open hand. The pain in my face had been bad enough, but this was excruciating. My head snapped back as pain exploded behind my eyes. I screamed again, this time in pain.

Bucephalus sprang right onto George's chest, every tooth bared and a vicious growl in his throat. He knocked George down onto the hay. With a curse, George tried to throw him off, but Bue was right on top of him. I saw the gleam of the knife blade as it came down towards Bue's back and I yelled to Bue but it was too late. Blood spurted as George slashed him along the side. Instead of running, however, Bue became more violent and sank his teeth into George's side. George slashed at him again and again, each time drawing blood.

Lymond had staggered to his feet and was trying to get to George, as much to keep the man from killing Bucephalus as to capture him. Lymond was too groggy—he fell across George's legs and held him down, but could do no more. In desperation, I jerked up the only thing I saw at hand—a bucket of oats someone had left by the stall door—and poured the entire bucketfull on George's head. He choked and sneezed, then tried to clear his eyes with the back of his hand. I swung again with the bucket and knocked the knife away. It went sailing in an arc, up and then down, and I thought it was going to hit Lymond, but it landed in some hay by his side.

Lymond quickly rolled over, grabbed the knife, and tried to get up, but he wasn't quick enough. George shook his head and glanced from me to Lymond, gauging which of us was the more immediate danger. He started to get up and I knew it was only a matter of a moment until he regained the advantage. I slammed the empty bucket down over his head and tried to hold it, but he was thrashing so that I couldn't, so I did the only logical thing: I sat down on the bucket with a thud and started screaming for help. George almost threw me off and I started to get up, but Lymond grabbed my skirt. "Sit!" It was a guttural command. I sat.

This was how Kenyon, DeWitt, and Woodbury found us moments later when they ran into the stables.

They quickly made short work of George, rolling Lymond off his legs. I moved and picked up the bucket. "I'm afraid I've hurt his neck," I said, looking at the red line made by the edge of the bucket. George was still choking.

"His neck will be in worse shape than that before it's all over," Lymond said. He was still trying to stand up but gave up after his legs buckled and he collapsed into the hay, propped up against the side of the stall. That blow on his head must have been worse than it looked. I went over to him and kneeled beside him to comfort him. He looked up at me and touched the side of my face with his fingers. "Poor Roxanne," he whispered sympathetically. "Does it hurt?"

I was suddenly aware of the throbbing pain in the side of my face and, to my complete amazement, began to cry. Worse, I couldn't seem to stop. I was embarrassed beyond words. I never cry.

Lymond put an arm around me and pulled my head to his chest. He must have known how embarrassing it was for me to cry in front of Kenyon, DeWitt, and Woodbury. I really didn't mind crying in front of Lymond. He put both arms around me and patted me as I sobbed into his shoulder. "Poor Roxie," he whispered in my ear. "Poor, sweet, Roxie."

I wanted to tell him I was neither poor nor sweet, but it was so wonderful to be held and comforted that I didn't. It felt so warm and right to be there, listening to him. The pain in my face was so bad, I was so overset about misjudging George, and the whole night had been such a disaster that it was wonderful just to curl up there, my face buried in Lymond's shoulder while he whispered to me.

Kenyon broke the spell. "Are you two all right? That's a nasty looking place on your head, Robert. Do you need a doctor?"

"No," Lymond answered, "but Roxanne might. She's been hit in the face."

I moved away from Lymond and wiped my eyes just in time to see Woodbury and DeWitt, assisted by some stable hands who had arrived, take Gage away. "Bucephalus!" I said wildly, looking around. "Bue was hurt. Is he dead?" I saw Bue's form lying in the straw and crawled over to him. He rolled his eyes towards me and got up, moving as slowly as I did. I hugged him, getting blood all over me, but I didn't care.

Kenyon had helped Lymond stand, and they came over to us. I could see Kenyon hesitate, then kneel to touch Bue. "Good dog," he said, lightly running his fingers along Bue's back. "It doesn't look too good, Robert," he said, looking at us. "He's losing a great deal of blood."

"Do something, Lymond." I could scarcely speak around the ache in my throat. "Please."

Lymond scratched Bue behind his ears. "He certainly saved us, didn't he?" Lymond asked as he ran his fingers along Bue's side. "Kenyon, I don't think we can wait for the doctor on this one. We need to send for him to attend to Roxanne, but Bue needs stitching now." He gave Kenyon a level look. "Do you think you can do it?"

Kenyon hesitated. "Please?" I whispered again, and he nodded. "I can't promise," he said.

"Just do what you can."

Kenyon called for the others to help him move Bue.

I suggested the kitchen where we would have water. We could put Bue on the table—at this point, I wasn't worried about what cook would think.

"I think that's a good idea," Lymond said, scratching Bue again. "We'll have you taken care of in no time, old fellow. It'll be all right." To Lymond's amazement and mine as well, Buecephalus lifted his head, looked for a moment as if he understood, then licked Lymond's hand. Then he looked at Kenyon and nuzzled his palm, almost as if he knew Kenyon was going to make everything all right.

Chapter 17

The doctor came while Kenyon and Holmwood were working on Bue. I was sitting at the table, holding Bue's head in my hands. He was still, as though he knew this pain was the only way to make him well again. I refused to allow the doctor to look at my face until I knew Bue was all right.

The doctor checked both Lymond and me. No bones were broken for either of us, but we were informed that we would hardly be presentable for several days. Lymond, he thought, had a concussion, and he was afraid my vision might be damaged. I tried not to show how much this alarmed me but Lymond knew. He reassured me as best he could and I asked him not to mention it to Aunt Hen or the other girls.

The doctor left laudanum drops for the pain. My face seemed numb right now, so I offered mine to Lymond, but he refused, insisting that I would need my drops later.

After it was all over, morning was breaking and I could hardly stand. Lymond had been right—my face had started throbbing unmercifully. I tried to resist, but finally mixed some drops and went to bed. It was a relief to sleep although I had the quaint notion that

I would wake up free of the pain. That was definitely not to be.

When I awoke, I blinked my eyes and my head felt unfamiliar on my body. My vision was blurred on the injured side and I had to move my head to see Livvy sitting by my bedside. I tried to rise, but the pain was intense. I moaned in spite of myself and touched my face with my fingers. It felt strange, all swollen and smooth. Livvy stood and tucked the blanket down. "Now, Roxie, just be still. I'll mix you some more laudanum drops and you sleep. You don't need to be up and around."

"Need to," I muttered. My jaw didn't seem to want to work properly. "Need to get up." I tried to rise, but let myself gingerly back on the pillows as the room began to spin around. It seemed easier to take the drops Livvy handed me, so I did. In a few minutes, I fell asleep.

It was late in the day before I woke and tried to get up again. This time Julia was sitting beside my bed. I very slowly opened my mouth and tried to speak without moving my jaw. "What happened?"

Julia laughed and propped a pillow behind me. "You've slept the day away, Roxie. Everything's fine, so you just rest. Could you eat a few bites? I'll get you some broth."

She tripped out the door and I tried to get out of the bed. It was slow work, and I had to hold on to things all the way, but I was determined to get to the mirror. After I got there, I almost wished I hadn't. My hair was frowsy and standing out all around my head and worse, my face was all swollen and purple. It felt better than it had, however, and I found I could move my jaw and speak, although my vision was still blurred. I took another look and realized it would be several days before I dared appear in public.

I made my way back to the bed and leaned back against the pillows wishing Julia would hurry. I was ravenous. I hadn't eaten anything in twenty-four hours.

The door opened and, to my horror, Lymond came in carrying a tray. Kenyon and Julia were right behind him.

"I'm . . . not . . . receiving," I said, forcing myself to say each word. My jaw just didn't want to work properly. Remembering how I looked, I tried to pat my hair down but I doubted it was any use at all. Lymond set the tray down on the table beside my bed and reached for a brush. "I think this may do a better job," he said. I reached for the brush and tried to brush my hair, but had no idea what I was doing since I couldn't see it. Lymond reached over and took the brush from my fingers and smoothed my hair for me. "I make an exceptional nursemaid, don't you think?"

"Mm." It did feel really good, but I certainly wasn't going to tell him that. I risked a look at him and noted that he didn't look very much better than I did. He put the brush aside and reached for the broth. "Do you want me to feed you or can you do it yourself?"

"Do . . . it . . . myself."

"I thought you'd say that," he said with a grin. Everyone sat down and watched me spill broth all over myself. Lymond reached over and mopped my chin. "Let me help you."

I shook my head and doggedly attempted to eat the rest of the broth while they sat there. Actually, I think I spilled most of it, but I managed to get enough down to take the edge off my hunger. Lymond took the bowl and put it back on the tray. "Bue?" I asked.

"He's fine," Kenyon said with a smile. He stood

and left, returning in a moment, leading a very still Bucephalus. Bue walked over to the bed and nuzzled my hand. It took him almost as long to get across the room as it had me. I scratched him behind his ears and almost cried. Bue nuzzled me again and went to his rug at the foot of my bed. He very carefully stretched out and sighed, his nose on Kenyon's boot.

"We're best friends," Kenyon said with a grin. "Or anyway, second best friends."

"I'm glad you said second best," Julia said, looking sideways at Kenyon. "I'd hate to think you placed Bucephalus above me." She turned to me, her face glowing. "Roxanne, we have something to tell you."

"I know." Speaking was getting easier. I sat further up in the bed and pulled the covers up around my neck. I looked at Lymond since I felt he probably could answer my questions more fully. "George been . . . charged?"

Lymond nodded. "He'll probably hang for the murders. As you deduced, he's the one who left the poetry on your pillow as well. He saw you in London and came down here to look around and see what was here. He couldn't find the scroll so had to come later with Boots."

Kenyon nodded. "Boots had become suspicious of him after Parrott's murder. Of course, we all had."

"Miss Hinchley affirmed that Parrott was planning to leave Gage. Gage killed him to prevent him from talking to any of us. It was just unfortunate that Gage had to do it when you were involved. It would have been much neater if he could have killed him away from the house. Oh, by the way, it was Miss Hinchley and Parrott you saw by the library window. It seems that was their trysting place." Lymond reached down and patted Bue on the head as he talked.

"Poor Miss Hinchley," Julia said. "She's completely bereft."

"Poor . . . woman," I mumbled. "Lymond, . . . scroll?"

"Woodbury found it in Gage's things. Uncle Harley, of course, is afraid to let it out of his hands." Lymond laughed and looked at me. "I hope you were planning to let him have it because he'll probably move in with you if you don't."

I must have looked as horrified as I felt because they all laughed. "Perhaps," Lymond suggested, "you could let him borrow it. All he really wants is to take the thing to London and wave it under Spencer's nose."

"If he can get away from Aunt Hen long enough," Julia said with a laugh. "I need to warn you, Roxanne, that Uncle Harley and Aunt Hen are planning a full-scale assault on the house to try to find the treasure. Uncle Harley has decided Papa probably hid it under the floorboards. He's going to ask your permission to tear them all up." Was I in error or was she absolutely sparkling? There was certainly something different about her. She looked at me and smiled broadly. "Also, Roxanne, you'll never guess: DeWitt has offered for Evelyn and she's accepted. They're planning to get married in London."

"Mmff." It was easier to way than "What!" Still, I had known something like that was in the wind. "DeWitt?" I mumbled.

"Are you ready for some tea now?" Lymond got the cup and teapot from the tray and poured. "As for DeWitt—I know what you're thinking," he said, with an amused glance at Kenyon. "DeWitt's one of my close friends and has worked with Debenham and the Home Office for years. This match is suitable in every way. Besides," he added with a laugh, "Uncle Harley's not only getting a son, he's getting a librarian."

I managed a smile and reached for my cup of tea. I had just brought it to my lips when Kenyon put his arm around Julia's shoulders. "We have news as well," he said as Julia smiled up at him. I'd seen that look before on Cassie—it was love. I strangled on my tea.

The coughing hurt my face, but Lymond hurt me worse by banging on my back. "Are you all right, Roxanne?" he asked anxiously.

I nodded, tears in my eyes. I couldn't have said a word if I had wanted to. "News?" I asked weakly, looking at the two of them.

Julia nodded. "I know it isn't what you wanted, Roxie, but Livvy and Kenyon just didn't . . . they just weren't attracted at all."

"You . . . were?"

"We both were," Kenyon said, looking fondly at Julia. "I've asked Julia to marry me and she's said yes. We'd like your blessing if you can. Robert can vouch for my character and means."

"Not . . . necessary." I looked from one of them to the other, not knowing what else to say. Julia looked at me anxiously. "It is all right, isn't it, Roxanne? We care very much for each other. I know you wanted Livvy . . ." She paused. "We just couldn't help it. Our attachment just happened. I tried to tell you once or twice, but never seemed to be able to. Then, at the end, I thought you knew."

I shook my head. "Didn't . . . know." I looked at the two of them, so very much in love. "Glad . . . for you."

Julia came over to the bed and took my hand. "Do you mean that, Roxie?" I nodded and she smiled happily. "We're going to be married as soon as possible."

"Wait until . . ." I tried to say, but she stopped me. "Of course we'll wait until you're presentable," she said with a smile, touching my face.

"Good." It was all I could manage. Julia bent down and kissed me, then stood up and looked back at Kenyon. "I've got to go tell Livvy. She told me it would be all right; Roxanne would understand." She dashed out the door. Kenyon looked at the door for a moment, then laughed and followed her.

Lymond looked around. "Here we are alone. Most improper, Roxanne." He scratched Bue behind the ears and leaned back in his chair. "This is a new situation for me—Roxanne Sydney unable to chide, berate, or belittle me in any way. I think I may enjoy this respite, brief though it may be."

I glared at him and he laughed. "Would you like me to recite some poetry to you, Roxanne?"

I made a face at him. "Attack, Bue," I said weakly.

Bue moved to get closer to Lymond, lifted his lip as though to bare his teeth, but instead, licked Lymond's hand. Then he put his muzzle on Lymond's leg and sighed contentedly while Lymond scratched him under the chin.

I could scarcely believe my eyes. "Bucephalus!"

Lymond grinned at me, his blue eyes almost dancing. "Face it, Roxanne. I've foiled you again."